Again and Again

Again and Again

A Novel

Ellen Bravo

She Writes Press

Published 2015
Printed in the United States of America
ISBN: 978-1-63152-939-9
Library of Congress Control Number: 2015932965

For information, address:
She Writes Press
1563 Solano Ave #546
Berkeley, CA 94707

She Writes Press is a division of SparkPoint Studio, LLC.

To all the survivors and other activists who make it
possible for nobodies to go against a somebody
and change the reality for everybody.

Contents

Prologue

Danforth University, Otsego, New York, Friday, August 18, 1978

Let her be from New York City. Let her wear black. Make sure she's smart and funny. Let her think I'm smart and funny, too.

By turning this into a mantra and keeping her eyes on the trees whizzing by, Deborah was able to drown out her parents' yammering in the front seat.

"You brake *before* the curve, Debbie," her father boomed from behind the wheel. "That's the ticket!" He'd begun mapping the drive from Cleveland to Otsego the moment the acceptance letter arrived, revising the official TripTik after frequent consultations with the atlas he kept on his desk.

"Mixers. That's what your cousin Rivka did: she went to every mixer she could find, and look at her—she met that Harold the third week!" Her mother, head turned slightly, hurled the words from the passenger seat toward the back of the car while keeping her eyes on the curves.

"Debbie has plenty of time to find someone."

"Thank you, Mr. Ann Landers. Oh my God, will you slow down? That truck is coming right at us!"

"Sylvia, please. You're killing me here."

Deborah shifted away from the pile of bedding wedged between her and the carton that held her brand-new electric typewriter and a tin of cookies, both presents from her grandmother. The plastic surrounding the dove-gray coverlet had left her back sweaty and her blouse wrinkled. Leaning against the back door, Deborah hoped the breeze from her father's window would air her out.

"Don't slouch, Debbie; it's bad for your complexion. Brains are good, but they'll only get you so far."

"And harping makes your skin glow?"

Listening to her dad come to her defense, always without raising his voice, Debbie wondered whether he did this out of love for her or to needle his wife.

The sun wove its way through the filter of trees and made patterns on Deborah's blue skirt. *Let her be from New York.* Danforth University had sent only her roommate's name, no other information. Deborah pictured Elizabeth Golmboch as a Manhattan sophisticate, willowy, maybe an English major, definitely not a virgin. She'd be striking but not vain, have lofty ambitions, never obsess over the mundane. Deborah's grandmother had warned her not to pin too much on any one person. Whatever happened at college wouldn't depend on who slept in the other twin bed in the room at Martha Hillerman Hall. But Deborah clung to these images like a sign. If the roommate worked out, Danforth would provide the transformation she longed for, from American Wasteland to World That Mattered.

Let her wear black.

The Timex on Deborah's wrist flashed 1:48. She'd hoped for something more chic when she graduated high school, but Timex was what her dad sold in his drugstore. "Digital, Debbie—you'll always know exactly what time it is," he promised, fastening the watch to her wrist as though it were a diamond bracelet. At that moment, she'd promised herself she'd morph into Deborah the second she arrived at college.

The room was empty when they finally pulled into the Hillerman parking lot and hauled the suitcases and boxes up to the seventh floor. But the south side had already been set up, the bed covered with an abstract quilt of various purples; Deborah could picture the quiet

Village boutique where Elizabeth bought it, maybe with her mother, maybe with her own credit card. There were no stuffed animals or froufrou pillows, no Yankee pennants like they'd spotted covering an entire wall a few doors down. Over her roommate's desk was an assortment of postcard prints, arranged not in rows, like Deborah would have done, but in an artful pattern.

"See, I was right, Debbie!" her father said. "The campus is magnificent. I told your mother they didn't airbrush that brochure, but she wouldn't believe me. And this isn't half bad for a dorm room." Her father, five feet eight with his shoes on, stood between the beds and extended his wiry arms. "Your brother had to be careful his roommate's *tuchus* wasn't in his face every time he turned around."

"So, where *is* the roommate?" Her mother opened the closet door on their side of the room as if Elizabeth Golmboch might have been hiding there. She checked herself in the full-length mirror, smoothed her slacks over her panty girdle, reapplied the powder meant to slim her nose ("like Barbra Streisand's, only shorter and without the bump," she liked to say), and tugged on the hair around her face. The heat threatened to restore its natural curl. How many fights had they had ("You have my features; why not learn my beauty lessons?") because Deborah refused to wear powder or let the beautician straighten her hair? "We want to take you girls to an early dinner. Your father is convinced we have to leave at the crack of dawn. If he's not back for his pinochle tournament, the Heights social scene will come to a grinding halt."

Her father might not have a clue about sophistication—Deborah had to talk him out of wearing his plaid golfing pants—but he did seem to get that she needed to be on her own. A better daughter would be grateful that her parents, however tacky, had traveled all this way to get her settled. A better daughter would have been glad to explore the campus with them, slurp the local ice cream, take photos of the Tamarack Gorge. Deborah just wanted them to disappear.

"Go on to the hotel, Mom. Dad deserves a nap for doing all that driving. And then you can wander around the campus a little. I'll put my stuff away. Remember, I have to be at a student-only orientation with the provost at four o'clock."

Her mother insisted on unpacking Deborah's clothes first and making the bed while her father stood on a chair to stow sheets and blankets on the top shelf of the closet. Deborah could have written the script: "How's she going to reach those?" "She'll stand on a chair, like I did." "And the next thing you know, our daughter will be trying to get to class on crutches." "Don't worry, Debbie, I'll come autograph your cast."

They'd been gone only ten minutes when a slight girl with fair skin and a pixie haircut walked in, wearing a wrap-around denim skirt and plain white blouse and brandishing a campus map. Her hair, an ordinary brown, was practical, rather than cute. She had features that were neat but unremarkable, what Deborah's mother would call a weak chin. A man with a similar chin lingered in the hallway, twirling a Milwaukee Brewers cap in his large hands.

"Hi, I'm Liddie Golmboch." The girl tossed the map on her desk and stuck her hand out. "You must be Deborah Borenstein. It's okay, Dad, come on in."

Even though Liddie was approximately the same height as Deborah, her dad had to stoop a little when he entered the room. "Horace Golmboch, from Saukville, Wisconsin," he said, nodding his head. "Very pleased to meet you."

Deborah had no idea where Saukville was, only that it was a long way from Manhattan. She could picture Liddie in ads for a 4-H club, her arm around the neck of a large calf, a straw hat shielding her skin.

Mr. Golmboch stuck his cap in his back pocket and looked around the room as if scanning for something that needed fixing. When he'd satisfied himself that everything was in working order, he cupped Liddie's head in his hand. "I need to get on back, Lid. Have to work on the Schmitz place tomorrow. And you need to get started here. But I'm so glad I got to see the Lutheran chapel. And to meet your roommate."

He turned to Deborah. "It's easy to get lost around here. I'm glad they gave you gals that map. Make sure my daughter shares the kringle her mom made. She was real sorry she couldn't get away. And I'm sorry we didn't get to meet your folks."

Deborah backed up slowly until she felt her bed with the backs of her knees and sank down on it. Okay, so you didn't have to be best friends with your roommate; there'd be other girls on the hall she could hang out with, someone else who could be her guide to a world of sophistication. This Liddie was probably very nice. At least she had a good eye.

While Liddie filled out paperwork for her work-study assignment, which turned out to be busing tables in the cafeteria, Deborah finished sliding her things into the dresser drawers and setting up her electric typewriter on the desk. They talked a little over a piece of kringle—it turned out to be a kind of Danish in a flat, skinny ring, apricot flavoring, unexpectedly tasty. Liddie hoped to get into the textile design program—she'd made that quilt herself. Deborah spoke of her interest in political science. But there wasn't much time; they'd been encouraged to get to orientation early. Just as they were about to leave, a girl with honey-colored waves stuck her head in the room and introduced herself as Nancy Minkin, their neighbor from down the hall.

"You two look normal. Can I walk with you to orientation?" Nancy's roommate turned out to be the Yankee fanatic. "When I told her I don't really like baseball, she nearly had a shit fit," Nancy told them. "'You're from Long Island!' she yelled. Her whole side of the room is Yankee decor, and if there's a game on, she's already announced, it *will* be playing loudly on her radio in our room."

Nancy talked nonstop all the way across the bridge and down to the arts quad. Having a small-town Midwesterner as a roommate was starting to look less alarming to Deborah, if this was what the New Yorkers were like. They made their way to Willard Broome Hall, where several hundred students were gathering in a large room made somber by heavy red drapes. Nancy broke away to hang out with a friend from her hometown. Some dean introduced the provost, both men right out of *Animal House* central casting, with hearty smiles and full heads of hair. Deborah was only half listening to the platitudes about "the greatest adventure of your life" and the need to "buckle down," when the provost made a sudden, dramatic pause.

"Look to your right and to your left," he bade them. Liddie was balancing on one leg on Deborah's right. On the left, a skinny black girl in khaki pants introduced herself as a physics major from Rochester. The provost peered at them over the lectern. "Now recalibrate your expectations. You may all have graduated at the top of your high school class, but you can do the math. Half of you will be at the bottom of the class here."

Deborah bit the inside of her lip and blinked hard. She tried to summon up the shimmer of the acceptance letter on her fingers, the fresh print smell of the course catalog she'd pored over all summer, the visions of stimulating conversations on the quad, but the sound of the provost's voice triggered the only sense still functioning.

Beside her, Liddie crossed her arms over her chest. "Thanks for the welcome, asshole," she muttered. Then she looped one arm through Deborah's. "I hear they call this building the Broome. From now on, I'm calling it the Willard, 'cause that guy will always give me the willies."

Deborah felt the gratitude whirl throughout her body like something injected into her blood.

Liddie had to miss dinner to attend cafeteria training. Deborah didn't mention the provost incident to her parents. But she described it in full to her grandmother in a letter the next morning. "Dear Grandma," she began. "I lucked out. My roommate's not what I pictured, but I think she's just what I want."

One

Washington, DC: Thursday morning, January 28, 2010

"Are you really going to let a *rapist* become a United States senator? Crap all over your life's work? It's crunch time, sister. Heroine or hypocrite—what's it going to be?"

As she spit out these words, Gillean Mulvaney was barreling her way into Deborah Borenstein's office, having opened the door so quickly, a whoosh of air blew several envelopes off the corner of the desk. Gillean stomped on them with her boots as she charged over to the visitor's chair and plunked herself down.

The woman hadn't said a word in the antechamber outside the office, where an intern from American University was filling in for Marquita Reynolds, Deborah's chief of staff. "I'm sorry, ma'am, but you need an appointment," the intern had said loudly enough for Deborah to hear.

"Ma'am, you can't go in there."

"Please, ma'am."

"Oh my Lord . . ." The intern, hand clasped over her mouth, trailed Gillean as she barged in.

Although Deborah had managed all these years to avoid meeting Gillean Mulvaney, she'd have known the reporter anywhere—the short, squat body; the reddish curls that looked unkempt by design, rather than neglect; the rapid-fire speech. And that voice, so gravelly from years of smoking, Deborah couldn't believe the woman had made it to her office without a tank of oxygen strapped to her back.

Mostly, Deborah was blown away that Gillean had found out about this story in the first place. Who on earth could have tipped her off? Deborah ground her feet into the floor beneath her desk and prayed her voice wouldn't wobble.

"Shari, this is Gillean Mulvaney," Deborah said. "She's a reporter, not an assassin. Ms. Mulvaney, if you wish to make an appointment . . ."

Gillean's eyes remained trained on Deborah as she pulled a cigarette from the pocket of her voluminous coat, holding it like a cocked gun. Obviously, she had as much regard for the DC smoking ban as she did for interns and potential sources.

"You listen to me, Deborah Borenstein," Gillean was saying. "I don't give a flying fuck about one more man in the Senate who can't keep his dick in his pants. I don't give a rat's ass about run-of-the-mill adulterers or family-values hypocrites. But this guy, Mr. William Harrison Quincy III—this one is a *ra-pist*." She drew out both syllables and held her thin lips together an extra beat on the "p."

Shari pivoted and ran out of the room.

"I've got a very busy morning," Deborah said, waving an embossed invitation to a briefing by Vice President Biden on the Violence Against Women Act.

"I know you know Quincy got his party's nomination. Amanda Pruitt told you yesterday."

Deborah straightened the pencils in the pot beside her computer. She wouldn't put it past Gillean to have planted a microphone in there.

"I also know you know he did it. What I can't figure out is why Breaking the Silence"—Gillean read from a brochure she must have grabbed in the reception area—"'the nation's largest organization fighting sexual violence against women,' hasn't already held a news conference to denounce the motherfucker. Did Quincy buy you off?"

"Look, my schedule is really tight today." Deborah watched Gillean scan the massive desktop, as if ready to pounce on an envelope stuffed with cash. Instead, the reporter's eyes took in the stacks of files in color-coded boxes: purple for CONGRESSIONAL ACTION NEEDED, scarlet for GRASSROOTS CAMPAIGNS, green for MAJOR DONORS, mustard-brown for FUNDER DEADLINE.

"Goddammit, he's going to win unless you stop him." Gillean scattered ashes as she punctured the air with her right hand. "I need you on the record. I need it now."

"I . . . really, I . . ."

Gillean ground out her cigarette in the BEST MOM EVER bowl Deborah's daughter made when she was eight. "Christ almighty, talk to me! Are you going to pony up or pussy out? Liddie Golmboch was your *roommate*!"

Just then Marquita marched in, all five feet nine inches of her, the intern tucked behind her. "Security is on the way," Marquita said. "I'm told it's much more comfortable to walk out on your own." Marquita had been the front line of defense since the day the organization opened, twenty years before. "I learned from the best in Senator Kennedy's office," Marquita told the search committee. "I can sniff out a woman in pain or a reporter in heat faster than most people can smell shit on a stick. Those who need help will get in. Those who need to be kept out won't have a prayer."

But not even Marquita Reynolds could have kept Gillean out today. Nothing could keep the woman from clawing her way to this story—nothing, except the silence of Deborah Borenstein.

"I don't know what your game is, lady." Gillean kept staring at Deborah while placing her surprisingly delicate hands on her generous thighs and pushing herself to standing. "But don't think you've seen the last of me."

TWO
Danforth University: Saturday evening, December 1, 1979

Her calendar page allowed no deviation—"LIBRARY UNTIL CLOSING"—but Deborah kept finding her head on her arms and spittle on the page. Normally, a description of the shunning of Bengali women after they'd been raped by Pakistani soldiers would have kept her riveted, but tonight her eyes wouldn't stay open. Deborah peeked through her hair to see whether anyone had noticed. The stacks were empty except for two graduate students sprawled in the far corner, playing chess, and a senior who seemed to live in his carrel, surrounded by index cards and a deflated Wise potato chip bag.

Had she missed the eleven o'clock chimes? Deborah pressed the light display on her Timex. Ten eighteen—the green digits flashed on and off like a frat boy mooning her. Here she was on a Saturday night, swallowing another sigh of self-pity. A year ago she and Brad would have been curled on his bed after a movie, maybe dinner first at the deli in town. The girls on her floor envied her for having a boyfriend already in law school—and in New York City, no less. "So you slog away now and schlep to New York once a month," Nancy Minkin told her. "You'll both graduate in eighty-two. Boom: marriage, a steady income. Instead of having to support him, you can make him a daddy right away!"

But Deborah didn't want to make Brad a daddy right away, and she was less and less sure she wanted to make him a husband. On her last two trips to NYU, all he could talk about was mergers and acquisitions. Brad's dorm room was dark and narrow, his suitemate, far from home, China or Korea or Japan—Brad didn't know which, and Deborah was too ashamed to ask—hovering somewhere just outside the door. "What happened to litigating a civil rights case before the Supreme Court?" she hissed in reluctant whispers. "When did you change your vision of the future?"

"My vision or yours, Deb?" he replied.

The potato chip guy balled up the bag and took aim. Deborah watched the plastic sideswipe the wastebasket and land on her boots. That did it. She shoved the econ text and Susan Brownmiller's *Against Our Will* into her book bag and dragged on her parka. Even the librarian failed to nod in Deborah's direction. She might as well have been invisible.

A new snowfall dusted her face as she walked onto the quad, adding another layer to the foot or more that had accumulated over the past two days. She used to complain about winters in Cleveland, but the weather over Thanksgiving had seemed mild in comparison with upstate New York. Still, as she trudged up the hill to the dorm, Deborah couldn't help admiring the drifts. "Admit it," Liddie once challenged her. "Without mud stains, snow has glamour, even brilliance." All the same, Deborah hurried to get to the warmth of Martha Hillerman Hall.

A few students dotted the lounge, but Deborah headed straight for the elevator to the fourth floor. She just wanted to pull on her flannels and wait for her roommate to come back from her date with Will Quincy.

"Why do you think a campus dreamboat would go out with someone like me?" Liddie asked that afternoon as she tried on various outfits from Deborah's closet.

"Maybe Will Quincy's smarter than he looks," Deborah replied. Actually, she'd been wondering the same thing. Deborah remembered her own reaction that first day in the dorm—Liddie's small-town-Lutheran-nice-girl exterior gave no hint of her wit and smarts.

You had to make her laugh to see her eyes crinkle and light up her face. The only relationship that lasted was with another design student, named Tommy Lannihan, who turned out to be gay—something Liddie figured out when they finally had sex. Other dates included a hotel student from Waunakee, Wisconsin, who announced proudly that he'd scoured the freshman rolls for anyone from his home state, and a guy in Liddie's biology class who needed help with dissection and saw that Liddie had a steady hand. Deborah and Brad had tried to fix her up several times, but Liddie resisted. "Blind dates remind me of church hand-me-downs," she said. "They never fit." She preferred hanging out with Tommy and his friends.

Deborah pulled off her boots and blew on her hands until they warmed up enough to unlock the door of their corner room. As she turned the key, she heard what sounded like the moans her cocker spaniel made one summer when his leg got trapped under the backyard swing. She must have left the radio on—good thing her father wasn't here to remind her they didn't own stock in the electric company. At least she'd remembered to turn out the lights.

Deborah dropped her book bag on Liddie's desk, closest to the door. The first thing she noticed when she switched on the lamp were several of the postcards Liddie had above her desk, a Vermeer and two blue Picassos, scattered on the floor. As Deborah bent to retrieve the one she'd just squished beneath her sock, she heard her roommate's bed squeak and noticed Liddie's leg, the borrowed black jeans around her ankle, thrust at an odd angle from her bed. The air held the acrid smell of male sweat.

Oh God, Liddie would die of embarrassment. Deborah quickly spun around and clicked off the lamp. But as her fingers reached the doorknob, she heard the moans again. Deborah had no real sexual experience besides Brad, and she was pretty sure she hadn't yet had an orgasm ("If you're still asking whether you have, then you haven't," her women's studies professor had told the class). Still, Deborah was certain those were sounds of agony, not pleasure. And there was something about the position of Liddie's leg, the dislodged postcards, a year and a half of rooming together—Liddie would never hop in the sack on a first date.

This time Deborah turned on the overhead fluorescent light, which illuminated what had to be Will Quincy's ass in the air and his arm, flecked with tiny gold hairs, bent across Liddie's neck. Deborah recognized the stranglehold from years of forced attendance at her brother's wrestling matches. She locked on Liddie's eyes, frozen wide with terror.

"Liddie!"

As Will lifted his arm, Liddie's moan turned into a rasping intake of breath, like the squawk of a machine about to burn out.

"Get the fuck off her now!" Deborah screamed. She pictured herself flying through space, tearing Will off the bed, ramming her knee into his balls so hard they would fly up to his throat and choke him.

In what seemed an unusually graceful motion, Will rolled off the bed on his own, pulled up his jeans, and slid out of the room, like someone who'd performed this maneuver on numerous occasions. Apparently, he'd never taken off his shoes. His eyes, an eerily light blue, looked right at Deborah as he grabbed the coat he had flung on her own bed and squeezed past her out the door. She caught a whiff of some fruity drink.

Liddie coiled into a fetal position against the wall and kept gulping in air. Deborah was at her bed in two strides, as if her legs had been transformed into the long and graceful limbs of her dreams. Frantically, she searched her brain for the words of the rape crisis counselor who'd come down last month from Rochester: "Talk softly, don't touch, offer support, don't tell her what to do."

Lowering her body onto the bed as lightly as possible, Deborah willed herself not to shriek or cry as she covered Liddie with the Danforth fleece presented to each student at orientation. "He's gone, Lid," she kept whispering. "I'm here. I won't leave."

The chimes were fainter up here. Shortly after they sounded, Liddie's body began to shudder as she kicked off the jeans still bunched around her ankles. Deborah jumped up to get her own fleece and tucked it around Liddie's feet, taking care not to touch her directly and cursing the stereo down the hall, which was blasting James Taylor's "Something in the Way She Moves."

When she finally rolled over to face Deborah, Liddie's face looked raw. There were abrasions on her right cheek and a scratch just under her right ear. Her voice was hoarse and weak. "He wanted to borrow my Rilke."

"Oh, Lid." Deborah pictured a late-night huddle where the same guys who sold term papers tutored newcomers in lines like this.

She rested her fingers on the edge of the crimson blanket, wishing she had one that didn't resemble blood. In the harsh overhead light, she could see a hideous bruise spreading across Liddie's neck. Deborah dug her teeth into her lip and begged God not to let her mess this up.

"I can call a cab to take you to the clinic, babe."

"There's no evidence," Liddie said. "You came before he did." She started to laugh, great guffaws that sounded like geese honks. Deborah pushed down her own panic as if it were a physical presence and resisted the urge to slap Liddie, instead putting just her fingertips on Liddie's shoulders and saying her name over and over. The laughter disintegrated.

Deborah struggled to keep her voice low and even. "There'd still be fluid. And you have bruises, Lid. There, on your neck." Liddie's hand swung up as if to hide the evidence.

"I bet your arms are covered with them." Deborah made no move to lift the covers and push up the sleeves of the borrowed blue velvet V-neck, one she knew neither of them would ever wear again. "I know he hurt you, babe." Deborah couldn't shut out images of the photos the crisis counselor brought, torn labia and battered vulvas—words Deborah had come to see as beautiful that should never be paired with such vile adjectives.

Liddie pulled the fleece up to her chin. Tears leaked from her eyes into her small ears, but her body was motionless and her voice steady. "My parents."

Deborah could almost see Mr. and Mrs. Horace Golmboch of Saukville, Wisconsin, standing awkwardly at the foot of the bed. Liddie's mom was an elementary school librarian, with a voice that promised stories and fresh-squeezed lemonade. She barely came up to her husband's shoulder. Last summer, during a visit to their home,

Deborah found Liddie's parents charming. Now she resented the hell out of them for crowding their way into this story.

"First thing they'd do is call my folks," Liddie said. "My dad would have me out of here in a heartbeat, scholarship or not. They never wanted me to go to such a big school in the first place."

Claire Rawlings, the rape crisis counselor from Rochester, had made a big point about the importance of medical testimony. Still, Liddie did have a witness. Not in time, not nearly fast enough—oh God, why hadn't Deborah left the library earlier?—but still, a genuine I-saw-that-was-no-kiss-and-I will-tell witness. Mr. William Harrison Quincy-the-Second-or-whatever number-he-was was a dead fuckin' duck. Deborah longed for some dramatic gesture—spray-painting his car (surely he'd have one) with "rapist" in lurid purple letters; handing out WANTED FOR RAPE flyers all over campus with a photo of Will from the Delta Omega registry or the rugby team. Members of the Stop It Now group were dying for an opportunity like that. But Liddie had to call the shots.

Back on her side, Liddie looked young, frail, diminished. Even her pixie cut seemed shorter. In the silence of the last few minutes, her breathing had taken on a rhythm—more plaintive, for being so soft and regular.

"Whatever you decide," Deborah said, "I'm here for you, Lid."

three

Washington, DC: Wednesday morning, January 27, 2010

Deborah wondered whether Marquita's stylist designed everyone's hair according to personality. The woman's braids spun across her scalp in dazzling precision, each swirl signaling style plus authority. She was waiting for Deborah with her hands on her hips and reading glasses on her nose—her only concession to turning fifty.

"I made one adjustment to your calendar for today," Marquita said. "Amanda Pruitt's coming at ten. You'll catch up with the accountant tomorrow." As most people knew and the others quickly found out, if you wanted to schedule something with Deborah, you had to go through Marquita. Deborah was no longer allowed to set her own appointments, not since the time in 1997 when she'd arranged a lunch date with a prospective donor for the same hour she was supposed to meet with First Lady Hillary Clinton. "You've heard of gatekeepers?" Marquita had announced. "Think White House. Better yet, think air traffic control. If it hasn't gone through me, it's not happening." That's when Deborah promoted Marquita from office manager to executive assistant. Two years ago, they'd changed her title to chief of staff.

Deborah already knew that Amanda wanted to see her. The head of Equality Unlimited, one of the nation's largest feminist organizations, had been calling both Deborah's cell and her home phone for the last twenty-four hours. They met informally every few months to catch up and often saw each other at meetings in between. But something was up; Amanda had left cryptic voice mails and finally took to heart Deborah's outgoing message. "The best way to reach me, really, is to call Marquita Reynolds at the office. Unlike me, she always knows where I am and where I'm going to be."

"I heard the word 'urgent' three times," Marquita said. She wasn't defending her decision, just explaining it.

In the hour before Amanda's visit, Deborah spoke on the phone to a grassroots leader in Chicago about their Keep Your Hands to Yourself! campaign to stop harassment on public transportation; a *Chicago Tribune* reporter about why that initiative should be a national model and why he ought to be speaking to the local leader; a trio of Senate aides working to increase funding for the Violence Against Women Act; and her daughter, Rebecca, who wanted Deborah to proof two college admission essays before the end of the day. "Don't start in on me about waiting till the last minute, Mom—they're not due till Monday. But my advisor just told us he wants to take a look before we send anything in, and I'd like you to proof it first. Can you squeeze me in, please?"

When the intercom buzzed, Deborah asked Marquita to free up a half hour of her afternoon. Rebecca had been adamant that she wanted to write every word herself—no consultants, no parents ghostwriting in the guise of "tweaking." She refused to parlay any connections or cachet her folks had, would not apply to Danforth or Tufts, their alma maters. Aaron had been hurt. "It'll be your thoughts entirely, Becca," he said. "We make our livings sprucing up words." On this front, at least, Deborah knew when to back off. She waited until she and Rebecca were alone. "See if you're open to having someone proofread for you. I never send out anything that hasn't been viewed by at least two other pairs of eyes—not since we printed twenty-five thousand copies of that brochure calling for new *pubic* policies."

The proofing would have to wait until after she found out what bee was in Amanda Pruitt's bonnet. Deborah moved from behind her desk to greet her guest. Unlike Aaron, whose income as a political consultant was more erratic than the needle on a liar's polygraph, Amanda's husband pulled in big bucks at a politics- and recession-proof law firm, one of the largest in the District. As usual, Amanda was wearing a suit, a new one of finely spun black wool—clearly some designer label, although Deborah never could tell one from another—and diamond stud earrings, small enough not to be ostentatious but sizable enough to say they didn't come from a department store. Who knew where she got time for the expert makeup? Deborah wouldn't be surprised if Amanda had some sort of personal attendant. Not that Deborah saw herself as shabby. She spent a decent portion of her salary on clothes, but they fell into the standard black-pants-or-long-skirt-with-fashionable-jacket category. Most days she added a little blush and mascara; she'd never gotten the hang of daily lipstick. Several staff at Breaking the Silence dressed in this fashion. Another group, the ones under thirty who ran marathons or did sweat yoga, wore pencil skirts and blazers from Ann Taylor Loft. The rest of the two dozen employees and interns showed up in jeans topped by T-shirts adorned with some meaningful statement—except for Marquita, who could walk out of Goodwill with a designer jacket and outshine them all. "You're a sales maven," Deborah told her, and vowed to find time for an apprenticeship someday.

"Good to see you, Amanda," Deborah said, grabbing both her guest's outstretched hands. Amanda wasn't really a hug-me kind of gal. "Let's go sit by the window."

Years ago Marquita pointed out the need for Deborah to think of her office layout according to the types of conversations her work required. "Chair opposite your desk for the typical guest—reporter, Hill staffer, someone seeking your support. No window behind you, fewer distractions for the guest, plenty for you if you need them: things to fiddle with, a silent intercom signal for me if you need to be rescued. Your chair swivels; theirs won't budge." She dropped into the burgundy leather side chair to demonstrate. Roomy enough to sit comfortably; no way to wriggle around.

Marquita then moved them both to the conference table. "Here's the place for weightier subjects, a small group meeting with funders or staff. Space for everyone to bring notebooks"—today that would be laptops—"coffee, snacks." She strolled around the table and tapped her index finger against her lip. "But what about girlfriend talk? You gotta have a place for that."

While Deborah surveyed the room, Marquita had pointed to the view of the Capitol from the window in the south corner, an area then occupied by bookcases bought on the cheap from the group who rented this space before them. "Right there. We haul all the reports and half the books outta here. A small couch, tasteful upholstery, a matching chair. That's where you'll hold someone's hand or plot earth-moving change." Marquita put in the furniture order that day.

Now Amanda started talking before they even reached that couch, still upholstered in the same deep-blue fabric but showing signs of wear. "This is big, Deborah. It's about an endorsement for the open Senate seat in Delaware." Amanda smoothed her skirt as she lowered herself into the chair, instead of sitting next to Deborah on the couch. Maybe they should have gone to the conference table.

"We've got the Republican male we've been looking for." Amanda pronounced the words as if they were a little naughty, like she was talking about a new sex toy. "He just won that primary by a landslide—did you read about it?"

News stories about Republican politics in Delaware attracted Deborah's attention about as much as reports of fly fishing. "No," she said. "Can't say that I have."

"I need to tell you how the cow ate the cabbage, darlin'. Feminists hear 'Republican' and shift immediately to enemy mode."

Deborah hated these kinds of blanket generalizations, especially when they lumped her in with everyone else. Still, after practicing for hours, she'd learned to keep her face absolutely expressionless. "Folk in DC will read you like a subway banner," Marquita advised two months after they started working together. "You, Ms. Deborah Borenstein, have got it bad—nostril flare, eyebrow lift, lip twist. You might as well just say, 'Man, you're pissing me off.' But I've been watching you. You're smart and you're tough. You can learn." Marquita's own smarts were a combination of street skills and on-the-job training. Her grandfather, one of the first black security guards at the Capitol building and a friend of Senator Ted Kennedy, got her an internship in the senator's office while she went to UDC Community College and raised a baby on her own.

Amanda was describing the candidate as an influential industrialist, "optic fibers or something like that, family business that was already lucrative and he made it even more so. But he's pro-choice, has been a solid supporter of women's issues, including donating to women's groups. And yes, he is a Republican. But he's like a Susan Collins, only more influential because he's a guy. This could be our ticket to persuading other Republicans to keep abortion legal—and, the way things are going, even to get backing for the Violence Against Women Act."

Normally Deborah would have broken in to ask questions or give an opinion. Today she was mildly curious how long Amanda could talk without a break. Deborah and Marquita had once made a bet on it; Deborah had never been able to restrain herself long enough to find out.

"The Democratic opponent is terrible—anti-choice, sticks his finger in the wind or up his ass to decide which way to go on funds for VAWA, voted for abstinence only, open to privatizing Social Security." Deborah wondered how much Amanda really cared about Social Security. Given her husband's pension and the heft of their portfolio, Social Security would amount to chump change.

The more Amanda went on, the more the whole thing sounded like a no-brainer. Despite Aaron's connections to the Democratic Party, Deborah got the importance of bipartisan support. Surely her colleague should know that by now.

Amanda hinged forward to signal she was about to divulge confidential information. "It's really important for Breaking the Silence to show it's nonpartisan. Some folks on the Hill have raised flags about women's groups whose PACs give money only to Dems. And you didn't hear this from me, but several big funders organized a private meeting making the same point."

A few years earlier, Deborah had been summoned to lunch with a foundation program officer who had engineered substantial grants for Breaking the Silence and had become a good friend. "We're getting heat from the IRS," the woman said over curried tofu salad. "The message was pretty clear: if we don't stop supporting what they see as 'blatant violations of the ban on partisan activity,' they're going to demand we pay out more of our principal."

"I know all about it," Deborah told Amanda. "But don't you think the IRS is going to back off under this administration? Surely that's part of 'change we can believe in.'"

Amanda sank back into her chair. "Foundations are gun-shy by definition," she proclaimed. "Plus, they're getting heat from some big donors."

Deborah sat up taller, wishing she were five feet eight and long-waisted, instead of five feet two and waist-challenged. "You know I don't kowtow to funders," Deborah said. "That's not how we make decisions around here." She didn't mention that this was the source of many heated discussions on the board, and that the view she championed was dangerously close to being overturned. "Anyway, we've supported moderate Republicans before."

"So you say, but everyone knows the kind of candidates Aaron works for." Amanda maintained her gaze as if she were waiting for Deborah's mask to crack. "Plus, I know you distrust corporate biggies, especially old money like this one. But I've met this William Quincy . . ."

Amanda's mouth kept moving but Deborah couldn't hear her over the pounding in her ears at the sound of Will's name. Delaware, blue blood, optic fibers—her antennae should have been up. She cursed herself for not paying more attention to state politics. Somehow, she managed to reach beneath the couch and press the intercom button Marquita had installed there "in case girlfriend talk degenerates into bitch slapping." So much for PC office lingo.

Marquita was at the door within seconds. "Sorry to interrupt, Deborah, but you have an urgent phone call."

"Back to you soon, Amanda." Deborah pushed herself up from the couch, vowing to make time for the gym classes Rebecca kept urging her to go to. "Email me the specifics, and I'll take it to the board."

Or not.

At this moment, only one person's opinion mattered to Deborah—Liddie Golmboch's—and she was as likely to serve on the board of Breaking the Silence as Deborah was to join a women's hockey league.

Four

Danforth University: Sunday, December 2, 1979

According to the Timex, it was 6:48 a.m. when Liddie's breathing evened out enough to qualify as sleep. Deborah never stayed up this late or got up this early—the slit in the curtains revealed a sky still plastered in darkness. Despite nodding off several times, she'd managed to keep her eyes open most of the night, smushed in the desk chair she'd moved to the side of Liddie's bed. For hours Deborah sat in silence, holding Liddie's hand, supplying Kleenex, adding or subtracting blankets as Liddie shivered or began to sweat, occasionally throwing out useless assurances that everything would be all right, wondering whether that would ever be true again. Before collapsing on her own mattress, Deborah carried the chair back to the desk so Liddie wouldn't trip over it when she managed to climb out of bed.

Mutilated creatures shuttled through Deborah's dreams—her cocker spaniel with his leg severed, chess pieces made of human flesh—until she heard a commotion up and down the hall. "Ten minutes to one! Last call for lunch! Drag your lazy asses out of bed!" God, it was that obnoxious freshman who'd managed to snag a spot on a sophomore floor. Deborah hated people who thought they knew what was best for you. She twisted to see whether the self-appointed hall monitor had interrupted Liddie's sleep as well.

All that greeted her in the other bed was a tangle of bedding.

Deborah jumped to her feet and made a mental list of places to search, chasing off images of Will returning to finish the job. As she pulled on yesterday's jeans, she struggled to remember the breathing tips they'd learned in self-defense class. In through the nose. Exhale through the mouth. More air out than in. But before Deborah managed to slow her pulse, Liddie was pushing the door open with her hip. Both hands gripped a child's purple pail filled with bathroom supplies, shoulders hugging her ears as if the bucket contained cement.

So much for medical evidence.

Deborah tiptoed across the room, set the pail on the floor, and wrapped her arms around her roommate as gently as she could. Liddie's body felt cold and stiff, like someone who'd stood under a shower so long, the water had turned to ice. After a moment, Deborah stepped away.

"Let me get you some sweats, Lid." As quickly as possible, Deborah assembled a turtleneck, her warmest hooded sweatshirt, and a pair of gray sweatpants and brought them over to Liddie. Dear, lovely Liddie, still as a statue, using just a finger to untie her flannel robe and let it drop to the floor.

Deborah had to flatten her heels on the floor and dig her knuckles into her thighs to keep from gasping at the sight of Liddie's bruises. Huge, ugly, all over her fair skin, some in the distinct shape of fingers, others giant splotches threatening to merge with each other. One stretched around her neck. Another looked like a marker, pointing toward her inner thigh.

After helping Liddie step into the sweatpants, Deborah tucked the flannel robe under her roommate's armpits. If she kept babbling, she might be able to pull this off. "Sit on the bed, Lid, and let me take some Polaroids of the bruises. Plenty of time, when you're feeling better, to decide whether or not to use the photos—at least you'll have them just in case."

Even before she was seated, Liddie transformed from statue to rag doll. Her shoulders and head rolled forward, causing the robe to fall beneath her small, pointy breasts. Deborah and Liddie used to joke about making a composite body, swapping some of Deborah's excess boobs and awarding both of them Liddie's perky shape.

Deborah forced herself to keep up a steady patter the whole time she was removing the Polaroid camera from the plastic storage case beneath her bed, loading the film, surrounding Liddie with pillows, adjusting the robe so that only Liddie's neck and arms were bare.

"You know, my dad sold me these at a discount," Deborah said. Last summer she'd convinced him to let her buy four cameras at cost. She'd let him think it was for theater purposes, although she'd dropped out of the Danforth stage crew when Stop It Now started. "You should have seen him giving me lessons in how to use them—like he invented the thing. 'It's all in the timing,' he said at least five times. 'Most people get overly excited and rip the cover off too soon. But it's also a mistake to leave it on too long. Use the stopwatch on your Timex. Make sure it's exactly sixty seconds.'"

Two cameras were stashed in rooms at Dorothy Beckett Hall. The group kept the fourth in their office at the student union. The assistant dean of Student Affairs, a guy in his late thirties with a ponytail who Liddie once described as "eager to be one of the gang, just a little older and with all the power," told Deborah he'd never seen an organization start as swiftly as Stop It Now. He'd asked a host of questions about what triggered it. "Was there an incident? Has some stranger been prowling around the dorms?"

"Our worry isn't strangers," she'd replied. "It's our dates."

The actual trigger was a conversation during an Intro to Women's Studies class the previous March in a chilly basement room in Goodman Parrish Hall. Professor Davis asked the twenty-five students, all but one female, to give a definition of what she called date rape. "Last Saturday night," answered Mae Driggins, someone Deborah barely knew. Tears rolled down another woman's cheeks. Speaking in a monotone, she described her shame in high school when she was raped while parking with her boyfriend on a lovers' lane.

"What'd you expect when you climbed into the backseat with him?" another student asked.

"Just making out," the woman whispered, "like the two other times we went there."

At first Deborah's thoughts focused on how lucky she'd been. No one had ever forced himself on her. Then she remembered a party her first year of high school, some guy she'd just met grabbing her breasts from behind and humping her in a dark corner of Shelley Novitske's rec room. Deborah had never told a soul.

She thought about her grandmother, who left Vienna in the early thirties and during the Holocaust lost every single relative still in Europe. "People knew what was happening to the Jews but they kept their mouths shut," she said. "Whenever you see evil, Devorah, you have to find a way to say, 'stop it now.'" In high school Deborah got involved in anti-apartheid rallies and demands for the city of Cleveland to divest any holdings in South Africa. She was just a participant, not a planner.

That day in class, two other students had been the ones to suggest they start a group. "I'll be part of it," Deborah said. "We have to stop it now." Someone applauded and urged them to take that as their name. Professor Davis promised to sponsor them. Within a week, Deborah developed a plan for dorm room sessions to bring in members. When Student Affairs asked them to name a chair, someone wrote in her name.

Since then she'd spent a lot of time thinking about the scope of the problem they faced and how to get the administration to pay attention. She'd talked with three students who'd each been raped by a date. She'd even pictured herself being called to the scene right after an attack. But never had Deborah imagined staring at the black-and-blue torso of her dearest friend.

The first flash from the Polaroid seemed horribly intrusive, followed by the grinding sound of the motor pushing the film out. Still Liddie just sat there, propped up by the pillows, eyes fixed on a book bag across the room. Deborah tried to capture as much of the bruising as she could in just four angles. White-backed photos piled up on her bed, the gruesome images emerging one by one. Deborah followed her father's instructions to the letter, clocking each print on her Timex, peeling off the covers, all the while chattering to Liddie as if they were sharing observations about classes or favorite foods.

"Hey, you guys, what's with the locked door?" The voice belonged to Nancy Minkin, who was still fussing with the doorknob. "I want to hear all about Liddie's date with Mr. Cool."

Deborah shifted her weight so she could get up from the bed without disturbing the pile of photos. *We're not guys!* she wanted to yell. *Mind your own fucking business!*

"We're just hunkering down, Nancy," was what she did manage to say, in a voice that sounded almost normal. "Back to you later."

"Oh my God!" Nancy's voice shifted to a loud whisper. "Is he still in there? You guys are too much!"

Deborah prayed Liddie's zombie-like state prevented her from hearing this. She'd have time later to set Nancy straight.

"Okay," she told Liddie, slipping the hooded sweatshirt over her head. "I'm off to forage for provisions. Back in a flash."

Deborah used the back stairs to run down to the vending machines and began pressing levers almost at random, stuffing bags of chips, sodas, and peanut butter crackers into her backpack. She took the stairs back up, hauling herself hand over hand up the banister, pausing on the fourth-floor landing to bring her breathing under control.

"Here you go," Deborah said as she laid the loot on a desk and offered the items one by one to Liddie, who hadn't moved an inch. With the tiniest turn of her head, Liddie declined them all.

Deborah sank down beside her roommate. "Talk to me, Lid."

"You mean, listen to you." Liddie's voice was still raspy and unnervingly flat, but at least she was talking.

"Oh, Liddie, I'm not trying to pressure you. Please don't feel that way. It's just that I really think we've got enough to nail that motherfucker. Don't you see, you have a *witness*. I saw how he imprisoned you with that stranglehold. I heard you crying. Most men get away with assault because it's their word against the woman's. We can stop him."

Liddie slid down the wall. "And here's what I really think: I'm a nobody going after a somebody. Nothing we do will make a difference."

Five

Washington, DC: Thursday evening, January 28, 2010

If she left after six thirty, the Metro ride home to Takoma Park took exactly thirty-one minutes from Deborah's office in Dupont Circle. Most days she was able to land a seat so she could spend those minutes reviewing briefing papers or scanning articles her staff clipped (how people absorbed documents on a BlackBerry or iPhone was beyond her). But today's pile of readings never even made it out of her tote bag. If that young guy from AFSCME—she never could remember his name—hadn't leaned over to remind her, Deborah would have ridden right through her stop.

Two high school students burst out laughing as Deborah crossed the green across from the Metro station. It took a while to realize they were laughing at *her*—she was muttering: "If you say no, Lid, I say no—I don't care if he turns out to be Dick Fuckin' Cheney." Deborah silenced herself the three blocks to her home, until she made her way to the back door. She surveyed the dregs of her garden, longing to plunge her face into something beautiful. Forecasters had been predicting a bad winter, but so far the snow had been scant. Still, the azaleas were at least two months away. Deborah vowed out loud to purchase a giant bouquet of anemones from the local florist on Saturday.

"Becca, baby, I'm home." Lamps were on in all the downstairs rooms, but no sign of her daughter. From the lights in back, Aaron appeared to be holed away in his office, a converted sun porch behind the kitchen.

"Down in a minute, Ma." It still surprised Deborah to hear her daughter's deep voice; she kept expecting the high tones and soft giggles of Rebecca's younger self.

Deborah was always telling her daughter not to shout up and down the stairs, but today she was anxious to switch her thoughts away from Gillean Mulvaney. "Did you see my email?" she called up. "The essays were nearly flawless—I caught only two typos."

Rebecca's essays had in fact moved her to tears, but Deborah would be careful not to lay it on too thick. At the age of six, Rebecca had heard her mother gushing over a two-year-old cousin's painting and had taken her aside at the first opportunity. "That painting was *not* beautiful, and you know it!" Rebecca said, fingers splayed across her bony hips. Deborah had made a point of going back to the toddler and picking up the drawing again. "I just love that color blue," she'd said this time. Nothing mattered more than having her daughter's trust. Deborah remembered her father patting Deborah's curls and telling her how beautiful she was, when every day the mirror showed features—the nose! the mouth! those eyebrows!—that were by everyone else's account too large. ("You'd be an interesting photography model," Mr. Donleavy, her high school drama teacher, told her once. "There's nothing diminutive about your face! Just stay away from TV.") So how could Deborah believe the other things her father said, about her intelligence and good sense?

In the essay, Rebecca had described years of dance lessons, early rising to practice in the basement, learning to push past exhaustion during late nights at the studio. "When I was fifteen," she wrote, "I figured out I had the will but not the gift. I wasn't going to be that glamorous ballerina I'd pictured for so long. Then, a year later, I came to see that dance should be like hiking or yoga—you don't need to be a 'champion' in order to claim it." Becca went on to say that she considered herself "trilingual, in English, Spanish, and dance," and that she wanted to use dance to teach those who had experienced violence to reconnect with their bodies.

"I grew up in a household where violence is seen as something to combat," she concluded, "a *jeté*, rather than a *plié*. Dance can help survivors soar again."

Deborah had never heard her daughter articulate any of this. The crisis over her lack of a "gift" had in fact been almost paralyzing for Rebecca, transforming their daughter into a sullen teenager cliché prone to sneers, tears, and screaming rants. For fourteen agonizing months, Deborah felt either clumsy or furious whenever she was around her daughter. Then one day Aaron, who remained much cooler about the whole thing, sent a "Rejoice—Becca's back!" text. By unspoken agreement, none of them referred to that period of time. It was absent from the college essay.

"Hey, *Mamele*!" Rebecca entered the kitchen in leaps and stood still long enough for a brief hug. The girl had inherited her mother's build, rather than the long limbs of her father. But her face held the imprint of her dad—flashing eyes, a straight nose with smallish nostrils, dimpled chin—and her hair had his tawny highlights. Deborah once confided to Liddie that she was attracted to Aaron because of his good looks but fell in love with him because *he* was attracted to *her* despite her looks—"a man looking for substance, instead of glam—what a relief!" What Deborah never confided was her other source of relief—that Rebecca had turned out to be so pretty. Feminists shouldn't care, but the world certainly did.

"Thanks for catching those typos, Ma. I always write 'out' when I mean to say 'our.' But I'm pretty confident I will never misspell 'public.' Since you told me that story, I type it *ver-y slow-ly*."

Deborah leaned her hip against her daughter's. "However you typed, sweetie, what you wrote in those essays was incredibly powerful. Made me *kvell*."

Aaron swept into the kitchen, dressed not in his usual jeans and sweater but in a dark-gray suit and electric-blue tie. Whatever grace Rebecca possessed clearly came from her father's side of the family.

"The college apps?" Aaron's eyebrows shot up, as if he'd just learned everyone in DC except for him had gotten free Super Bowl tickets. "When do I get to read them?"

"Read as in proofread, Pa. No comments, no suggestions." She crossed her arms across her chest and looked up at him.

"I can do that." In reality, Aaron had a hard time reading the newspaper without a red pen in hand, but he'd lost this battle with Becca long ago.

"Not one red mark. I totally mean it."

Deborah watched Aaron compose his features as he crossed over to the refrigerator and took out the salmon he'd been marinating. They both tried hard not to show Becca how freaked they were about the idea of her leaving next year. Even though the real reason he worked at home was financial, not parental—since he'd left the PR firm that failed to make him a partner, his revenue didn't justify DC office rents—Aaron treasured the time with his daughter.

"I'll bake the fish, babe," Deborah said. "If you hand me the couscous, I can get that together, too."

"Call me when dinner's ready, okay?" Rebecca hollered as she ran out of the room. "Gabriel García Márquez is waiting in my room, and I don't want to add another minute to his solitude."

As Deborah poured water into the pot and waited for bubbles to form, she decided not to tell Aaron about Gillean Mulvaney just yet. The kitchen contained enough emotion for the time being.

Along with the box of couscous, Aaron held out a bottle of their favorite red wine. "Actually, Ms. Borenstein, I came in here to tell you some good news." He passed her the box and anchored the wine bottle with both hands on the wooden top of the island, as if to keep himself from jumping up and down. "I have a big gig, a US Senate race."

"That's fabulous!" Deborah sent a silent thank-you to the heavens as she hugged Aaron with one hand while stirring couscous in the pot with the other. "Who's the lucky candidate?"

"The DSCC tapped me to lead the Senate campaign of Andrew Plale in Delaware. It'll be a tough race, but I think we can pull it off. Plale has paid his dues—served in the state legislature, two terms in Congress, appeals to moderate voters. He's up against some gazillionaire who'll no doubt try to buy the election. But our guy . . ."

Deborah dropped the empty couscous package on the floor and swooped down to retrieve it before her face gave her away.

“Anyway,” Aaron was saying, “we’re opening a DC office, setting up a war room. I’ll have to spend time in Delaware, but campaign headquarters will be right here on K Street. We’re starting opposition research as we speak. Soon as I have the skinny on the other side, I’d love your help with the women’s groups.” His phone beeped with a text.

“Damn, I have to go,” Aaron said. “Wine when I get home, okay?” He pulled her close for a proper hug and spoke into her hair. “Thanks for sticking with me through the tough times, sweetheart. I think this is the one that’ll bring me back.”

As the back door slammed shut, Deborah heard the hiss of water against the lid of the pot. By the time she reached out to lower the flame, the couscous had already boiled over onto the stove.

SIX

Danforth University: Monday, December 3, 1979

Deborah scrunched the hood of her parka around her face and stomped her feet as she waited behind snow-laden bushes for Will to come out of Simpson Hall. Before Saturday night he'd likely had no idea who she was, but she didn't want to take any chances today, not after he'd stared right at her. She'd never forget that icy stare—"bedroom eyes," that was his fucking *nickname*, he'd probably been told that all his life. Six months ago Deborah would have been flabbergasted to learn that someone so handsome was involved in a rape. Surely a guy like that could get any woman he wanted. Now she understood that "what rapists wanted" required a category of its own.

"It's the difference between winning and vanquishing," Professor Davis had told them.

"Yeah, but isn't it still about sex?" someone asked.

"Actually," Professor Davis replied, "it's about power and humiliation."

Deborah knew today's mission was probably foolish, but it might be her only shot. Liddie wasn't budging on pressing charges or even going to the student health center. Somehow Deborah had to scare Will enough to get him to leave Danforth in exchange for not being prosecuted. It wouldn't be enough, not by a long shot, but it would be some measure of justice. And Liddie would never have to see or hear of him again.

Although she had no troops and little ammunition, Deborah figured she had two things going for her: some intel and the gift of gab. For starters, she knew Will Quincy was in Liddie's art history class in Simpson Hall Monday Wednesday Friday at 9:00—that's how they'd met—and that he was the only male in the class. This meant there was a chance his frat brothers wouldn't be coming out of the building with him. In fact, Delta Omega members had a reputation for scheduling no classes before noon. One of the Stop It Now core group, Janie Dembrowski, had a half brother who'd pledged there. Adam Dembrowski boasted about the seniors who helped underclassmen select their courses to maintain this perfect schedule. "If God meant us to go to class early," Adam said, "He wouldn't have created hangovers."

After Deborah finished snapping the photos the previous day, Liddie alternated between a near-catatonic state and what appeared to be sleep. The RA on their floor bought the story that Liddie was suffering from a bad flu and wrote out a permission slip for Deborah to bring food from the cafeteria. She carted back apple juice, a gallon of chicken soup, packs of Saltines and oyster crackers and melba toast, mashed potatoes, whatever comfort food she could carry. So far Liddie had consumed little more than water and some bouillon with an occasional Saltine, the crackling of the paper reverberating in the painfully quiet space. When Deborah offered to tell the flu story the next day to Liddie's professors and pick up assignments, Liddie hadn't refused—meaning, she didn't shut her eyes and point her chin ever so slightly to the right, the way she did each time Deborah offered any sort of nourishment.

At some point Sunday evening, it started snowing again. Deborah slipped on her parka and took a walk all the way down to the gorge. Better to be buffeted by icy fingers of wind than by Liddie's silence. Deborah longed to talk to other members of Stop It Now, but she worried that someone like Janie Dembrowski would demand they take action against Will, regardless of what Liddie wanted. "One woman says, 'No way, my parents would kill me if they found out I'd been drinking,' and five more get raped by the same asshole," Janie would argue. For the first two months, the group had this debate over and over. Finally, Deborah insisted they take a vote. Janie decided to stay involved even though she lost—but Deborah never shared information about any rape they heard about where the target chose not to go public.

On the way back from the gorge, Deborah had to spin out of the way of a runner who was so in the groove, he never saw her on the path. One foot slid out from under her, and she landed hard on her tailbone. "Dumb-ass motherfucker! Selfish goddamn prick!" Deborah shrieked her rage at the unknown racer, at a universe that didn't give a fuck about fairness. The cold seeping into her jeans finally drove her to get off her ass; that's when she came up with the idea to confront Will after class the next morning.

She also decided to end things with Brad. When he called as usual that afternoon at two o'clock, she told him she couldn't talk because Liddie was ill. In her heart, she already knew what his response would be when he found out what had happened: "Oh, puh-leeze. How stupid could she be?"

At 9:52 a.m., Will Quincy emerged from Simpson Hall. He was wearing a sheepskin shearling jacket, nothing faux about it, the light color showing off a tan that meant he was probably on the slopes all during Thanksgiving break. His hair, Robert Redford dirty blond, was covered by an extrathick stocking cap, deep brown, no doubt made to order. Deborah's heart nearly stopped when she saw Will was talking to a female student who looked up at him with her mouth open. "Wow," she said, "thanks so much. I'd love to. Uh, I have to go back in for archaeology class. Thanks again. See you Saturday."

The second the coed went back inside the building, Deborah crossed the path so she was walking right next to Will. Given how easy it would be for him to outrun her, especially with her sore tailbone, she had planned her remarks to get his attention right away.

"I imagine going to jail is not high on your list of 'things I want to do before I graduate,'" she said.

Deborah had prepared herself for swearing, spitting, even shoving. The one thing she hadn't anticipated was being laughed at. Loudly.

Last month Professor Davis, the faculty advisor for Stop It Now, had helped them role-play how to handle hecklers as the group prepared for a presentation at the Broome. Deborah memorized the key points: Pay attention to body language. Stand tall, shoulders back. Keep your voice steady and devoid of emotion.

"Laugh all you want, William." Deborah hoped that name conjured visions of parents or grandparents. "I hear prisoners reserve a special welcome for rich-boy rapists with pretty eyes. Most of them couldn't care less about the rape. It's the rich part that gets them."

Will turned his body and looked her up and down. "Hey, I get it. Really, I do. You're jealous that your roommate's getting some and you're not. Don't despair. I know guys who'll take a blow job from anyone."

Deborah longed for dagger-like fingernails like Nancy Minkin's, so she could rake them across that disgustingly smug face.

"Or maybe you're just jealous that Liddie has the hots for guys and not for you," Will said. "Well, I hate to disappoint you, sister, but your dream girl is no virgin and she's certainly no lesbo."

All the way back to the dorm the night before, Deborah pumped herself up with comebacks to whatever snide remarks he might throw at her, including that old Ginger Rogers line "Too bad your mother never had any children." But here in the thick of it, Deborah knew she had to stay focused on one thing only—getting Will to see the likelihood that their side would prevail.

"Rape is forced, nonconsensual sexual intercourse," she told him in a voice that might have been instructing him in the earth's axis of rotation. "In this case there is a witness, there are photos of the injuries, and there is a university that does not want bad publicity. Listen very carefully. You are being given a get-out-of-jail card. All you have to do is leave Danforth. You can say you want to explore the world, travel for a semester, finish at some other school. In the scheme of things, that's a minor inconvenience. And much, much better than you deserve."

Deborah had spent most of the night in bed with a flashlight working on this speech. She struggled with whether to describe it as a onetime offer, to make it seem as if it were coming directly from Liddie. But before Deborah could utter another word, Will leaned down until his face was only inches away.

"Liddie wanted it," he whispered. "She wanted it bad. Such a shame you had to come back early and interrupt us." He turned on his heel and began an easy lope across the quad.

Seven

Washington, DC: Friday, January 29, 2010

The executive committee conference call was set for two o'clock Eastern time. That morning Deborah had to fend off phone scoldings from Catherine Snyder in DC and from Angela Treat in Boston, the board members Gillean had set her sights on. The woman was like a goddamn metal detector—she'd zoned in on the two biggest donors on the executive committee, the ones most aligned with the view Marquita described as "build the buzz."

"The funders love publicity," Catherine liked to say. "They want their money to translate into influence—something visible they can point to. We need more high-profile stories featuring quotes from our director. Deborah Borenstein must both represent and become our brand."

Marquita, like Deborah, preferred the organization to build its base and promote local leaders.

Deborah had confided in Marquita right after Gillean stormed out the day before. They would have talked on Wednesday after Amanda Pruitt's visit, but there were Becca's essays to proofread and a letter of inquiry due to a new funder. By the time Deborah came up for air, Marquita had taken off to drive her dad to his weekly poker game. "He throws his little money away like the big damn fool he is,"

Marquita once said. "And I chauffeur him there, like the bigger damn fool I am."

Now she huddled with Deborah on the girlfriend couch, preparing for the conference call. Deborah had convinced Catherine and Angela to let the whole executive committee discuss what to do about Gillean Mulvaney's demands for information.

"I feel like Play-Doh," Deborah said. "People are pulling me in so many different directions, it'll be a miracle if I don't end up in useless little shreds."

"Get over yourself, DB. If you wanted simple, you shoulda picked another line of work."

"You don't know the half of it. Guess who's been hired by Quincy's opponent—Mr. Aaron 'I Need a Serious Gig Yesterday' Minkin."

Marquita raised her right eyebrow. "Did the campaign know about your connection with Quincy?"

"I can't see how. But it won't take long for Gillean Mulvaney to find out this new development, and once she does, she'll get to Aaron faster than . . . than some expression I'm too zapped to recall." Deborah lifted her hair off her neck. Her new, layered look was flattering ("Finally, you're calling more attention to your cheekbones and eyes!" her mother had so kindly pointed out), but she missed being able to shove her mane into a ponytail.

"He already assumes I'll help him get women's groups on board because he needs a win and he knows I know that. Argh!" Deborah let out a mini-version of the office scream, usually reserved for bad rulings in rape cases. She'd made sure she was asleep when Aaron came home last night and slipped out of bed long before he woke up. But starting at noon, he'd been leaving text messages on her cell every fifteen minutes.

"Save the pity party for later," Marquita said. "We need you to focus."

Deborah shook her head back and forth in a futile attempt to erase the faces that haunted her, faces as vivid as if she'd seen them last week: Will Quincy's smirk on the quad, Liddie's empty eyes the day after the rape.

"You know you can count on Yomara and Della," Marquita was

saying. "And you get a vote, too, if it comes to that. For today, at least, you should be okay."

Yomara Vasquez in Brooklyn and Della Wells in Chicago, the other two members of the executive committee, represented the younger activists Deborah had been cultivating over the past five years, most of them women of color. They favored trips to high schools and community colleges, followed by home visits, along with creative use of new media. The results were a mix of educational activities, leadership circles, public policy work, and in-your-face confrontations about street harassment and sexual assault featuring Twitter feeds and videos on YouTube. They didn't rake in big donations, but they garnered lots of small ones. In those cities and four others, local chapters of Breaking the Silence had grown a cadre of male activists who made it a priority to reach out to youths in congregations, sports venues, wherever, and get them to sign a pledge: "I will treat all women with the same respect I would want for my mother or my sister."

Deborah and Marquita agreed the best tactic was to let Yomara and Della make the case, having Deborah speak only when necessary. The question remained: Would it be overkill to have Marquita on the call as well?

"I want you on as a member of the leadership team," Deborah said. "There's precedent for it. You don't get a vote, but no reason you shouldn't have a say."

Marquita crossed her arms under her breasts and hugged her sides.

"Excuse me," Deborah said, "but do you have any idea when the real Marquita is showing up? Because if she has something to say, she'd spit it out." *Even when it rips you to pieces*, Deborah thought but refrained from adding.

The cell phone played Stevie Wonder's "I Just Called to Say I Love You"—Aaron. Deborah silenced the ringer.

"All right, let me lay it out for you in black and white." Marquita, arms still crossed, leaned her elbow on the arm of the couch. "Catherine and Angela see me as your little sidekick. Neither of them has ever talked to me alone. As in, *never.* They don't think I have a life separate from you, much less a thought. Whatever comes out of my mouth, they're going to think you wrote the script."

"And I should cater to that view why?"

"I'd be happy if you just saw it."

It took a few rounds for Marquita to agree to join the conference call but strictly on her terms. She would facilitate and try to maintain a neutral stance, intervening only to make sure everyone had a chance to express herself. While she was laying out that role, Deborah wondered how much she had contributed to the sidekick stereotype. On a page in her notebook devoted to Things to Think About, Deborah wrote "blind spot" in a large rectangle.

For the hour until the call, Deborah drafted handwritten notes to seven donors, had a mentoring session with the intern Shari to evaluate her resume, and made arrangements for dinner with Aaron at their favorite Indian place in Cleveland Park—he'd be careful about raising his voice there. "Stuck in meetings," she texted. "Indique @ 7 xoxo."

At two o'clock, Deborah pushed the phone closer to Marquita's chair and pressed the speaker button.

"As I understand it," Marquita told the callers, "we're trying to resolve a difference of opinion about how to handle an inquiry to the ED from an investigative reporter. The reporter also contacted Catherine and Angela. As usual, comments on this call are confidential and each of you is encouraged to speak with respect but without reserve. Deborah, why don't you start?"

Deborah began by thanking everyone for taking the time to join the call. "Gillean Mulvaney thinks I can corroborate an anonymous source implicating an industrialist named William Quincy in a 1979 rape at Danforth. The target of the assault was a very close friend of mine. Without going into any detail, I'll just say that the incident caused this woman considerable harm." Deborah pressed her hand to her stomach, as if the guilt roiling there might be audible otherwise. "Out of respect for her privacy, I did not and will not speak with Ms. Mulvaney."

Marquita asked Angela Treat to go next.

"I get that many people would feel this way, Deborah." Angela, whose parents were founding members of Jack and Jill of America and had sent their daughter to elite private schools and camps for black girls, spoke colloquially only to patronize. "But the willingness to name names is what makes our organization different. We've urged countless women who've contacted us to come forward. The concept is embedded in the way this organization announces itself to the world. For our executive director to remain silent in an instance like this would be a breach of the highest order."

Catherine jumped in, even though Marquita had not called on her. "Let's be clear what's at stake here. The man is running for political office. We're talking about being responsible for having a rapist in the US Senate." Gillean Mulvaney must have sent Catherine her talking points.

"May I go next?" Yomara was great at conveying strong emotions without breaking a sweat. "Every time I go out to speak, I make this point: We help women break the silence when that's *empowering* to them. I show my video on the hypocrisy of the media who dump shame on the person raped, rather than the rapist. We will never go back on that."

"But that's exactly what we'll be doing if Deborah refuses to speak up now," Catherine said.

Marquita had written "Interruption Log" on a sheet of paper. She drew a check under Catherine's name. "We'll come back to you after Yomara finishes and Della has a chance to speak," she said. "Yomara?"

"To me, it's like saying because we believe in nongendered roles, we won't allow our daughters to slip on a dress or play with dolls. You can't punish women for the culture not moving fast enough. Whether or not to step forward and name names has to be left to each individual."

"Abso-fucking-lutely," Della said. Deborah tried to picture Catherine's lips pinched with distaste. "If women don't decide freely, how does that build power?"

"Did your college roommate decide freely that her former rapist should end up in the US Senate?" Catherine asked.

Deborah filed away the information that Gillean had told them Liddie was her college roommate. Catherine hadn't heard that on this call.

"The woman involved is still my very dear friend."

"So you've talked to her since Gillean came to see you?" Catherine's voice had become shriller with each utterance.

"Well, no, but . . ."

"And who made you God in this situation?"

Deborah mouthed a silent scream. Marquita quickly reminded everyone of the ground rules. "It sounds like we have consensus that the woman involved should be the one to decide whether or not this story comes out," Marquita said. "Deborah, are you able to reach her and report back to us by next Monday, February first?"

This was not the outcome Deborah had anticipated.

"I'll be glad to talk to her, if she's reachable," Deborah said—knowing full well Liddie had built her life so she'd have no reason to travel from her small Wisconsin town. "Let's plan another call on Monday."

Marquita ended by getting each person to agree they would not discuss the matter with anyone for the present and would not mention it in emails, even to each other. Who knew how low Gillean Mulvaney would stoop?

"I find it difficult to believe that she has the ability to hack into our system," Angela protested.

"Oh, she doesn't need to do it herself," Deborah said. "This is someone who would have no compunction about using hackers—and certainly seems capable of lining them up."

Marquita reminded the group that they had adopted this same policy in other controversial situations. And that was that.

Except for dinner with Aaron. And the call to Liddie. And the inevitable follow-up from Gillean Mulvaney.

Eight

Danforth University: Friday, December 7, 1979

By Friday Liddie still hadn't returned to classes or to the cafeteria, although she had been nibbling at the soup and crackers Deborah brought back every day. The assignment folders grew fatter on the desk. Mostly Liddie slept or knit; a prodigious pile of Christmas gift scarves, one for each of her fourteen first cousins, blossomed on the floor next to the bed.

On top of everything else, Deborah had taken on sentinel duty, dishing out daily reports and keeping at bay inquiring friends and authorities, most notably Nancy Minkin ("Whaddaya mean I can't see her? I'll wear a mask!") and Nora Jankowski, their RA ("As a dorm leader, I'm concerned for Liddie's health and also for the danger of this flu spreading to others on the floor"). Today Nora was particularly insistent about speaking to Liddie directly.

"Like I told you," Deborah said, "Liddie's been checking with her doctor at home. She's had this kind of virus before. There's not much you can do besides resting and keeping well hydrated. Apparently it's not airborne, and we're both being very careful. She uses only the bathroom stall you designated for her." Nora had plastered a sign on that door: AVOID CONTAGION. USE ANOTHER STALL.

Nora, a broad-shouldered woman from Skanteatales, New York, held on to her elbows as she peered down at Deborah outside the dorm room. "Luckily, no one else has gotten sick yet, but that's not the only problem. Liddie's profs have been very accommodating, but exams are *next week*! If she's not well enough to take them, she has to have an *official doctor's note*. We all care about Liddie. But we've also *never* had a Martha Hillerman student *flunk exams*."

Liddie seemed oblivious to the noise in the hall and to the deadlines. Deborah, on the other hand, was ready to pop. All week she'd tiptoed around the elephant in the room, an amazing feat considering that she left those confines only to squeeze in her own classes, gobble down meals and bring soups back for Liddie, and sneak calls to Claire Rawlings, the rape crisis counselor in Rochester.

Deborah made the first call on Tuesday morning. "I really need your help," she told Claire after filling her in. "I just want to support Liddie, but I'm in way over my head."

"Funny how that works, eh?" Claire had moved from Toronto when her husband got a job at the University of Rochester. From what she'd told them, the Canadians seemed way ahead in building an effective movement against sexual assault. "Easier to think of rape survivors in the abstract. Real ones are so much messier."

According to Claire, the skipping-classes thing was understandable. There was no way Liddie could go to Art History three times that week without running into Will. And even though the rest of their courses didn't overlap, even though the campus was huge and you could go a whole semester without seeing someone you knew if he didn't sit in the same classroom or live on your floor, the possibility of a Will sighting lurked everywhere. Deborah herself had already spotted him, less than twenty-four hours after her failed ambush.

"She's completely collapsed!" Deborah said in her second call on Wednesday.

"She's been raped," Claire replied.

By Thursday's call, Deborah was feeling desperate about how to keep all the secrets and spin all the lies. "I'm freaked out that she might blow her scholarship," Deborah confided. "But I'm also worried about my own grades, and I don't want to lay that on Liddie."

"Which is why you're standing in a pay booth in the bitter cold, calling me," Claire said. "So give yourself some credit. You're doing fine."

"I haven't told you the worst thing." Deborah hunched over in the booth, fingering the roll of quarters waiting to be fed into the slot. "Half the time I just want to shake Liddie and scream at her. If you only knew her—she's tough as nails and really perceptive. I can't bear to watch her give Will this much power!'"

Claire, who never sighed or scolded, now said twice, "I need you to listen carefully." Deborah pictured that round, shiny face nodding slightly to reinforce the point. "Liddie's not giving this guy anything. The problem is that women in this situation have entirely too little power to begin with. Confusing those two things only adds to the feeling of having no control. Don't be mad at yourself for what you might think—but keep following your better instincts."

Deborah unleashed tears of frustration, relieved to have this one outlet where she didn't have to hold it all together. "But we have *evidence*, Claire. We have exactly what most women lack."

"Yes, and that's great, and Liddie may decide to come forward because of that. But, as you know, there's no guarantee. The system is not on our side here."

"Isn't that just why we need Liddie to press charges?" When she'd visited Danforth, Claire had stressed how important it was for groups like theirs to get a win and then use it to force the administration to take more action to prevent assaults in the first place.

"Right now we have to focus on what Liddie needs. She needs information about her options, and she needs support for whatever decision she makes."

Liddie, however, wasn't asking for info or support. By noon on Friday, Deborah decided she had to at least open the conversation. First she went through her usual mantra of *I know you need some breathing room and I don't want you to feel pressured and above all I want you to make up your own mind*. She prayed it didn't sound canned.

Liddie's knitting needles kept up their clacking.

"Look, Lid, I'm sure you heard Nora—we're approaching D-day. Tell me what I can do to help."

"Nothing, DB."

This had been Liddie's answer to every topic Deborah brought up that week: "What do you want to eat?" "What else can I bring you?" "What do you need?"

Deborah scooped up the pile of scarves, a cornucopia of colors and patterns—burgundies looped with bright orange, violet criss-crossed with pale yellow, none of them strictly perpendicular. "These are absolutely gorgeous, Liddie. You have so much talent, and you're so close." The textile design major was very selective. Liddie would be one of only twelve students chosen—it was why she had come to Danforth—but blowing off finals would wreck that faster than Nancy Minkin's nails unraveling a design in progress.

"It's okay." *Click-clack.* "I know what's what." *Click-clack.* "I'm going home."

Deborah hugged the scarves to her chest in hopes of keeping her voice at a normal register. "Home for winter break or home for good?"

Liddie's sigh sent a flutter through the yarn. "Will graduates in June. I can come back next year."

Deborah moved to her own bed and made a show of smoothing the scarf fabric, some blend that felt like cashmere. All week she'd been thinking of her roommate as absent, tucked away somewhere, when in fact Liddie had been present all along, stitching plans as she put together those scarves—just not the plans Deborah had hoped to hear.

Surely Liddie knew the prospects as well as Deborah did. Each night Deborah was awakened by Liddie's low moans or twitching limbs; each morning when Liddie went to the bathroom, Deborah quietly took a pair of sweat-soaked sheets down to the washer and threw another set on the bed. Will or no Will, even if Liddie got an apartment off campus, Danforth would always be the backdrop to those long nights of tormented sleep—unless she changed the ending to this story.

"For some women," Claire had said, "speaking up changes everything. Keeping silent just reinforces the notion that the victim is to blame. But for others, it can be disastrous—if no one believes you, if you bring a charge and lose, it can feel like being attacked all over again."

Deborah's nails were bitten down to the quick. Talk about a catch-22. The college didn't think sexual assault was a problem, because there were so few reports. And women would never step up until they believed their complaint would be taken seriously.

"I can't bear to see him drive you out of here, Lid. He's the one who's gotta go."

"You mean press charges." The needles had fallen silent.

"That's an option," Deborah said, as if the file folder on the desk were full of choices, instead of assignments, and this was merely one.

For the first time all week, Liddie climbed out of bed and stood face-to-face with Deborah. "I know you want to slay the dragon, but let's move out of Mythology 101 and into That's Life in the Big Bad World. I'd been drinking that frat-party punch, knocking it back—everybody saw me. I let him kiss me; in fact, I was wildly flattered that he wanted to. There may be hay sticking out of my hair, but even a dumb girl from the sticks oughta know what a guy wants when he starts talking about coming up to your room to see your Rilke. No one will believe me. Except you, of course, and your mighty Amazon warriors. Something the administration would no doubt use against me."

Deborah didn't know it could hurt to breathe. "C'mon, Lid."

Liddie kept her eyes trained on Deborah's. "C'mon, what?"

Back in Cleveland, Deborah had a younger cousin, Lyle, born with what his mother called "developmental delays." He was a total brat, but Deborah's parents made sure she and her brother never reacted to his antics, not even the time he smashed the transistor radio she'd saved up for with her babysitting money. Deborah's insides were twisted with the same kind of resentment over having to bite her tongue now—and the same kind of guilt for even harboring that thought.

"You know that's not fair."

"Of course it is." Liddie, who'd looked pale and unsteady when she first got up, straightened her spine and assumed the role of the universal bureaucrat: "'Miss Golmboch, is it not true that your roommate heads a group that focuses on sexual assault? Are you to have us believe that Miss Borenstein, who distributes flyers all over campus with this information, wouldn't have supplied you with the phone number of the police or the health clinic?'"

"But I'd explain all that, Liddie—how I wanted to take you and you refused. We'd get Claire Rawlings to come back down here, and Professor Davis—they'll testify about how few women report a rape, and why. I understand you're worried about your parents, but they don't have to be told—the proceedings can go forward with complete confidentiality. No one has to know unless you want them to."

Liddie sank back down on the side of her bed. "You think Will isn't going to flood the room with his fraternity brothers?"

In her ear, Deborah heard Claire's low-key phone voice: "Don't overpromise. Be a good listener."

"It's bad enough to be stupid that night," Liddie said. "Bringing charges for the principle of it would make me an official idiot." She looked up at Deborah with cheeks hollowed out by the week's liquid diet. "I don't think I can bear to lose twice."

Deborah reached out and lightly held Liddie's hand. "This isn't about standing on principle, Lid. I believe in my gut that you can win—I'd never say a word if I didn't. Plus, there's so much at stake for you. Will they really hold your scholarship till next year if you just disappear?"

She felt Liddie's hand tremble.

"Listen. I don't care if *you* invited *him* out, put your tongue down his throat, and were grinding up against him. The kiss, the alcohol—none of that gives anyone the right to rape." Deborah found herself speeding up, as if the faster the words came out, the more likely they were to convince Liddie. "But that's not even the main defense here. It's not your word against his. I walked in, I heard you gasping for air, I saw him, I witnessed that stranglehold. And we have photos, Liddie, with dates on them."

"And you've argued how many cases, Madam Litigator?" Liddie snatched her hand away.

Deborah resisted the urge to wheel around and march out of the room. "I know I'm not an expert, Liddie, but we've been researching this for the last six months. Look, I hate that motherfucker. I do want him punished. But most of all, I don't want you to sacrifice your dreams because of what he did."

Liddie dropped down to the mattress. Her eyes, normally hazel, had turned a dull brown, the flesh beneath them sunken and baggy. She held up her palms and shrugged, like a child being asked to choose between missing her best friend's party and giving up her favorite doll.

Deborah pulled over her desk chair and talked softly about the complaint procedure. "You're right, they'll want to know whether you went to the clinic or called the police, and why not if you didn't. But Claire Rawlings has expertise on this—she has three years at the Rochester Rape Crisis Center; she's appeared in two other cases."

Thankfully, Liddie didn't ask what Claire's win record was. Deborah knew—zero for two. She also knew that Liddie's reasons for not seeking help were absolutely typical. The university hadn't done a fucking thing to educate students about rapes like this, not a word on how to avoid it or report it, much less a single step to stop it. Still, the last thing Liddie needed right now was for Deborah to get on her high horse.

Liddie's sigh seemed to boomerang around the room. "It seems so much easier just to let it alone," she said.

Deborah leaned in close to Liddie but did not touch her. "There's one other thing, Lid. I'm positive you're not the only one Will's done this to. Just the other day I saw him hitting on a student who looked like she wasn't even eighteen, had to be a first-year. Who knows how many rapes you can prevent if you get him out of here?"

Liddie's breath quickened as she buried her face in her hands.

An hour later, she walked with Deborah down to the office of the dean of student services.

Nine

Washington, DC: Friday evening, January 29, 2010

As soon as the host led Deborah to her husband's table at Indique, she knew that Gillean Mulvaney had hit her mark. For starters, Aaron was seated in the back corner of the restaurant's second story. Usually he chose a table close to the door, even if he had to wait (he called it "client watch"); in the summer months, he'd find a table on the sidewalk patio. Also, he'd clearly arrived early and already ordered his favorite dishes, lamb vindaloo and chicken biryani—normally Aaron made fun of men who made decisions for their wives. The wine bottle on the table was half empty. Both the text and email lights on his BlackBerry were flashing. His eyes were not flashing. His limp tie was slung over an adjoining chair.

"She called."

Deborah slid into the chair across from her husband and unbuttoned her coat. Although she opened her mouth, Aaron waved a slice of garlic naan to signal he was just getting started.

"Unlike you, my beloved, I am eager to share every detail of my life. So let's see, where did we leave off?" Aaron chewed the same way he did everything, with gusto. "As I told you last night, I went to meet with my team. Very good group, includes that guy we call Spacey 'cause he looks just like Kevin Spacey, receding hairline and all, headed up Doug Hollander's campaign, along with the usual suspects—no pun intended!—plus two interns from the D Triple C, social-networking whiz kids." Aaron paused only to drain his wineglass, which he promptly refilled.

Deborah remembered the first time she'd heard someone say "D Triple C"; she'd thought it was a crude way of referring to some woman with large breasts. Aaron was the one who explained it meant "Democratic Congressional Campaign Committee."

"Anyway, they'd already begun doing opposition research before they hired me. You should see the file on this William Harrison Quincy III. Goes all the way back to prep school, Exeter, big sports guy, not so great in the grades department but then who cares? Legacy at Danforth, auditorium named after his granddaddy. You overlapped with him a couple of years, but it's a big place, I'm thinking, not likely someone you'd have hung around with—fraternity guy, lacrosse, scads of family money."

The spicy scents from the lamb were beginning to turn Deborah's stomach. She pushed the dish to the center of the table.

"Funny, though, in the back of my mind, I started thinking about that story of what happened to your roommate at college. I dunno, something about the wealthy ancestors, the frat house, lacrosse—'course, that coulda fit a lot of guys, but an antenna went up, you know what I mean?" Unlike Deborah, Aaron's appetite seemed to grow with the story. He scooped up some chicken on his naan and shoveled it into his mouth.

"Over all these years, I've learned to trust those instincts, play any hunches, leave no stone unturned—that sort of thing." When Becca still let them read her papers, Aaron circled any cliché for immediate attention. "So I put in a call to my sister. I know we never discussed the incident with her, all her resentment that you hadn't confided in her from the beginning, blah, blah, but you know, she and I had talked about it a couple times over the years, just the two of us."

The clatter of dishes and voices of other diners disappeared into what felt like the bellow of those last words. It was Nancy Minkin who'd encouraged her brother to seek Deborah out when she moved to DC. Nancy was the only woman on their floor Deborah had told about the incident, but as far as Deborah knew, Nancy had never mentioned it to her family—though not because she didn't want her parents to worry or because she thought the whole thing was too sordid. Back in 1979, Nancy had her own reasons: "Don't worry," she'd promised Deborah, "I'll never breathe a word, certainly not to my folks. All they'd hear is that men are allowed up on the floors, a fact I've bent over backward to keep from them. Boom—the parents ship me off to Bryn Mawr or some other all-girls school. Virginity trumps husband hunting any day."

After Deborah and Aaron became a couple, she had talked to him about the assault, avoiding Will's name—she'd vowed never to speak it again if she could help it. She actually planned the conversation, saved it not for a quiet dinner or an after-sex embrace but for a winter hike at Rock Creek Park, where she laid out in some detail what happened and how the whole episode had transformed her life. In all these years she had never discussed the issue again with Nancy, not at family get-togethers or on the phone or over email. Deborah didn't know what bothered her more—that Aaron had felt the need to talk to his sister about it, or that he'd failed to mention those conversations to his wife.

"Anyhoo, Nancy confirmed the name of the rapist interrupted—or would that be rapist interrupt-us? Whatever, he's the very same guy I'm up against now who wants to represent the great state of Delaware in the Senate of the United States of America." Aaron's face remained relaxed, as if he were sharing amusing observations from a campaign kickoff party. "Not that Nancy had a clue about his candidacy. Reads the Style section, thank you very much, television stays tuned to those home-decorating foodie-guru channels. So I didn't say a lot about that, just pumped her for some backstory on the guy. And she went on and on about what a hunk little Will Quincy had been, how all the girls had a crush on him, such gorgeous eyes, the whole schmear." Aaron paused for a giant helping of dal.

Deborah shifted in her chair. "Aaron, for God's sake . . ."

"Yeah, she said no one on your floor could believe Liddie had snagged a date with him. Not that Liddie was a loser or anything, Nancy hastened to point out, just that she wasn't a looker and rich playboys didn't usually go for scholarship gals whose work-study included clearing trash off tables in the cafeteria, that sort of thing."

Deborah didn't realize she'd been swiveling her water glass until she upended it. Aaron grabbed his napkin and one from an unused plate on the table to sop up the water before it cascaded onto his wife's lap. She could hurl the water from the other glass in Aaron's face, Deborah assured herself. She could tell him to shut up, or she could simply get up and walk away. For right now, she threw her own napkin at the damp tablecloth and waited for him to get to the real point of this exercise.

"You know Nancy—she piled it on about how she'd been worried sick all week when Liddie never came out of her room, how hurt she was that you'd excluded her, given all the times she'd been there for the two of you, yada yada yada, and of course how devastated she was every time she thought about what poor Liddie had been through. And this is interesting . . ." Aaron twisted in his seat and signaled their server, a skinny guy with a wilted ponytail who happened to be two tables away, to refill their water glasses. Her husband had the sixth sense of a spy—or a political operative.

Aaron waited until the server confirmed that everything was satisfactory—"Tip-top!" Aaron insisted—and moved on. "Nancy said she never knew exactly what happened. Her guess was that you and your group must have pushed Liddie to file charges, which Nancy thought was 'totally hopeless.'" Aaron dabbed the air with fake quote marks, a practice he typically disdained. "Whatever the case, clearly the guy walked. My sister hated to see a guy like that get off scot-free."

You didn't have to be a genius to see where this was going. The thought of Gillean Mulvaney sitting down to schmooze with Nancy Minkin at her brother's request made Deborah peel off her jacket and keep her arms locked at her sides to prevent the sweat stains from showing. "Enough!" she said, feeling her jaw contract with the effort of not raising her voice.

"Almost caught up with my day, toots. So here I am, my hunch confirmed, wondering what to do with this information, when lo and behold, in walks the grande dame—okay, maybe not so grande, but you get my drift—of investigative reporting, Ms. Gillean Mulvaney herself. The kind of person you're not likely to forget or disremember. Which is why I was so knocked-off-my-ass surprised—not when she told me her reason for being there, but the fact that she'd hand-delivered this very news directly to you just yesterday and you hadn't bitten, nor had you said word one about the visit to me! I tried to cover that up. You know me—didn't want her to think the wifie had disrespected me by neglecting to share such a huge piece of news. Not that I care what Gillean Mulvaney thinks."

An older Indian couple took the table next to theirs. Aaron leaned closer to her and lowered his voice to a whisper. Deborah glued her eyes to his Adam's apple and imagined herself stuffing her napkin right down his throat.

"What I do care about, Deb, is winning this goddamn campaign. What I care about is making sure we don't lose the Senate because a motherfucking rapist buys his way into the chamber, when a word from my *wife*—that would be the woman married to the campaign director of this guy's opponent—could stop him before he even gets out of the gate."

Aaron's lips were now so close to her head, the whisper felt like a rod of molten heat jammed straight into her ear. Deborah snapped her head back and shifted her chair closer to the wall. She could feel the slightly embossed wallpaper behind her ear.

"This isn't about you, Aaron."

"Oh, it's about me, all right." For the first time, Aaron stopped fiddling with his food. His face had folded into a grimace, as if the meal were setting off an ulcer. "It's about standing up for me and for our marriage. But it's also about standing up for principle."

"Gillean Mulvaney has as much connection with principle as I have with pig roasts."

Aaron shoved both hands into his mop of hair, still thick, still a rich, honeyed brown almost untouched by gray. Deborah had been dyeing her hair for nearly ten years.

"I get it, Deb. Gillean's on a tear and she's not going to stop till she has what she wants. So she's not goddamn Saint Teresa. Who gives a fuck?" Aaron's sigh seemed to leave him deflated, as if he could no longer sustain that level of outrage. The Indian woman, face hidden behind her napkin, turned just her eyes to glance at him. "Look, babe, if you don't speak to her, she'll find someone who will. Why not get the credit? It'll mean kudos for the organization. Donors will love it. It'll strengthen your hand against whoever on the board wants to rein you in. And yes, sure, it will mean a lot to me." For the first time that night, Aaron gazed into her eyes. "Is that such a bad thing? I need this. Even more, I need you."

For Deborah, Aaron was always hardest to resist when he appeared vulnerable. She reached for his right hand, stroking the knuckles back and forth in sync with her breathing so she could keep her voice low.

"And what I need is for you to hear me, sweetheart. You already know what I'm about to tell you. You know how much I'm rooting for you. You know how I despise that snake. Picturing him in the Senate makes me want to puke." Deborah swallowed hard to keep back the bile that rose in her esophagus every time she heard Will's name.

"But I have one overriding interest here," she said. "It's Liddie. Any version of the story where we make this public—all I see are TV anchors thrusting microphones and camera lenses in Liddie's face, hollering questions, camping beside her dogwood trees, and Will making snarky comments about how she wanted it, begged for it . . ." Deborah shuddered so hard, Aaron reached over and wrapped her jacket around her shoulders.

"You don't have to mention Liddie's name."

"Exactly. I don't have to, because Gillean Mulvaney already has it. And because Will would name her in a heartbeat."

Suddenly Aaron stood up, all six feet of him, to slide his wallet out of his pocket. The server had crept up behind them with the check and a Styrofoam box for the leftovers on Deborah's plate. Aaron quickly transferred the rest of the food before taking his seat and pushing his chair even closer to her. The server was reciting tonight's specials to the couple at the next table.

"Trust me on this, hon. This is my job; I know how these things work. I can get Gillean to leave Liddie's name out if that's your condition. No sweat. Whatever William Quincy III wants to say, he has handlers and they'll make him keep his mouth shut. This is the kind of story you don't touch other than to say, 'We regret our opponents are resorting to outrageous falsehoods about the distant past, rather than programmatic remedies for the future. We will not dignify the story with a response.' Hell, I could write the goddamn press release."

The sky, already dark when she'd arrived here, seemed pitch black against the streetlights out the window. There was snow in the forecast, but not a flake had fallen, unlike that day on the quad when she'd hidden behind mounds of snow, waiting for Will. How to translate to Aaron the sounds from that day: Will's cackle, his voice loaded with sarcasm, his too-close whisper? These had made up the soundtrack of Deborah's nightmares for thirty years.

"I was there, Aaron. I saw this guy at work. Handlers or no handlers, he'd find a way to leak something about Liddie, knowing she'd never respond to the smears. And even if you're right, there's no way to convince Liddie that reporters wouldn't get wind of her identity. She's worked so hard to establish that sanctuary."

"Have you even talked with Liddie since this thing broke?" Echoes of Catherine Snyder—Deborah half expected to see the board member walk up to their table. "Is this really the PC thing to do, becoming her spokesperson without her permission?"

Deborah swallowed hard. "I'm calling her this weekend. But God help us, Aaron, this is Liddie we're talking about. You've met her."

"Just that once."

"Don't play games with me. You've been hearing me talk about her for years. You know what she went through. You know how guilty I feel to this day."

So much for the whispering. The woman at the next table put down the menus and gazed right at them. Aaron stuffed his tie in his pocket, slipped on his coat, and grabbed the Styrofoam box.

Deborah yanked her arms first into her jacket and then her own coat and followed him down the stairs. On the Metro they both buried their heads in documents; neither spoke while they trudged home from the station, breath visible in the frigid air. Still silent, Aaron locked the back door behind them, transferred the leftovers to a glass container, hung up both their coats in the hall closet, and led her to the living room couch as if she were a child or a pet. Turning on a single lamp, he sat so close, the corner of Deborah's jacket was wedged under his hip. She wriggled it free. Luckily, Becca was staying at her friend Louisa's house in hopes the snow would come by morning—the dad hailed from Minnesota and had equipped the family with snowshoes.

Aaron began with a calm voice and blank expression, although his fingers were tightly interlaced. "Look, I respect your concern about Liddie. I do. All I'm asking is that you respect what I know about PR." For a full five minutes, they went back and forth about whether or not Will would follow the template Aaron had laid out. Deborah wouldn't have been surprised to see him whip out his laptop and run through a PowerPoint.

Outside the gauzy curtains, Deborah could see flakes starting to fall. She rubbed her hands together—they really needed to reinsulate this old house. "Aren't you the guy who's always telling me, 'It's not about what's real—it's about what the public *thinks* is real'? I don't want to argue PR theory! What matters to me is what Liddie wants."

Aaron lifted her chin with his thumb and index finger. She remembered the first time he'd done that, on an early date when she was describing a dressing-down she'd received from another congressman's chief of staff. "You're a treasure," Aaron had said. "He's a scumbag."

With his other hand now, he tucked her hair behind her ear. "Don't you see, Deb, a win for Plale would be a huge break for me. I need you to go public with this. You don't have to do it for Gillean—fuck her. If you don't like her, I can arrange for you to leak the story to another reporter. Do it for me."

Deborah took his fingers off her face and held them in her hand. "Please, babe, don't make this a choice between you and Liddie. You can run this race without resorting to dirt from the past. . . ."

"Really? Is that what you called Anita Hill's allegations against Clarence Thomas?" Aaron wrenched his hand away and rose from the couch. "How many dozens of those cases have you argued on national TV? And you were able to argue them, I might add, because your devoted husband was home cleaning up after kiddie messes and teen meltdowns, chauffeuring to dance practices and God knows what else while you were hanging out at the White House and flitting around the country. Well, it's my turn now, sweetheart. The last thing I need is for you to sabotage this by keeping quiet."

"Sabotage?"

"Undermine, undercut, ruin, destroy. Take your pick."

Although later she wouldn't remember how she got out of the room, whether she held her back straight or peeled her limbs off the couch, Deborah somehow managed to stumble upstairs and into Becca's bed.

Ten

Danforth University: Friday, December 7, 1979

Liddie's decision to take on Will Quincy turned out to be like one of the puzzles Deborah's father liked so much, where you had to untangle one set of metal pieces in order to reach a second set, and then a third. First Liddie had to work through her own misgivings. Then she had to make sure she could take her exams at a later date and hang on to her scholarship. The next hurdle was filling out the complaint form. All those pieces, of course, would lead her to the most grueling challenge of all: the preliminary hearing before the university's judicial administrator.

After talking with Liddie that morning in the dorm, Deborah called and confirmed that the dean of students could see them. "All right, okay," Liddie said, as she put on regular clothes for the first time all week. "If the dean agrees to give me an extension on my exams, I'll fill out the form and you can deliver it. But otherwise, forget it. I'm not going through that . . . that *process* if I'm going to flunk out anyway."

Deborah knew Liddie had read Stop It Now's literature; no need to explain the steps to her. After hearing the case, the JA could refer the matter to the University Hearing Board or dismiss it altogether. In the case of a dismissal, the person bringing the complaint had the right to appeal to the hearing board. The complainant could also go to the police.

A meaningless set of options. If the JA threw out the charges, Liddie would never move on to those other steps.

"We've worked hard with the JA, Lid. He's promised us that these proceedings will be kept as dignified as possible."

"Oh, I have a pretty good picture." Liddie pantomimed stabbing herself in the eye with her knitting needles.

"Lid! Stop!"

"You mean, stop it now?"

Deborah busied herself piling up the knitting and trying to avoid staring as Liddie pulled on a pair of jeans—she needed a belt to hold them up—and a wool sweater with an extralarge turtleneck. The bruise over her throat had turned a nasty shade of green. All week Liddie had worn some version of the turtleneck-sweatshirt combination that Deborah assembled for her the morning after the rape; she dressed in the shower stall early in the morning, before walking down the hall back to their room. Deborah suspected Liddie couldn't bear to see her own bruises.

Liddie started muttering about coats. "We need different jackets. He might see us. Jackets with hoods. Big ones."

The solution was Nancy Minkin. She alone on their floor had two parkas, both with roomy hoods. They decided Deborah would tell her about the assault but not about pressing charges. Nancy had been a good friend and on more than one occasion had proven herself to be a mensch, staying up with someone flipping out on speed, taking the rap for a six-pack discovered in their lounge. She'd also proven herself a keeper of secrets. The previous year rumors had flown that her roommate attempted suicide, but Nancy had refused to say a word about it.

"You're lucky you've got Brad," Nancy said after she pledged never to mention the episode to anyone, especially to Liddie. "It's a jungle out there."

On top of the sweater, Liddie wound a plain scarf around the bottom half of her face; Nancy's parka hood hid the rest. They headed out into a day of spectacular brightness, sun bouncing off the snow in what felt like a mockery of their mission. By the time they walked from the dorm to Willard Broome, Liddie had to hang onto the banister with one hand and Deborah's arm with the other to make it up the three flights to the dean of students' office.

Deborah had met Dean Gordon Biddle only once before, at a gathering for the heads of all the student organizations. He had ruddy cheeks and soulful eyes, as if ready to celebrate or commiserate at a moment's notice. He boomed a "Hello, girls" as his secretary led them in—you'd think they were there to discuss decorations for homecoming weekend—and invited them to the chairs in front of his massive desk.

By this point, Deborah was sweating under her own parka and couldn't wait to tear it off. She kept her eyes on Liddie, who left her coat on, scarf pulled just below her chin, hair shooting up in static clusters. Liddie remained standing in front of the chair, fingers lightly touching the desk. Her voice was soft but clear: "I've been raped. I'm going to file a complaint with the judicial administrator. I'm unable to take my exams. I'd just like a short extension, so I don't lose my scholarship." Deborah tried not to gasp as Liddie's legs buckled and she sank into the chair, the parka poufing out around her like a loose sausage casing.

"Are you all right, Miss Golmboch?" The dean's entire face had turned red. He poured water into a glass and held it out to her.

"It's her first time out in nearly a week, Dean Biddle, and she's hardly eaten in all that time." Deborah seized the glass of water and placed Liddie's hand around it. "Just give her a minute."

On the slow, silent trek over here, Deborah agonized over whether the meeting would be too much for Liddie and thereby derail the complaint filing. This mini-collapse could help convince the dean. But if he started in with a stream of questions about doctor's notes and medical records, Liddie might change her mind.

To Deborah's continued amazement, Liddie's voice emerged from the folds of the parka, anticipating just those questions: "I have no doctor's note. I couldn't face it. Deborah can verify the rape and my state of being over the past week."

Dean Biddle shaded his eyes with one hand, as if to deny his visitors the opportunity of influencing his decision. The top of his head revealed comb marks and a perfectly straight part. "Why don't you get some rest, Miss Golmboch? Let me think this over, and I'll get back to you by the end of the afternoon."

They made another wordless journey back to the dorm, this time on the bus. Liddie shed her parka and slid into bed, resisting any offers of help—"I'm just tired; I'm not feeble," she said. "You don't need to hang around." Deborah soothed her hurt by remembering what Claire had told her just yesterday: "Be glad for every time she rolls her eyes or snaps at you. It means she's taking back a sense of control."

Collecting her books, Deborah claimed she had a date with the library, then headed straight back to Dean Biddle's office. Liddie had set the ball in motion. All Deborah would do was make sure no one erected a barrier along the way—although how she was going to pull that off, she had no idea. Twice she stopped in her tracks, once to get her breathing under control and once to summon up all the acting experience she'd had—mostly observed—in high school.

Dean Biddle scowled as she reentered his spacious room. The place smelled of some kind of cherry pipe tobacco—Deborah noticed a circular stand full of pipes that adorned his desk. She waited for him to direct her to a chair, but he kept his eyes on some report he'd been reading. After a few minutes, she simply dropped into the seat nearest to him.

"I'm sorry to bother you, sir," Deborah said. "It's just that . . . well, if Liddie were in better shape, she'd have told you herself, but she's a mess. I mean, you could see that. Essentially, she's lost the last six days. Our RA could confirm this, although she thinks Liddie's had the flu. Like most women who've endured a rape . . ."

The dean's ears turned scarlet. "Look, I understand these issues are delicate," he said. "Still, I'm reluctant to give Miss Golmboch special treatment. We do have procedures we're obliged to follow. There's no doctor note, no record of any kind from Heller Clinic or any family physician. I remind you that I'm deliberately not getting involved in any way with the complaint of untoward sexual activity."

Deborah bit back the impulse to enlighten him about the difference between sexual activity and sexual violence.

"It's also highly inappropriate to be having this conversation with a roommate, rather than the individual involved." The dean rubbed the bridge of his nose.

"Don't you see, sir, it's a catch-22. Liddie would still be sitting here herself if she weren't in such a bad state. But that's exactly why she needs some"—Deborah pulled at the wooden pegs on her borrowed coat as she searched for the right word—"*consideration* from you."

Dean Biddle swiveled his pipe stand.

"It's not like she's been a slack-off. You just need to look at her record to know how hard she's worked and how highly her professors think of her."

The dean lifted his lower arm and examined his watch. "Is there anything else?"

Deborah slipped her arms out of the parka and pulled her chair a little closer. Several times after the orientation session their first year, Liddie had come to Deborah's rescue. She'd bolstered Deborah through the humiliating put-downs in the poli-sci department, all the male professors who resented her budding feminism. "They're scared, DB," Liddie said. "They're watching their little fiefdom slip away." And when Deborah's grandmother, the one person in the family who was rooting for her to find her own path, suffered an aneurysm, Liddie called the airlines to find a flight, rode the bus with Deborah to the airport, and waited six hours until the plane took off, relishing every one of Deborah's anecdotes about her grandmother, never once saying, "It'll be all right."

Deborah leaned her arms on the desk and propped her chin on her palm, partly to look like she knew what she was doing, mostly to keep her hand from shaking.

"Actually, I'm here in a dual capacity, as the witness to Liddie Golmboch's assault but also as the president of Stop It Now. I'm really hoping you're able to expedite things so Stop It Now doesn't have to get involved." Deborah pictured old movies with Lauren Bacall and tried to imitate a confident gaze.

The dean finally looked her in the eye. "Really, Miss Borenstein,

I can't see how it would do anyone the slightest bit of good to make this a cause célèbre."

"I agree," she said, and sat back in her chair. Somewhere she remembered learning about the pregnant pause.

Dean Biddle pulled the most ornate pipe out of the stand, inserted a pipe cleaner into the curved stem and dragged it back and forth a few times, dipped the pipe into a can of tobacco adorned with Prince Albert, and took his time packing the stuff down with a special tool made of what looked like sterling silver. Deborah used to like to fill her father's pipe for him. The image of Dean Biddle threatened to spoil that task for her for a long time.

"All I can do is ask her professors," Dean Biddle said, after holding a lighter to the pipe and drawing in deeply. "The rest is up to them. And to her, of course. She'll still have to buckle down and meet their high standards."

Deborah jumped to her feet, wiped her hand on her jeans, and stuck it out to the dean. "Thank you so much, Dean Biddle. It will mean the world to Liddie." With his permission and Deborah's earlier story to each professor about Liddie's flu, the extensions ought to be a done deal.

He waved his pipe at her. "This will have no effect on the hearing. As you know, the judicial administrator's office is completely autonomous. They'll take an objective look at any allegations, hear from both sides, weigh all the evidence."

Deborah chewed on the inside of her lip and uttered another thank-you. No use trying to convince the guy that Liddie was telling the truth. He'd become a minor character in this story.

By the time Deborah raced back to the dorm, Liddie had already received a call from the dean informing her that he'd contacted her professors and all had agreed to give her until February 1 to make up her exams. The onus was on Liddie to make the arrangements.

"That's great, Lid. You were really impressive in there."

"Yeah, yeah." Liddie had gone back to her knitting. She checked the length of the scarf she was working on, this one in full-throated blues and greens.

Deborah snuck a glance at her watch: 2:19. She hated to push, but if the complaint got delivered by five o'clock, Liddie could get notice of a hearing date before the end of exam week. Deborah shifted from foot to foot.

"Let's get this over with," Liddie said, without lifting her eyes from the needles. "Where's the form?"

Deborah had two dozen copies of the complaint form from the judicial administrator's office stacked neatly inside a special folder, along with Stop It Now's handout "The Four Steps to Healing from Sexual Assault." Professor Davis let them type their flyer in her office and she ran off small batches of copies in the Sociology Department whenever she got a chance. Each member of their group maintained an identical folder. Just last month, in an effort to increase reporting, they persuaded the JA's office to let them distribute complaint forms to students who contacted them. Randall Peters, who'd been a Binghamton city attorney before he'd landed this job, listened carefully as they made their case. "Our office must avoid any appearance of advocacy," he'd said, gazing at them over his reading glasses. "But we certainly have no objection to making the complaint form more familiar."

Since that time, Stop It Now members had learned of three "incidents," a word that made Deborah cringe. ("Would multiple assaults be a 'co-incidence'?" she'd demanded of Claire Rawlings.) To date, none of those three wanted to file, all for the same reasons that held Liddie back: "It was a date, everyone saw us, I was an idiot." Mae Driggins, who represented Stop It Now in the Black Student Union, let out a long sigh when Deborah asked if they'd had any reports. "They think we're all hypersexual sluts," Mae said. "Who's going to listen to us?"

But Liddie's situation was different. Deborah Borenstein would bear witness and send Will Quincy's ass if not straight to jail, at least off the boardwalk of privilege he'd swaggered on since the day he was born. When that happened, without mentioning any specifics, Stop It Now could broadcast the win in an effort to convince others to come forward as well.

The following Wednesday, Deborah needed only a short pile of coins for her call to Claire Rawlings. "Mark your calendar," Deborah said. "The JA will hear the case January seventeenth. A new year. A new decade. A new day for women at Danforth."

Eleven

Washington, DC: Saturday, January 30, 2010

Deborah waited until ten o'clock Saturday morning to make the call, considering the time difference with Wisconsin. Years ago, when Becca first discovered the concept of time zones, she informed Liddie, "You're an hour slower than us."

In fact, Liddie wasn't slow at all, especially in the mornings. She'd always been an early riser. Her loom faced east so she could have natural light streaming in during the most productive morning hours. And Richard was out of bed before sunrise to feed the goats and chickens and take the dogs for a run.

Still, any earlier than ten might sound like a crisis call.

In Becca's room the previous night, during the wee hours, Deborah realized she had to have this conversation with Liddie face-to-face and got busy making arrangements. Midwest Airlines was making her use forty thousand miles, but she had a seat the next day on the eight thirty plane to Milwaukee and a rental car lined up so she could get to Random Lake by eleven o'clock Central time, with a return flight that evening. This call was simply to let Liddie know she was coming.

As she waited for the clock to move forward, Deborah curled up with her laptop on the futon in her study and scrolled through the most recent additions to Liddie's website, Random Acts of Beauty. Liddie decided on that name back in the early 1990s, when she'd first moved to Random Lake. "The designs I come upon at random," the designer—known as E.V.—explained first in a brochure and now on her website. "The acts are intentional. And the beauty, that's a gift for us all."

Deborah last visited the site in November, to order Hanukkah and Christmas presents for staff, friends, and family members, and to flag items for Aaron to choose among. Liddie had created an ingenious registry that wasn't limited to engaged couples or expectant parents. Anyone could identify gift ideas for herself. Typically Deborah would highlight some wearable art—a knitted sweater or crocheted scarf or jacket with woven panels—along with household items like the exquisite teal-and-purple runner now on their dining room table, the one-of-a-kind hand towels in both bathrooms, the batik pillows on her couch, the flying-woman wall hanging in her office. She never knew which prospect Aaron would select and therefore was always surprised; Aaron knew his gifts were always on target.

Since she'd married Richard, a decade ago, Liddie had gone back to quilting and added those to her offerings. Deborah clicked on a dozen new designs, some with large swirls of purple and burgundy, others blending quiet pastels with fanciful animals—bashful hippos or strutting chickadees. One of these would definitely be on her birthday registry in March.

Richard picked up on the first ring. In all the years those two had been a couple, Deborah couldn't remember a time when Liddie had answered.

"Well, if it isn't our favorite gal from the big city!" Richard's voice was a lovely baritone. Deborah pictured him singing to the animals he tended—arias during birthing, lullabies when he had to put down a pet.

Because much of her work was done over the phone, Deborah liked to imagine the face that went with the voice. Sometimes she was spot-on, could put names to folks flown in for a meeting before she heard the person speak, based solely on her telephone impressions. More often she was dead wrong, and such was the case with Richard.

Liddie had introduced them by phone a couple months after she'd started seeing him, in 1994. In Deborah's mind, he was taller than Aaron, lean but muscled, floppy hair, Wilford Brimley mustache. When she met Richard on a visit the following year, Deborah had to bite down hard to keep her jaw from flapping—five feet six with work boots on, hairline already deeply receded, no facial hair, and a body that most would describe as stocky but that Deborah quickly came to see as sturdy. Richard Blankenship was the sturdiest anchor of a man Deborah had ever met.

"How's Wisconsin's premier vet?" Deborah hugged one of Liddie's pillows. "We could use you here in DC, you know. Very bad case of hoof-and-mouth disease."

"Tell you what, young lady. I'll gather a crew of veterinarians, you let us bring those forceps we got for large animals to clamp shut some jaws, and you got yourself a deal."

God, Deborah thought, it felt good to laugh. "Done," she said.

"I bet you want to speak with my beautiful wife. Hold on." Deborah could hear the wooden clatter of the loom in the back of what Richard called their great room. She imagined him walking over to Liddie and holding out the phone, pausing to lay his cheek against hers as gently as if she were a newborn calf.

The loom fell silent as Liddie's voice came on, sweet and steady. "Hey! It's still January and my birthday's not for two weeks. Everything okay by you?"

They tried to talk on the first Sunday of every month, as well as on milestone events like birthdays, anniversaries, and winter and summer solstice, the only holidays Liddie celebrated. In the early years, Deborah had traveled to see Liddie several times. Even after she'd moved to DC, the goal had been at least one visit a year, but work kept Deborah in a whirlwind and some years she didn't manage to get away. She regularly invited Liddie to come to DC as well, including for the wedding in 1985 and Becca's bat mitzvah a few years ago. Once, Deborah sent an open-ended Build Your Own Vacation, like those choose-your-own-ending storybooks Becca liked so much as a kid. However she made the ask, Liddie never took her up on it. "I don't venture very far," she'd say.

Deborah fingered the embroidery on her pillow, one of Liddie's early creations. She'd wanted to be casual, refer to some last-minute gig in their neck of the woods, claim she was coming up early so she could see them. But Liddie deserved more.

"There's something I want to check in with you about, Lid," Deborah said. The window in her second-floor study showed off several inches of fresh snow—enough to draw Becca and Louisa out on snowshoes that morning, not enough to cancel flights the next day. "For perhaps the first time in history, we have more snow than you. I'm taking advantage of a brief window to get there and back."

Liddie's voice remained steady. Deborah imagined one hand resting on the shuttle of the loom. "Can you stay over?"

"I'd love to, but Monday's crazy busy. Have to leave tomorrow evening."

A slight intake of breath on Liddie's end. "Wow, there and back the same day. Something weighty, eh?"

In the background, Deborah heard Richard's booming laugh and yips of pleasure from their chocolate lab, Charlie Brown. She could see them wrestling in the airy kitchen, the woodstove crackling in the background, remains of Saturday breakfast on the table—oatmeal and berries, maybe an omelet. Deborah had never been to their home in the winter, but Liddie had described it in letters, her neat cursive on blue stationery, the kind that comes in packets with a silky ribbon, letters she continued to send long after Deborah switched to email.

"It'll be good to see you, babe." And that was mostly true. Deborah provided her arrival time. Liddie mentioned some construction on 43 North, said it shouldn't be a problem on a Sunday.

Despite the fact that her weaving lay before her, Liddie sounded fully present on the phone. Long before Deborah ever heard the term "mindfulness," she associated that concept with Liddie. No multitasking for her, not like Deborah, who Aaron berated for checking her BlackBerry while walking on the street—"some rapists *are* strangers, and they look for distracted women"—and lampooned for brushing her teeth while peeing. When Liddie talked to you, you felt like yours was the only voice in the room, no matter the background noise from radio or television, no matter how many other people were in the area. This was a trait that had disappeared during those lost years but revived as Liddie came back. *Please*, Deborah prayed, *don't let my news throw Liddie off course.*

"Since I'll see you soon, I'll let you go now so you don't rack up a big bill," Liddie said. Unlike most people, who used this as a polite way to say, *I'm done*, Liddie was entirely sincere.

"Allow me to fill you in on an invention of the modern age commonly known as cell phones. I know you like the other kind, where you hold a little receiver piece in your hand and ring up the operator to place a call, but you should try this—minutes are free all weekend." This was an old joke between them. Deborah used to be surprised that someone so technologically savvy—Liddie's website was one of the earliest Deborah knew of and became more sophisticated and user-friendly every year—remained so out of touch with mobile phones. Then Deborah figured out how few people Liddie spoke to. Orders and distribution for Random Acts of Beauty were all arranged online. Before that they went through Liddie's mother, who still drove down once or twice a week from her home in nearby Saukville to do the packaging and shipping. Richard and Liddie's circle of friends remained small. Her world was devoid of blather.

Deborah switched the phone to the other ear. She was remembering those frantic calls years ago to Claire Rawlings, stopping first to get rolls of quarters at the bank counter, once having to stomp her feet to keep from freezing while someone in the phone booth smooched long-distance with her boyfriend. The last time Deborah had been in touch with Claire was a couple years earlier, after she'd seen Claire quoted in an article in the *New York Times*. The former rape counselor had gotten a PhD in women's studies and become a professor at the University of Rochester.

Deborah felt her heartbeat quicken. Besides her and Liddie and Nancy Minkin, Claire was the one other person on their side who knew about Will Quincy. Professor Davis had died of ovarian cancer several years after Deborah graduated from Danforth.

"Earth to Deborah!" Liddie was saying. "Have I lost you?"

"You'll never lose me, Lid. I'll see you tomorrow."

Instead of nestling on the futon or climbing back into Becca's bed, Deborah stood up and dragged out her yoga mat. She'd heard Aaron shoveling the walk hours ago; he left right afterward. *Breathe*, she told herself, taking in long inhalations and blowing them out until her heart slowed down.

Folded over in child's pose, she told herself things would be okay. Unlikely that Gillean would know about Claire Rawlings. Even less likely that Claire would take any action on her own. She'd been at that hearing. She'd counseled Deborah during the aftermath.

Claire knew the stakes.

Twelve

Danforth University: Thursday, January 17, 1980

Deborah had hoped for a hearing room that resembled the Harvard Law School Library—mahogany-paneled, with roomy leather chairs, green-shaded lamps, oversize portraits of men with formidable eyebrows. Not that she could distinguish mahogany from maple, and not that she'd ever seen the Harvard Law School Library other than as a backdrop in *The Paper Chase*. Still, a setting with that kind of grandeur made justice seem a more likely outcome.

But yesterday, less than twenty-four hours before the hearing, Liddie had been notified by phone that the proceedings were being shifted from Ogden Hall, home of the judicial administrator's office, to an antiseptic classroom in Goodman Parrish. Deborah made noises about needing to buy some of her favorite pens and went off to the arts quad to get a peek. Nothing but a few rows of student desk chairs with metal seats. Not a single item on the walls. The desks looked onto a chalkboard with lines of Greek in the right-hand corner, cited below in English as a passage from Aristophanes' *The Frogs*.

"The JA just wants to keep it low-key," Dean Biddle assured Deborah when she rushed over to inquire. "Avoid attention. Make sure the thing doesn't turn into a circus." That's why the hearing had been set for the Thursday before classes began.

Dean Biddle seemed much more concerned with the impact of the "thing" on the university's image than he did with Liddie's well-being. Deborah was dying to ask why the dean was in the loop about a neutral hearing being handled by a supposedly autonomous branch of the university. But he'd held tight to his office door while answering her question and never invited her in. Clearly, nothing she said was going to change the venue; the last thing she wanted was to delay things. Deborah thanked him for his time and hurried back to the dorm to check on her roommate.

Liddie's chin and cheekbones were dagger-sharp when her dad dropped her off the day before. "Take care of this gal," he told Deborah, his hand gently steering his daughter into the dorm room before he drove straight back to Saukville. "Don't let her blow away." Deborah was not surprised to learn that Liddie stuck with the flu story while she was home—she needed some explanation for the weight loss and lack of appetite, not to mention the incompletes. Like Deborah's parents, Liddie's waited each semester for the arrival of the letter containing grades, but the spectacle in each of the two households was entirely different. Deborah's mother wanted to make sure she wasn't goofing off—"especially now that you're a single girl again," she told her over the holidays. Liddie's parents, on the other hand, were absolutely certain that their daughter would "do them proud" and couldn't wait to see the evidence.

As soon as the squeak of her dad's work boots was no longer audible in the hall, Liddie began sliding neat stacks of socks and underwear into her dresser drawers, fitting sweaters smelling of lavender in the plastic container under her bed—Deborah could see Mrs. Golmboch stroking each item as she packed them—and spreading new knitting projects over the desk. Liddie had yet to take out her book bag—Deborah doubted she'd cracked a textbook all vacation—and seemed to have made no move to schedule her exams. But that was okay. "It's perfectly natural for her to put off academic catch-up until after the hearing," Claire Rawlings told Deborah when they talked over the break. "One hurdle at a time."

Deborah had to dodge some hurdles of her own while she was home. She tried to participate in holiday cheer, but most of the time she hunkered down in her room, pretending to get a head start on the new semester or trying to catch up on sleep after those two brutal weeks. "It's normal to be blue because you don't have a boyfriend," her mother said, encouraging Deborah to attend mixers at the temple. Her brother kept offering her pot. On New Year's Eve, when the rest of the family each shouted out a wish just before midnight, Deborah mumbled something inane about world peace. Her real wish was written on a tiny piece of paper and buried in her pillow: "Victory ➔ L back."

Deborah began preparations for that victory before leaving for vacation. Step number one: trying to arrange for Claire Rawlings and Professor Davis to testify as experts in the field. As soon as the JA received Liddie's complaint, he mailed a form asking for names of witnesses, with lines for contact information plus a large rectangle entitled "Detailed Justification for the Presence of This Individual." The form arrived in a plain brown envelope. Liddie stared at it for a full five minutes before Deborah grabbed it out of her hands and tore it open.

"I thought maybe, you know . . ." It took Liddie another five minutes to name her fear—that someone had snapped photos of her making out with Will at the fraternity party.

Deborah shuddered at the demons hovering over her roommate. She was also infuriated by the implication that these materials were somehow shameful and had to be disguised. Later that day, she vented for five minutes to Claire on the phone. "Brown paper wrapping—what the fuck! I'm all for confidentiality, but couldn't they use a university envelope, something generic? This made it look like *pornography*, for God's sake."

In his infinite wisdom, the JA decided only one of the two "interested parties" could make an appearance. "There are no accepted standards for experts in this arena," JA Peters wrote Liddie in their last communication before she went home. "We can allow one such party to speak. A second testimony would be duplicative. Please be advised that this is simply a preliminary session determining whether or not to pass the complaint to the University Hearing Board."

Liddie dangled the letter like a piece of rotten fruit in front of Deborah, who was pulling off her boots after returning from the last of her exams. Freshman year they'd started a tradition of celebrating their "final finals" with a party in their room, feasting on corned beef and rye specially packaged by Deborah's dad, a kringle baked by Liddie's mom, and a bottle of wine secured by an older friend. When this semester's packages arrived, Deborah quietly passed them on to Nancy Minkin.

"You choose," Liddie said, pointing her chin at the letter and going back to her knitting.

Professor Davis was the one who insisted on Claire as the stronger advocate. "I'm the academic, but there's no recognition of my work as a field of study," she said. "Claire knows the research as well as I do; plus, she has several years of practical experience. That's more likely to get their attention."

And so, a little before ten o'clock on the day of the hearing, Deborah made her way to Willard Broome Hall to meet Claire, who was driving down from Rochester. The plan was to go to Professor Davis's office to rehearse for the two o'clock session. Claire was waiting right inside the double doors at the Broome, shivering in a black skirt and panty hose, wearing snow boots but carrying a plastic bag that no doubt contained a pair of pumps. They'd used a quick shorthand about what to wear—"I'll be in my Sunday go-to-meeting clothes," Claire had said. No need to explain the importance of not appearing like wild-eyed men-haters. Deborah herself had picked out a pair of camel slacks and matching turtleneck as a Hanukkah gift, along with a preppy navy blazer. Her mother assumed it was for the Christmas afternoon mixer at the temple, which Deborah had gotten out of only by feigning a stomach flu.

Under gloomy skies promising more snow, Deborah and Claire walked the short distance to Professor Davis's office in Vilas Hall. If Claire had taken on the role of older sister for Deborah, Professor Davis—who'd never once said, "Call me Margaret"—was like an unmarried aunt, the one who took you to museums and science exhibits, taught you to eat goat cheese and beet salad, encouraged you to aim high.

The two experts had been working on this case over the holidays, redlining each other's drafts and compiling background material.

Claire would give a "brief but pithy" overview of the grim statistics on reporting and seeking medical help. They encouraged Deborah to stick to the facts: where she'd been, why she'd come back to the room early, what she'd seen, how she'd tried to convince Liddie to go to the clinic, why she'd taken the Polaroids. And Liddie—Liddie would read her statement.

Last night Deborah had encouraged Liddie to write out a longer form of what she'd said in her complaint. On a sheet of notebook paper, Liddie neatly printed fifteen sentences: "On December 1, 1979, I went to a fraternity party with Will Quincy. I was flattered that he'd asked me out. We kissed. I had several drinks. We talked about the poet Rilke, and he asked if I had a copy he could borrow. I said yes. We went to my room. Instead of stopping at the desk, Will pinned me to my bed. I said *no*! We didn't kiss. He pressed his arm against my neck, his knee against my thigh, tore off my jeans, tore me again and again. I tried to yell, but his arm cut off my voice. My roommate walked in, and she did yell. He left. I will never be the same."

Deborah copied the statement after Liddie fell asleep and showed it now to Claire and Professor Davis, who both bent their heads over the crinkled page, Claire's hair dark and tucked behind her ears, Professor Davis's prematurely gray and scooped up in a loose bun.

Professor Davis looked up first. "They should tattoo that last sentence on his chest."

Claire's eyes were wet. "On his nuts."

Deborah folded the paper and shoved it back in her book bag. It was all she could do not to round up a group of Stop It Now members to attach this statement with permanent glue to the front door of the Delta Omega house. Claire grabbed Deborah's hand until she regained her composure.

"Okay, so let me be sure I have this right," Deborah said. "Because this is a preliminary hearing, it's not going to be like Perry Mason—no cross-examination, no ganging up on the witness, right?"

"That's what the procedural rules say." Claire was back to business. "The JA asks clarifying questions, but his tone should stay neutral and objective. No badgering. And it's his job to get each party to stick to factual statements, rather than diatribes against the other side. Still, we should be prepared for anything. You never know what someone like Will Quincy is capable of."

Professor Davis promised to treat Claire to lunch—the gas and other expenses for this trip were all coming out of the counselor's modest salary—while Deborah went back to the dorms, stopping at Loon Lodge to pick up turkey sandwiches for herself and Liddie, mayo and mustard on the side. Liddie had returned to solid foods, but Deborah hadn't seen her swallow more than a few bites. As for Deborah, she'd be lucky if she made it through the hearing without projectile-vomiting.

After what was indeed a failed meal, Deborah hid in the bathroom stall for ten minutes doing one of the theater breathing exercises she'd learned in high school—in through the nose, out through the mouth, hands lifted up on the inhale and stretched out on the exhale. She'd always felt as if they were offering a blessing when they did that. Only now did she understand that the blessor and the blessee were one and the same.

Liddie looked like she could use some blessings herself. Her hair had lost all its luster, and her cheeks had the pallor of an invalid. For the hearing she chose a bulky sweater and long black skirt, the waist folded over twice to keep it up. Deborah brought along her book bag with the file she'd compiled, sheets displaying the photos, plus a copy of the complaint and of Claire's remarks. Liddie brought neither book bag nor purse. Today they wore their own coats—there was no way to avoid seeing Will.

As they walked down the corridor at Goodman Parrish, Deborah wondered whether the building was really dingy or just seemed that way compared with the imaginary mahogany-paneled room. She had no idea how Liddie had imagined the space—they'd kept discussions of the session to a minimum. Deborah had assured Liddie she would not mention the hearing to Stop It Now, would do no publicity of any kind.

Claire Rawlings had already arrived and welcomed them to the other two desks in her row. Randall Peters, the JA, was seated at the front table. Deborah had expected him to be robed, but he was dressed in a brown suit with a carnelian tie and white shirt. He kept his eyes on the items in front of him, a short stack of papers, a legal pad, and several pens and pencils, which he kept lining up. The implements with which he would record and decide.

Someone had erased the board.

Deborah, seated in the middle, slid her chair closer to Liddie's so that their knees touched, a feeble attempt to brace themselves for seeing Will. Liddie had her hand wrapped around the sides of her desk. Two minutes later, they heard what sounded like a dozen people entering the room. A glance at the floor revealed six he-man feet and one startling pair of high heels.

Claire had warned them to expect a fraternity buddy as witness, but there appeared to be two of them—like Will, scrubbed and clean shaven, decked out in charcoal blazers with the Delta Omega crest and lighter gray pants. More alarming was the woman who accompanied them, midthirties, wearing a pin-striped suit, carrying a sleek leather briefcase, and sporting a Farrah Fawcett hairdo, every flip deliberate. She looked like she belonged in a fashion magazine.

"Why do *they* get three 'interested parties'?" Deborah scribbled on a note card to Claire. "And who the hell is she—expert against concept of rape by a known acquaintance?"

Claire's writing was tiny and quick. "Looks like lawyer. Think, 'I pulled myself up by my high heels, and so can you.' We shoulda known. Quincy family = big donors. Bet administration agreed to make exception."

The JA, a short, tidy man in his early forties whose face remained a blank slate, was asking each person to state his or her name and title. The complainant's side went first; the fancy-schmancy woman went last. Claire had pegged it right—the woman introduced herself as Lucinda Baxter, attorney-at-law. JA Peters proceeded to remind everyone of the rules, the importance of sticking to facts and avoiding judgment-ridden terms. "This is not a courtroom," he said, rolling a pen between his two hands. "There will be no badgering of witnesses or cross-examination. Attorney Baxter is here not to ask questions of the other side but to share expertise and views on evidentiary material, in the same way the complainant has brought someone to share expertise on other matters relevant to the case." Deborah assumed

Lucinda Baxter intended to discredit the studies they'd brought. What could she possibly have up her sleeve—a statistically significant sample of women who enjoyed being ravished?

Randall Peters called on Liddie first. She pushed herself to standing and pulled her statement out of a pocket in her skirt. "On December 1, 1979, I went to a fraternity party with Will Quincy." Deborah could have recited the rest from memory. Liddie read it hunched over, both hands on the desk. Her voice never wavered and remained low, except for the "*no*," which she held for a long beat, and the "tore me again and again," which was nearly inaudible.

This morning, the book of Rilke poems had been lying on Liddie's desk when she took her shower. Skimming through the table of contents, Deborah found a short poem titled "Again and Again" and read the lines: " . . . again and again the two of us walk out together / under the ancient trees, / lie down again and again among the flowers, / face to face with the sky." Deborah had to spin around to keep from getting the page wet with tears. One more reference that would never be the same for Liddie.

Now it was Deborah's turn. "Avoid subjective words," Claire reminded her this morning. "Let the facts speak for themselves, just as Liddie did. Let the pictures speak." Deborah had rehearsed her remarks with Claire and Professor Davis and several times on her own. None of that prepared her for how hard it was to bite back all the barbed words that flooded her mouth now. She did her best reciting what had happened and holding up the sheets on which she'd pasted the Polaroids.

Claire was brilliant. Unlike Deborah, who felt herself rocking back and forth like a fourth-grader giving her first speech, and Liddie, who had to brace herself against the desk, Claire remained steady and rooted, alternating between statistics and examples of women she'd met over four years of working with rape victims. "Every reaction we've heard from and about Elizabeth Golmboch—her worry about her parents' response, her fear of being blamed, her wish to avoid further pain and humiliation—all these are typical behaviors following a rape, particularly one by an acquaintance." Claire held up a folder of articles on the subject that she had prepared for the judicial administrator. When he removed his reading glasses and waved her to the front, she delivered the folder and the photographs to his table.

Deborah began to keep a scorecard on the back of the receipt for the turkey sandwiches. She gave them one point for her testimony, three for the Polaroids, three for Liddie's statement, three for Claire's.

The speaking order for the other side was not as she expected. Rather than Will going first, the person Deborah came to think of as Frat Boy One, Norman Kuehn—"K-u-e-h-n, pronounced 'Keen'"—was their starter. He looked like a linebacker and rose with difficulty from a desk sized for the average person.

"Your Honor . . ."

"Mr. Kuehn, I'm not a judge. Please address me as Mr. Peters."

"Sure. Mr. Peters, I'm here because I want you to know that everyone at that party saw Liddie drinking and coming on to Will. Several guys say they heard her invite him to her room, and everybody knows what that means."

The JA stopped writing. "Mr. Kuehn, I must remind you that you are here to state facts, not opinions. Please limit your remarks to what you yourself saw and heard."

Deborah added another point to their column.

"Sorry, Your Honor . . . I mean, Mr. Peters." Norman Kuehn unbuttoned his jacket. "I saw Liddie Golmboch pawing at Will . . ."

The JA stared over his half-rimmed glasses and repeated his admonition about judgment-laden terms.

"Okay. Sorry. I saw her kissing him hard and long and pressed up against him. She seemed quite happy. I mean, she was grinning and she was laughing."

Liddie's knee against Deborah's started to shake.

Frat Boy Two was named Stuart Mulligan—"everyone calls me Skip." Although he was as big as Frat Boy One, he seemed more accustomed to moving out of the chairs. Probably dropped in to class now and then. "Glad to be here, sir. I want to say that I myself with my own ears did hear her invite Will to her room."

Peters wanted specifics—this had to be a good sign. "As close to the actual words as possible, Mr. Mulligan. Did you hear Ms. Golmboch initiate the idea of going to her room?"

After three variations of that question, Frat Boy Two finally conceded that maybe Will had brought up the idea. "But I can swear on a bible that she did say she had the book and that Will could come over to get it. And everyone knows . . ." The JA's throat-clearing ended that sentence.

Deborah wished Peters had asked the frat boys how much *they'd* had to drink. But never mind. Another point in Liddie's column.

Will Quincy waited to stand until Frat Boy Two had returned to his seat. Deborah realized Will wasn't nearly as big as his fraternity brothers. Lacrosse, like rape, apparently benefited from speed and agility, rather than bulk.

"Thank you for the opportunity to speak and the commitment to due process," he began. Deborah remembered Will's smarmy voice that day on the quad. This I'm-such-a-good-boy tone now made her want to gag. "Rape is a very serious charge, sir. The mere accusation can be enough to ruin a person's reputation. So let me say this unequivocally. I would never engage in sexual relations if they were not absolutely consensual."

Deborah wondered if the JA could see the tremor in Liddie's legs.

"To be perfectly honest, I thought Liddie was okay, but not really anything special. I wasn't particularly attracted to her. But when she made a big deal out of having a copy of Rilke in her room, and then when we got there she pulled me onto her bed . . . well, you know, I'm only human. I admit it was awkward when her roommate came in. I was embarrassed—the roommate seemed a little possessive and started yelling at me, so I felt the best thing to do was to leave. A couple days later, that same roommate, Miss Borenstein, accosted me on campus . . ."

Deborah's pencil slipped into her lap.

"Accosted, meaning . . . ?" Peters asked. His forehead wrinkled.

"She was waiting for me outside Simpson Hall on the Monday after my date with Liddie. She told me I'd be sorry, that she was going to make my life miserable. I tried to step away, but she ran after me. It was really uncomfortable."

Deborah waited for someone to object. But this wasn't a Perry Mason movie; she was going to have to do it herself. "Objection, Mr. Peters. That is not what happened."

"After everyone has spoken, Miss Borenstein, you'll have a chance to comment on anything you've heard here," Peters told her. "If you're finished, Mr. Quincy, we'll move on to Attorney Baxter."

Claire passed Deborah a note card, one they'd written ahead of time. "Breathe. He's a snake. Breathe." Claire had added another line: "JA only cares about what happened Sat. nite."

Between breaths, Deborah tried to convince herself that this was true. Will had completely misstated what happened between them. But even if she'd used those exact words, so what—it didn't undercut her testimony or Liddie's. Might even help. She wouldn't award them any points, but she wasn't taking any away, either.

Lucinda Baxter was the only person who made her statement standing not at her seat but directly in front of the JA. Briefcase in one hand, she walked up to the front table and touched the sheets with the Polaroids. "May I, sir?" Peters removed his glasses and nodded.

"These photos do seem alarming—but one has to ask, are they authentic?" Baxter put them back down on the table and clicked open her briefcase, whose top immediately popped up. One by one, the attorney pulled out what looked like yearbooks. "In my hand are the yearbooks from Cleveland Heights High School, years 1976, 1977, and 1978. As you will see on the pages I've marked, Miss Deborah Borenstein was a member of Thespians on the Heights each of those years, specializing in"—and here she opened one of the books to a page marked with a scarlet square of paper—"productions and stage makeup."

Despite Claire's efforts to restrain her, Deborah was on her feet. Stage makeup! The most she'd ever done was rouge and face powder, a beauty mark! Who needed bruises in *Oklahoma* and *Bye Bye Birdie*?

"Please, Miss Borenstein." The JA held up his hand. "You will have another opportunity to speak in just a moment."

Deborah saw points stacking up on the other side. Her pencil skittered somewhere on the floor.

"The possibility of fabricating evidence becomes more likely, Mr. Peters, when combined with the reality that Miss Borenstein has an ax to grind." Once more, Lucinda Baxter, tilting slightly forward on the toes of her three-inch high heels, popped the lid of her briefcase.

Liddie jolted in her seat at the sound. This time, the attorney drew out a thin booklet.

"This document, sir, entitled 'Stop It Now,' is a screed against men, written by Miss Borenstein for a militant group she organized. I offer one excerpt as evidence of the kind of strident sexism it contains, and I quote: 'All men have rape fantasies. All men are potential rapists. All men are capable of wielding the penis as a weapon of war.'"

Deborah could hear Claire scribbling but was simply incapable of doing anything other than keeping herself upright in her seat.

"Judicial Administrator Peters, as someone who has worked hard to reach my position in life, I must say this kind of document offends me and many other women. But the sentiment isn't limited to writing. As part of my preparation for today's session, I interviewed the dean of students about whether there'd been any publicity or threat of publicity regarding this proceeding, in contravention of the rules. Dean Biddle mentioned that Miss Borenstein had paid him a visit and made statements implying that her militant group would take action if Miss Golmboch were not awarded an extension to take her exams."

Lucinda Baxter added the slim booklet to the pile of yearbooks and tossed the Polaroid display on top, as if she were about to start a bonfire. "Given the lack of any independent medical analysis, the likely fraudulent photos, and the motive for false accusation, I respectfully submit that these charges be dismissed. I trust the university has appropriate procedures for filing complaints for perjury and slander, which Mr. Quincy will avail himself of."

Surely there had been oxygen in the room when the session began. Deborah managed to rise from her seat. She managed to speak without moaning or screaming. She addressed the nature of the plays she was involved in back in high school, actors without a single bruise, how limited and amateur her role had been. She sat down again without collapsing. When the others left, she walked out with them. She allowed Claire to accompany Liddie back to their room.

And then Deborah walked to the gorge, curled up against a fallen tree, let the snow pummel her, and howled.

Thirteen

Washington, DC:
Saturday,
January 30, 2010

"Taa-daa!" Becca appeared at the door of Deborah's study, cheeks rouged from the wind and hair wild, just sprung from a stocking cap with Obama '08 across the front. "Look out the window and admire my snow family!"

Deborah swiveled her chair to gaze at the yard below, glad for the chance to turn her back so she could blink several times at the mention of "family." Outside stood three snow figures of varying heights. The tallest wore an old red scarf of Aaron's. The middle and smallest ones had snow ears adorned with pipe-cleaner hoops.

"Love the earrings!" she said, turning back to Becca. "And look at you—you're like an ad for healthy living. How was the snowshoeing?"

"Food first," Becca said, turning to cross the hall to her bedroom to dump her stuff. "I'm starved."

Deborah had just taken the kettle off the stove when Becca pounded down the stairs. "Hey, who's been sleeping in my bed?" she asked.

"Would you rather have lemon ginger or green tea?" Deborah held up both boxes.

"C'mon, Ma. All these years of having to make my own bed—I know your hospital corners when I see them."

"Stop acting like we were breaking child labor laws," Deborah said. "You were at least seven."

Making housework a form of play had been a gift from Aaron beginning when Becca was a toddler. She used to love sorting her toys by shapes or colors and dropping them into containers. "Night-night, puzzle!" she'd say. "Night-night, lion!" Her first official chore consisted of standing on the vacuum while Aaron ran around the room, making sure he didn't miss a spot. He would bypass a whole corner just to hear Becca shriek the phrase he'd taught her, "Go back, slacker!"—though for the first year or so, she'd pronounced it "smacker." At age four, Becca began measuring ingredients for pancakes after being hoisted onto a stool. She was helping cook by the time she was in second grade and for several years had been preparing an entire meal once a week, usually on Sundays. Hers was not the neatest room, but she'd always done her share of chores. "We should invite more people to dinner," Becca said one day shortly after her eighth birthday; they'd just scrubbed floor to ceiling in preparation for a visit from Marquita and her honey, Malcolm, a DC social studies teacher. "Then the house would always be clean." On the spot, Aaron invented "Guess who's coming to dinner?" They'd take turns naming a famous pretend guest, mostly living but sometimes historical figures; Pippi Longstocking and Harriet Tubman made the list as well. Aaron would blast old favorites on the stereo—Pointer Sisters, Creedence Clearwater Revival, Aretha Franklin—and get them into the swing of it.

Becca pulled the orange juice bottle out of the fridge and filled a tall glass. Citrus fragrance floated through the kitchen. "Seriously, did you have company?"

"No, I fell asleep in your room."

Looping one leg over the other, Becca leaned back against the counter and glared at Deborah, who was sitting at the island wringing out her teabag with a spoon. "Did you and Dad have a fight?"

"It's no biggie, Bec. Just one of those need-a-time-out things adults run into every now and then." Deborah toasted her daughter with her mug. "I'd much rather hear about snowshoeing. How'd you like it?"

She gazed at her daughter's lovely throat as Becca guzzled the rest of her juice. The thought of someone like Will Quincy manhandling that throat made Deborah's chest so tight, she had to bury her face in her tea and breathe in the steam. For the first time, she realized her daughter was nearly the age she and Liddie were when Will smashed into their lives. Suddenly the proportions of the room seemed dizzyingly out of whack, as if the island no longer sat in proper alignment with the floor and the windows.

"Give me a break. Ms. 'The Best Part of Winter Exercise Is Coming Back Inside' wants to hear all about my day in the snow?" Becca turned back to the fridge and emerged with fists full of avocados and tomatoes and a container of tuna salad. She laid her haul on the counter.

Deborah banished the ugly images and tried to picture her daughter out in the snow. In fact, Rebecca had written an entire essay for senior English on snowshoeing. Deborah came upon it one day on the bed when she brought up dance costumes from the dry cleaner. "I love the smell of the air," Becca had written. "The quiet, broken only by the satisfying crunch of the snow. The feel of my lungs expanding. The rhythm of my legs. Even though I'm completely rooted to the ground, it's like I'm dancing." Deborah longed to mention this, but Becca would go apeshit if she knew her mother had read it.

"I'd actually stay outside just to watch you."

"Whatever." Becca scooped tuna from the Tupperware and piled it on a chunk of bread, licking the residue from her fingertips. "What am I, some exotic species?"

"C'mon, Bec. You know what I mean."

"Why do you do that?"

"What?"

Becca rocked back and forth on the balls of her feet. "Ask questions when you already know the answer. I've adored snowshoeing since that first time at Liddie's. It's *nifty*. Okay?"

Deborah's chest tightened again. Becca had been fifteen and in the throes of her depression, skulking around Liddie's beautiful home with jaws locked tight like a toddler refusing to swallow medicine. Deborah remembered the waves of worry and embarrassment that had swept over her. And then Richard said the magic words: "Hey, Miss

Rebecca, take a look at these." In the back closet was a pile of snowshoes, kept at the ready for Richard's gaggle of nieces and nephews. "You might fall on your butt a few times, but in the silence you'll hear sounds we never listen to: birds whispering and the wind in the tree limbs. You'll see the trees aren't naked, just dressed in sky. Take your pick of those snowshoes—we've got all sizes. Dogs need a run." When they returned from their trek, Becca was laughing for the first time in months. She helped Richard cook dinner and romped with Charlie Brown, Richard's new puppy. The spell broke the second Deborah's rental car pulled into the airport, but Deborah would always associate snowshoeing with the beginning of getting her girl back.

"You should have been Liddie's daughter," she sighed. "She and Richard are the Imelda Marcos of snow footwear."

Becca sliced the avocado and piled it on top of the tuna, adding the tomato at the last minute, as Aaron had taught her. Liddie's name seemed to relax her a little. "How is Liddie? I miss her."

Deborah swallowed her sigh. There was no point in disguising the destination of Sunday's trip. "Actually, I'm going on an impromptu visit to see Liddie tomorrow, just for the day, before they or we get too much snow."

Becca used her fingers to mop up the tomato juice running down her chin. "A same-day journey to Wisconsin?" she asked. "What's up with that? Does this have something to do with the whole separate-bedrooms thing?"

"I haven't seen Liddie in a long time, and her birthday's coming up." Deborah rose from the stool to get Becca a plate. "Here you go, darlin'. *Oy*, that's Louisa's mother's plate—we need to return it. So, how was spending time with Louisa? What's she's thinking about doing next year?"

Becca had been holding her sandwich over the dish. Wiping her hand on her jeans, she dropped the sandwich on the plate and plunked the plate on the wood top of the island. "Really, you want to know all about Louisa? Okay, she's freaked out because she thinks her ass is too big and her bush is too thick and she's scared to shave herself and would rather walk naked through the hallway than try a bikini wax."

"Oh, Becca." The pain in Deborah's chest spread so fast to her stomach, she had to hang onto the counter to keep from doubling over.

"Should we have a little talk about hypocrisy?" Becca's dark eyes glowered. "You want to know all about my life, but you won't fill me in on yours. I smell something big. What's Daddy think about all this?"

Deborah moved closer and put her arms around Rebecca. "I hear you, sweet girl. If only I'd been as smart as you when I was your age." Her daughter's body remained tense and inert. "It's not that I don't want to talk about it—I'm just not capable right now. But I will be soon. I promise a long conversation after I get back. Is that okay?" She stood back to look again into Becca's eyes, which were now filled with tears.

"I don't know if it's okay," Becca said. "I don't think you do, either."

Fourteen

Danforth University: Monday, January 21, 1980

The single sheet from the JA's office was lying on Deborah's desk when she came back just after noon from her first day of classes. This time the communication did not arrive in a brown paper wrapper. It was jutting out of an official envelope with the university seal—as if the contents were announcing a scholarship or a prize. "In re: complaint LC972," it began. Amid the jargon about complainants and respondents and impartial proceedings stood the only words that mattered: "The judicial administrator finds no conclusive evidence that a nonconsensual sexual act took place as alleged on the fifth of December, 1979. The complaint as rendered is dismissed."

Somewhere on the page there must have been information about appeals and options and criminal and civil courts, but Deborah's eyes couldn't take in anything beyond the section marked "Conclusion: The JA will not pursue charges against the respondent. No mention of this proceeding will be included in the respondent's university record."

Deborah had spotted the letter the second she walked in the door and dropped her book bag on the floor in order to read it. A week ago, it might have gotten lost on her desk in the cascading heap of reprints, study notes, and paper drafts, but the desktop was newly cleaned, all the clutter from last semester filed or thrown away, this term's textbooks lined up according to course and secured by Danforth bookends, a gift from her dad, who bought a set for their house as well. Her typewriter rested in its case beneath the desk. The letter stood out like a stripper in a room full of nuns.

Deborah pulled the door shut, locked it, and flung herself on her bed. She wanted to scream profanities and pound the walls, but the truth was, she couldn't muster the rage. She knew this was coming, knew it the way you knew you didn't get the part because you lacked the height or beauty or self-confidence—or, worse, fucked up the audition by giggling or sweating too much. Nothing would reverse the outcome. And this time, it wasn't just her ego on the line.

She and Liddie had still not exchanged a word about the hearing. Deborah tried to raise it when she came back Thursday from the gorge, soaked through to her underwear. Liddie held up her knitting needles like a cross before a vampire. "It's over," she said. "Let it be over." The weekend passed with minimal conversation. Liddie covered her bed with pages of material for the exams she was scheduled to take on Monday, but every time Deborah glanced over Liddie was dozing, curled up in the back corner of her mattress, the sheet having long ago come undone. Her hair became so greasy, occasionally a page would stick to it. When she was awake, Liddie subsisted on tea from a small electric kettle and packets of Saltines, whose crumbs mingled with notebooks and texts. The room had begun to smell like the high school gym after wrestling matches.

Saturday evening Deborah gave up and went to see *The Electric Horseman* with Nancy Minkin. Tactfully avoiding the rape and knowing nothing about the hearing, Nancy chattered nonstop about visiting her brother, an intern with a consulting firm in Washington, DC.

"I'm telling you, Deborah, he's a catch," she said. "You guys have a lot in common, always absorbed with current events. He's really smart. And did I mention he's really cute?" Deborah somehow mustered enough "that's interestings" and "uh-huhs" to keep Nancy from asking probing questions.

Liddie's exams would keep her away until late afternoon—assuming that was where she'd gone; her towel hung unused from the hook on the door, as it had for the past four days. As soon as Deborah could manage to put her feet on the floor, she dug out the roll of quarters at the bottom of her book bag and took the stairs two at a time down to the back entrance. She filled her lungs with the cold and kept her eyes on the naked branches and graying snow until she arrived at the phone booth outside Loon Lodge. A steady stream of students were heading up to the dorms, some hurrying against the wind, others dragging. Deborah spotted a couple she knew only as Sally and Solly, laughing as they shared a Danish and licked the crumbs off each other's lips. Who the hell were they to deserve a life that was still normal? Deborah turned her back so they wouldn't recognize her and stop to chat.

Claire answered right away, as if she'd been expecting the phone to ring. She let out a whoosh of air after Deborah delivered the news. "How's Liddie? How are you?"

Deborah divided the coins into four equal stacks. "Haven't seen Liddie. She's supposed to be making up her exams, but who knows if she is? I can't imagine she didn't expect this. She always knew we didn't have a snowball's chance in hell. I'm the one who believed in tooth fairies."

Claire was telling someone in muffled tones that she was not to be disturbed. "Sorry about that," she said. "Okay, we need to be pragmatic here, figure out next steps. This decision screams out for an appeal to the Hearing Board." Claire began methodically ticking off the flaws in the proceedings. "First, there's the dean of students allowing that Quincy family lawyer to be part of the proceedings. I'm sure he pressured the JA on that one; dean's office is supposed to be neutral—clearly a violation. Then there's the JA letting Baxter discredit the Polaroids without giving our side a way to rebut. I mean—"

"Wait, Claire."

But Claire didn't wait. Deborah listened as the never-rattled, always-grounded Claire Rawlings allowed her voice to rise in volume and pitch. "It drives me nuts that she got away with that! I tried to jump in three different times. I wanted to hit home what you said—there's no way an amateur could have made up bruises like that. Plus, I wanted to point out how easy it would be for an expert to determine this one way or the other. But Peters wouldn't let me in. He just glared at me over those ridiculous half glasses and did one of his regal head bobs. You were too shaken up to notice, but I can describe it in the appeal document."

An operator's voice demanded additional coins. Deborah pulled off her glove and plunked twelve quarters into that slot. Afterward, her fingers were too cold to bend.

"I'm sure we can prove the authenticity of the photographs to the Hearing Board or, for that matter, in court. I already contacted someone who's an expert on photographic evidence. And how on God's green earth did Lucinda Baxter know about those Polaroids? How dare the JA's office tip her off!"

In an effort to steady herself, Deborah grabbed onto the shelf; two piles of quarters pinged across the narrow floor. "Claire, stop, please. It's my fault. It was me. I handed Will our game plan. That day on the quad. I did it." Tears dampened the remaining coins. In reply to Claire's questions, Deborah laid out her efforts to convince Will to take a leave of absence. "Liddie seemed to have made up her mind not to file. I didn't want him to ruin her life." Deborah turned out her pockets in a vain attempt to find a Kleenex. She swiped at the snot leaking over her upper lip.

Claire's voice returned to normal. There was no "How stupid could you be?"—but also no "Don't worry, it's not your fault." Instead, Claire told Deborah she'd call Professor Davis and arrange a meeting for seven o'clock that night. "I've already filled her in on the hearing," she said. "I'll set out as soon as I finish up a few loose ends. Bring Liddie. We'll figure . . ." The operator's voice drowned out the rest.

Deborah went straight back to the dorm room and, except for a speeded-up bathroom break, did not emerge until she had to leave for the meeting. After putting fresh sheets on her own bed and organizing her sweaters into two plastic bins, Deborah relined the books on her desk by height, instead of topic, and then huddled in her chair. staring at the same ten lines of *The Changing Face of the Constitution*. She felt as if a scarf were wrapped tightly around her neck, blocking the airway. If only Liddie would charge screaming through the door, hollering at Deborah, hurling balls of yarn around the room.

But there was no sign of Liddie, no one to ask where she might be—and no reason to believe she'd return as the familiar, no-bullshit, swift-tongued version of herself. Deborah dashed off a quick note and looked for a place to pin it on Liddie's pillow or blanket, finally taping it to the bedpost: "Back by 10. Please wait up."

Deborah took the bus and walked another four blocks to get to Professor Davis's place. She lived just off campus, the second floor of an old brick house on Erie Street. Claire had already arrived when Deborah rang the bell. Both women came to the door and looked over her shoulder.

"No Liddie," Deborah said, climbing the stairs. "She never came back after her exams."

"You left before she did, right?" Claire said.

Deborah nodded, wondering whether they'd have the whole conversation huddled in the doorway.

"That means the letter from Peters must have arrived before nine o'clock. Does your mail always come so early?"

Only now did it occur to Deborah that the envelope had to have been hand delivered. She pictured some rosy-cheeked student intern rushing off on errands like this for Randall Peters, someone who'd attended orientation sessions on how to give the letter the proper push under the door, oblivious to the explosion it would unleash upon landing.

"Please come in, Deborah," Professor Davis said. "Let's sit down, and we'll make an assessment." After hanging Deborah's coat in a closet, the professor led them through a modest-size living room with built-in wooden cabinets and braided rugs on the floor. On the mantel Deborah noticed several framed photos of Margaret Davis with another woman. The professor, her face always serious in the classroom, was grinning in every picture, and her hair was either loose or gathered at the temples with combs. Deborah had never seen it down before.

"I thought we could use a little sustenance," Professor Davis said. At one end of a large dining room table, a platter of gouda cheese, apple slices, and assorted crackers awaited them. The table looked just like the one Deborah's grandma used to have, dark wood and giant claw feet. Mint tea was steeping in a ceramic pot with matching cups. Nestled between the two other women, Deborah filled a small plate with food and searched for a way to thank Professor Davis for the sheer normalcy of the scene.

But a different set of words tumbled out of her mouth. "I'm thinking of resigning from Stop It Now," Deborah said. "Someone has to be accountable for something." She'd forgotten to shove tissues into her pocket and had to use one of Professor Davis's cloth napkins to wipe the tears from her cheek.

Claire exchanged a glance with Professor Davis. "I can think of three people who'd be overjoyed to hear that—Will Quincy, Dean Biddle, and that fancy lawyer. "

"You know, Deborah, you were also assaulted in all this," Professor Davis said, her hand resting lightly on Deborah's shoulder. "Will invaded your room in more ways than one. And Claire told me what happened in the hearing—those people were vicious to you, as well as to Liddie."

Claire's voice took over, as if the two of them were actors who'd practiced a scene and knew how to jump in without any pauses. "That may be the way lawyers work, but none of us had a clue there'd be a lawyer in there. I'd have prepped you entirely differently if I'd known."

"You know we think Liddie needs counseling," Professor Davis added. "But please consider getting some for yourself as well. I wish I knew someone to recommend, but we're checking with everyone we're aware of."

A belt of anxiety fit itself around Deborah's waist. She didn't want counseling—she wanted punishment, wanted something she cared deeply about to be snatched away. "Don't you think I need to step down?"

Claire leaned in closer, both hands spread on the table. "I don't mean to sound harsh," she said, "but you're going to have to lick your wounds later, kid. Our job right now is to think about next steps, both for Liddie and for stopping sexual assaults on this campus. It might feel good to throw yourself on a dagger, but it's not going to do one blessed thing to solve the problem. Drink some tea and let's get cracking."

Professor Davis smiled at Deborah and lifted a small notebook that had been resting on her lap. "We need you, Deborah, now more than ever. Regardless of whether Liddie decides to appeal, we need to talk about the JA process and what has to change. I thought we could throw out some options and bring it to the Stop It Now meeting—it's set for Thursday night, right?"

Deborah took a gulp of tea and tried to absorb the direction the conversation had taken. She wished her grandmother were still alive—she'd have an expression for this, some Yiddish wisdom about not staring so hard at the pimple on your cheek that you miss the floodwaters rising up around you.

"First item: admitting materials related to a campus organization in an effort to discredit the integrity of a complainant or a witness." Professor Davis held up a copy of the pamphlet.

"Oh, God." Deborah reached for the document. "That was the first thing I ever wrote, inspired by Susan Brownmiller. We handed it out one time, when we were trying out the idea of dorm circles. Guess what—women students don't really give a shit whether most men are capable of rape. We spent the whole night trying to convince them that forced sex *is* rape, whether you know the guy or not." In fact, the topic of whether or not to use that brochure still produced heated theoretical discussions within the Stop It Now core group. Deborah couldn't remember why that had ever seemed important.

Professor Davis pushed herself back in her chair. "Deborah Borenstein, you're allowed to think whatever you want. Having strong views does not mean you'd make up a story about a rape. It's outlandish that they made such an accusation. Unconscionable."

"And what about Lucinda Baxter lobbing in that so-called threat to the dean!" Claire added. "If this university had denied an academic extension to a rape victim, your group would have every right to protest. Calling it a threat makes it sound like Stop It Now was going to do something illegal, set his office on fire or hold him hostage."

"I hadn't planned to say anything about the group," Deborah told them. "I was so frantic about that extension, and he was being such an asshole, so who-the-hell-do-you-think-you-are-to-come-into-my-fortress, with his perfect little part and fancy little pipes. The guy couldn't bear to mouth the word 'rape,' like the *word*, rather than the act, was the problem. So I mentioned something about hoping Stop It Now wouldn't have to get involved." Deborah raked both hands through her hair. "I'm such an idiot. I thought he was a non-factor in all this, that we needed him only for the extension."

"Oh, he's a factor, all right." Professor Davis refilled their cups. "I heard he has his eye on the provost position. No surprise he's looking out for donors."

Deborah breathed in the mint vapors, which were having no effect whatsoever on the gnawing in her abdomen. "The thing is, I went back there on my own, after going with Liddie. She was a mess—we had to stop every ten steps for her to catch her breath. I mean, she was great with Biddle, really stood her ground, you should have heard her. But she could barely keep her head up. He told her to go rest, he'd think it over. It was such a simple thing to ask for—he could so easily have said yes."

Deborah couldn't meet their gaze. She kept her eyes on the piece of gouda Claire was molding to her apple slice. "And that's when you made the comment about Stop It Now?" Claire asked. "When Liddie wasn't there?"

Deborah nodded. Her hair felt heavy on her neck. "The truth is, I had mixed reasons for going. I did it for Liddie. If she couldn't take her exams, that was it—they'd yank her scholarship, she'd be gone. But it was also about the complaint. She said she wouldn't file if the dean said no. That comment—I just said it to get him to act. I've never breathed a word about this case to Stop It Now. Even if Biddle had denied the extension, I wouldn't have taken a single step without Liddie's agreement."

"Did Liddie know you went back?" Professor Davis asked.

Deborah could feel the other women's eyes on her. "No." She stared at Claire's apple, abandoned on the plate. "She didn't know. I didn't say."

Somewhere in the kitchen, a clock ticked loudly. When Liddie had first set up her side of the room, she'd also had a clock with a noisy tick. After two days of no sleep, Deborah begged Liddie to leave it in the bathroom and use Deborah's clock radio instead. Liddie agreed, but all first year she called Deborah Miss Princess with the Pea.

Once again, Claire set her hands on the table. She wore a Timex like Deborah's, a thin gold wedding band, nails neatly clipped. "We have to keep our eye on the prize here, Deborah. What Margaret said is absolutely true. You had a right to say the group would object if a rape victim were denied time to make up exams. The JA never should have allowed that comment to be used as an attack on your integrity. Think what a threat that is to civil liberties. The student ACLU chapter, the Black Student Union—lots of other organizations on campus would be outraged about this, I'm sure."

Deborah's tears spilled onto her place mat. "The fatal blow was the photos. If I'd just kept my mouth shut, they'd still have done the lawyer thing and gone after me and the group—Liddie predicted they'd use that against her. But those Polaroids, they were our proof. Baxter might have said we faked them, but she wouldn't have known in advance, and she wouldn't have dug up that stupid theater background to rest it on. God, they let me help with makeup because I couldn't get a part in the play."

This time it was Claire who touched Deborah, two fingers on her forearm. "What you did, Deborah, was a mistake. What they did is systemic. You can beat yourself up or you can work to change the system. Right now, the person we have to focus on is Liddie. If she's up for doing an appeal, I feel sure we can win. That has to be her choice. But whatever she decides, we have a lot of work ahead to change the way this campus handles complaints. And we need you in order to do that."

Deborah felt as if she'd been dangling from a giant hook and had suddenly been set back on the ground. She wasn't sure she deserved to be let loose, especially not by these women.

"How do we keep this confidential if we bring it to Stop It Now?" she asked.

Claire and Professor Davis started talking at the same time. Each nodded at the other to continue, and both fell silent. Claire used the opportunity to finish her cheese and apple slice.

"The group can talk about this situation without needing any details of who was involved," Professor Davis said. "We just tell the outlines—someone was raped by a date; Deborah became aware of it; the woman didn't want to go to the clinic; Deborah offered to take Polaroids of her injuries, which were extensive; the other side brought in a lawyer, who insisted the photos were doctored based solely on the fact that Deborah had been on the stage crew in high school and is an activist against sexual assault. We want to demand procedural changes that will prevent such an outcome in the future."

Claire knocked the crumbs from her cloth napkin onto her plate. "That's one arena. But we also want the administration to *take this issue seriously*, build it into orientation, take a look at what some other schools have started doing, pay attention to prevention, for Pete's sake. What Stop It Now has been saying over and over."

"*Yes*," Deborah thought. "*Again and again*."

Professor Davis offered to type up their suggestions and bring them Thursday night. Deborah was used to being the list maker, but all she could do was pile the remaining food on the platter and wander in the direction of the ticking clock. She was washing plates when Claire came to offer her a ride back to the dorm.

By the time Deborah walked in the door, her Timex read 9:47. Liddie was rolled up in a ball in the back of her bed, exhaling the labored breaths that meant she was asleep. There was no note on Deborah's pillow or desk. She vowed to sleep lightly so she could hear Liddie get up, but when someone knocked on the door at 7:02, Liddie was already gone.

This time the delivery person was not a student intern but a slick-haired guy in a trench coat who shoved a letter into her hand and said, "You've been served." No university seal on this envelope, just BAXTER, BAUMGARTENER AND LOHAN, ATTORNEYS-AT-LAW in the upper-left-hand corner and a green sticker in the bottom right, branding the letter as certified.

The guy had an exceptionally long neck, which he extended past Deborah's shoulder so he could peer into the room. His breath on her ear was hot, despite the weather, and smelled of onions and sausage.

Seeing no sign of Liddie, he shoved an identical envelope into his leather carryall and disappeared.

The envelope was fatter and the letter more legalistic than the JA's, but the key words were familiar enough from TV—the firm intended to file charges of perjury and slander both through university channels and through a "private right of action" unless Deborah signed an agreement never to repeat these accusations against one William Harrison Quincy III. A return envelope, folded crisply in thirds, was included.

Although she spent four hours scouring the campus, stopping at every building housing Liddie's classes, traveling over to the textile department on the ag quad, Deborah never found her roommate. The process server was more successful. By the time Deborah got back to the dorm, Liddie was on her bed, surrounded by the same piles of sweaters and underwear that she'd only recently put away. "It's signed, in the mail," she said, her voice flat and barely audible. "My dad's on his way."

Deborah felt as if someone had taken her roommate and stabbed her with a hypodermic needle, numbing Liddie all over and leaving her an outsider in her own life. She let Deborah strip the bed, help with packing, bring back some chicken soup. Deborah kept up a one-way conversation, none of which she could remember afterward. By midnight, Liddie was gone.

It took three weeks for Stop It Now to secure a meeting with a glowering JA, another week and a half to get a response to their proposal, four more weeks and a picket line to schedule a second meeting, a month after that to get a watered-down version of changes to the procedures, nearly a year for establishment of a task force to review possible education and prevention efforts.

According to a note from Mrs. Golmboch, it took only five days for Liddie's parents to check her into the psychiatric unit of Sheboygan Memorial Medical Center.

Fifteen

Washington, DC: Saturday, January 30, 2010

As Deborah stepped onto the porch, she had to shield her eyes from the sunlight bouncing off the snow below. Up and down the block, neighbors were wielding shovels and kids were bombarding each other with snowballs. Despite four inches of white stuff, the air seemed mild. Mrs. Lee next door lingered out front with her infant strapped in a carrier. The baby was sticking out its tongue to taste the snow that fluttered from the trees.

Deborah felt like she was watching a Frank Capra movie—if only her daughter weren't missing it all. She'd tried enticing Becca out of her sulking: "Come with me to the store. We can get real cocoa, the kind you make with milk on the stove. And when we come back, I'll help you add a snow dog to your creations in the yard."

"That'd be a first," Becca had muttered. "Not interested."

Deborah sighed. Becca had a right to know what was going on, but Deborah had no idea how much to tell or when. And she had no clue what to do about Aaron. Still, dammit, it was a gorgeous day and she, Deborah Elizabeth Borenstein, deserved to enjoy a little walk to the store. As she hiked the canvas bag onto her shoulder and made her way down the steps, a snowball landed on her boot.

"Sorry, Mrs. Borenstein!" Mr. Symanski leaned on his shovel and pointed to his youngest grandchild, a three-year-old who had landed smack on his well-padded backside after lobbing the snowball. "It's his first real snow, and his aim's not so good yet. He was trying to get me!"

"May this be the worst thing he ever does!" Deborah waved at the little boy, who had fallen back down after trying to push up with just his left hand to avoid squishing the new snowball he'd made and stashed in his right.

Against the backdrop of shovels scraping and kids squealing, Deborah heard the high-pitched whir of tires spinning in the snow. She turned around, expecting to see a neighbor trying to shepherd a child to a birthday party or some other event that refused to cancel.

Instead, Deborah took in the wide-mouthed grimace of Gillean Mulvaney, rocking back and forth behind the wheel as if sheer willpower could de-ice the snow beneath her tires and allow her to park two doors down from Deborah Borenstein's house. You didn't have to be much of a lip-reader to make out the expletives punctuating her efforts.

Already a cigarette butt had been hurled outside the window into the previously unblemished snow on the tree lawn.

Deborah was so startled, she froze and watched as Mr. Symanski lugged his shovel over. "You got to keep your foot off the brake, lady," he was shouting to Gillean. "You've made a real groove here. Hold up—let me dig you out, but don't even try parking. When I tell you, you need to gun it and take off."

The first shovelful of snow was all it took to propel Deborah off the sidewalk in a quick jog around to the back door. Once inside, she locked the door and shoved the safety bolt into place, then ran to do the same to the front door.

"Jeez, Mom, what's going on?" Becca's voice rang out behind Deborah as she used both hands to draw the living room curtains. Just an hour ago she'd flung them open to embrace the afternoon light. "You didn't even take off your boots! If that was me, you'd be apeshit."

Later, Deborah would mop up the tracks she'd left, eager to remove any trace of Gillean Mulvaney. But the image of that face behind the wheel, beet red from exertion and fury, grafted itself onto the television screen and the pages of Deborah's book and the inside of her eyelids when she tried unsuccessfully to fall asleep that night.

Even if she could exorcise the image from her brain, Deborah thought, would she find Gillean tailgating them to the airport the next morning? Hauling a bedroll to the office lobby to stage a sit-in? Squeezing her hefty hips into the adjoining seat on the Metro?

Was this to be Deborah's new life?

Sixteen

Washington, DC: Saturday, January 19, 1985

The day was wicked cold, unlike any Deborah had experienced in her three winters in DC. When she and Aaron first arranged a Saturday hike in Rock Creek Park, the weather had been much milder. This front hadn't seized the area until the previous night.

"I give up," Deborah said, as she opened Aaron's car door and the wind whipped her hair into her eyes and mouth. "Where's your extra hat?" Aaron used both hands to cover her head with the wool cap he'd been wearing and then scooped a second, thinner version from the backseat for himself. Deborah felt her heart contract. That Tuesday she and Aaron had toasted their ten-week anniversary. If this relationship was going to work, he'd have to want to stick around after seeing her with hat hair—and after hearing her tell Liddie's story and its impact on Deborah's life.

Ten weeks. The blink of an eye. And yet in some ways Aaron Minkin had been a presence in her life for years.

Nancy Minkin never abandoned the idea of fixing up her brother and Deborah. At Nancy's urging, Deborah called Aaron as soon as she came to DC in 1981, the summer of junior year, to intern for Rep. Jarvis Kaminofski from Binghamton. Aaron dropped off a welcome packet he'd prepared, complete with a cheat sheet of DC insider talk and initials ("Going to 'the Hill' doesn't mean Jack and Jill grabbing their pail," he wrote. "It refers to 'Capitol Hill,' atop which sits the Capitol building, where the members meet—although what counts for a hill here in the District would make Otsegons crack up. People also use that phrase to mean the buildings where House and Senate members have their offices, which are on flat ground. Go figure. There's also no easy code for place names. 'GW' means George Washington University, but George Mason University isn't 'GM.' Hang onto this list, and you'll be fine.")

Deborah had been in a staff meeting when Aaron stopped by with the packet. When she phoned to thank him for the tips, he asked if she'd like to grab a drink sometime with him and his girlfriend. Deborah declined the invitation. A quick call to Nancy brought these details: "We just found out about her. She's a Penn State grad who works in his office on events planning. It won't last—she likes country music, for crying out loud. I give her two weeks before she lands someone with a lot more dough than my brother makes."

The following spring, right after her twenty-second birthday and just before graduation, Rep. Kaminofski offered Deborah a permanent job. Liddie sent her a needlepoint that read, "On your way! Period, full stop!" The reference came from a fake telegram Liddie had sent their first year at Danforth, when Deborah's professor proclaimed that women didn't make good political candidates because they teared up too easily during their periods. "Run for office," Liddie had written. "Period, full stop."

By the time Aaron called to invite Deborah for coffee—"that's code for a date," he said—she was already going out with an aide for the congressional rep from Ashtabula, Ohio. Nancy Minkin wrote, urging her to reconsider, but Deborah was too busy getting used to her new life to give it much thought.

She finally met Aaron in person two and a half years later, at a Mondale-Ferraro victory party turned wake at the Capitol Hilton. Deborah was decked out in a T-shirt that read, ONE SMALL STEP FOR A WOMAN, ONE GIANT LEAP FOR WOMANKIND. Just when she was about to go home to mourn in private, an eager lobbyist for the AFL-CIO pulled on her sleeve. "Hey, here's a guy you should meet," he said, pointing at Aaron. "He's what you feminists call *evolved.* And he's unattached." Deborah had seen a snapshot of Aaron, but it was a family photo in which he'd been crouching down, embracing a nephew. Aaron in the flesh looked slightly familiar and jaw-droppingly impressive at the same time.

"Kramer Books just expanded its coffee shop," Aaron said when he heard her name.

"I'd love to," she replied.

"Coffee" quickly became their code word. The first time they had sex, two weeks later, Aaron asked if she'd ever tried French press.

For Deborah, getting to know Aaron was like moving up from the kids' table. He was familiar with all kinds of people in Democratic circles. In his job at an up-and-coming political consulting firm, Aaron had his choice of having a hand in the campaign for Sen. Howard Metzenbaum, a liberal lion from Ohio who was a shoo-in, or an uphill congressional challenge in West Virginia. He chose the West Virginia race. "Paying my dues," he said.

Their relationship moved quickly, as if to make up for that lost time. Aaron had been living in a house near GW with three other guys. After two months of spending every spare minute with Deborah, meaning late nights and most of the weekends when he was in town, Aaron found them a one-bedroom apartment on U Street with a whisper of a garden. They were due to move in February 1. Deborah had never expected to be this joyful.

"I'd fallen into a rut," she wrote Liddie, "like all my women friends who are straight. Half complain about guys who can't pick up their socks; the other half develop complicated charts about who cleans the toilet and who scrapes the pans. Till now I've been moving from one camp to the other. But Aaron is a different breed, Lid. He loves to cook! He prefers order to mess! And he knows how to *listen*!

"Of course, he's not perfect," she added. "His car radio is tuned to sports talk. He doesn't see dirty glasses orphaned on shelves after a party. But he's eager and open. The first time he came over, he wandered into the kitchen and asked my roommate what he could do to help. My mother thinks there may be something wrong with him. I think I'm in love."

When they were together and not having sex—Deborah slightly tipsy with delight at finally learning what all the fuss was about—they cooked or tried a variety of restaurants, they went to movies, they laughed at each other's jokes, and they talked and talked, mostly about their work, about colleagues and politics. They hadn't spent much time yet on their pasts.

They hadn't talked at all about Liddie.

Aaron had seen Deborah pick up the phone to call Liddie, knew they were best friends, but Deborah had been waiting for a time with no distractions to tell him the whole story. Somehow it didn't blend with pad Thai or a postorgasmic lull.

Now, after a half hour of brisk walking, mostly uphill and mostly in silence, Deborah warmed up and the wind died down, as if to make way for her story.

"I want to tell you something that's been pivotal to my life," she began. She and Aaron both kept their eyes on the ground to maintain their footing but continued to hold each other's gloved hands as Deborah laid it all out—the horror of walking in on the assault, the pain at seeing Liddie wither away in the aftermath, the clandestine phone calls to Claire Rawlings, the awful confusion over what to do, the bungled encounter on campus with the rapist (she would not utter his name), the blow of the hearing, the heaviness of that thin JA letter in her hand, her own guilt.

As she was talking, Aaron lifted her hand and held it tightly against his chest.

"Remember that night I woke up covered in sweat?" Aaron had told her she was moaning and rocked her slowly until she went back to sleep. "I don't know what triggers the nightmare. There doesn't seem to be any pattern. Sometimes I go for months without one; other times I might have the same horrid dream three nights in a row."

He led her to a smooth spot overlooking the creek and gathered her into his arms. "I've known motherfuckers like that," he said, freeing her hair from the cap and caressing it over and over. "No better than animals stalking their prey. I hate him and what he did to your friend, and to you."

Deborah wept tears of relief that Aaron didn't blame Liddie, didn't call her stupid or impossibly naive. She drank in his interest as she described the organizing her group did afterward and how committed she was to ending violence against women. Kaminofski was one of the congressional leads on a bill to fund programs for women who'd been assaulted. "If you really want to keep hanging out with me, you need to know all this," she told him, her eyelids heavy with frozen tears. "It's part of the package. That includes Liddie."

Aaron tucked her hair back in the hat, which carried the slightly spicy smell of his aftershave. "I started to fall in love with you that first night at the Mondale-Ferraro party when I noticed the mascara running down your cheek," he said. "I could only be with someone as passionate as you are."

As they started hiking down the winding path, Aaron asked a lot of questions about the work she'd done in college and the prospects in her job with the congressman. Then Deborah brought the conversation back to Liddie and the struggle she'd had to get on her feet—the short stay in the psych ward and the year after that in her parents' home. Deborah gave only the broad outlines of her visits during that time, leaving out the details—the weekly notes she sent, each prompting a brief reply from Liddie's mom: "Thank you, dear. We remain hopeful." The sour smells on the Greyhound bus to Saukville. The sound of Mrs. Golmboch swallowing tears that first trip as they drove back from the hospital in Sheboygan. The visits when Liddie was home, more responsive but often unable to track the conversation, as if whatever meds she was on created some echo or distraction in her head.

"And now?" Aaron asked. They were walking through a stand of birch trees, whose bare limbs were decorated with tendrils of leaf filaments. Aaron plucked a few off Deborah's hat.

"Liddie enrolled in the technical college in Sheboygan, first one class and then full-time. Her last semester she started having panic attacks and wound up seeing a shrink. He thought she was paranoid and stuffed her full of pills. I flew in to see her that spring . . ."

"Wait, I lost track—were you here already?"

"Yes. This was eighty-three, almost a year after I started with Kaminofski. Anyway, by then she'd decided to throw out all the meds. She told me, 'I'm not sure which was worse, being informed that I can't accept reality and need to "get over it" or being labeled paranoid and encouraged to get stoned. It's like someone telling you, "Nothing will change, but you won't care so much." I'd rather feel even if it feels bad.' She finished her degree and got a job at a local greenhouse in Saukville—she's still there. And she still knits gorgeous things, for gifts or charity. The bright spot in her life is this German shepherd her dad got her." Deborah grinned. "She told me, 'Finally, something live and male I like to touch!' That's so Liddie."

Aaron didn't laugh.

"Why so quiet?" she asked, reaching for his arm.

"I don't know. There's something . . ." Aaron waved his free hand in the air as if it held a net that could catch the right words.

"Something what?"

"It's just—it sounds like she has a loving family, and you've been a great friend. I don't get why it's taking so long for her to get over it. Did something terrible happen to her when she was a kid?"

Deborah stopped in her tracks and waited for him to realize she was no longer by his side. "You sound like one of those defense lawyers," she said when he turned around to see what had happened. Deborah grabbed her crotch, rolled her shoulders back, and lowered her voice. 'So my client pulled out his dick and masturbated all over the plaintiff's clothing. Big deal. Most women would just tell him to go to hell. Surely it was plaintiff's family history that caused her to overreact in this way—if we are to believe the, shall we say, histrionic testimony we heard today?'"

Aaron's face fell in on itself. "C'mon, Deb, you know me better than that."

"Do I?" Deborah's breath caught in her throat.

"How could you compare me with someone so despicable?"

"How did this become about me?"

"That's just what I was thinking." Aaron's voice was moving from plaintive to angry.

"Jeez, Aaron, next to 'what was she wearing' and 'why was she drinking,' probing about someone's childhood is the most common kind of victim-blaming bullshit out there."

"I'm not *blaming* anyone. You're the one who's blaming *me*, and I don't even know what for!"

Their first official fight lasted two and a half hours, much of it in bruised silences, all the way home from Rock Creek Park and in separate rooms at her apartment. Just before they were set to leave for dinner with friends, Aaron knocked on the door of Deborah's bedroom. She opened it immediately and collapsed into Aaron's outstretched arms.

"I'm so sorry I offended you," he whispered, as she wept on his shoulder. "Listen to me, Deb. Listen good. I love you. I'm in for the whole package. I want to be the person who banishes your nightmares forever."

Seventeen

Random Lake, Wisconsin: Sunday, January 31, 2010

A whirlwind of brown fur flew at Deborah and nearly knocked her over as she climbed out of the rental car. Charlie Brown was still a puppy the last time she saw him. Standing on his hind legs, he now easily matched Deborah in height. His tongue burnished her face.

Despite the fact that she'd barely slept and had to force down some tea and toast that morning, Deborah had begun smiling as soon as she negotiated the lane to Liddie and Richard's place. All other seasons their three acres of land were a riot of color—giant mums and peonies and tiger lilies, rows of red and yellow peppers, bowing purple eggplants, three kinds of lettuce competing for attention, leaves of scarlet and gold. Even in winter, a stand of spruce trees graced with snow shielded the house from the road until it seemed to rise up at the end of the lane. From the outside the structure looked like a typical Wisconsin farmhouse, except for the large bay windows in front and on the side. You had to look closely to notice the solar panels on the roof, but Richard had stood in this very spot and pointed them out to her, along with what turned out to be the tops of skylights—all part of the renovations he'd overseen throughout the years.

As Richard darted out of the house to corral Charlie, Liddie stood in the doorway framed by holly wreaths. Deborah was pierced with a déjà vu of Liddie in the doorway of their room in Martha Hillerman Hall, holding up a WOO-HOO! sign after Deborah won the freshman essay contest in political science. Gone were the pixie haircut and unlined face of that young Liddie, still the image Deborah carried in her mind. Now Liddie's hair hung in a long braid flecked with gray—not white or silver, just gray. Just Liddie. She was wearing jeans and a knit sweater in shades of mint, a design Deborah recognized from the website. Richard had on flannel, although Deborah knew he wore Liddie's creations when he wasn't mucking the barn or preparing to deliver a colt.

Deborah filled her nostrils with the smell of wood burning in the kitchen stove, something much more fragrant than whatever she and Aaron tossed into the fireplace at home. She felt a glimmer of understanding for what Becca meant about the air being clean and bracing out here, as opposed to DC, where cold just meant creaky joints and disrupted plans.

"Hey, Charlie Brown, let's get this gal inside!" Richard had his fingers resting on the scruff of the dog's neck; the slightest contact from the master seemed to quiet the animal. With his free hand, Richard gathered up Deborah's elbow and led her to Liddie, who looped her arm through the other elbow. Together they whisked Deborah into the kitchen, lit through with sunshine and filled with a bouquet of food aromas—something eggy with mushrooms and spinach, freshly baked bread, and oh, heaven, one of Liddie's mother's kringles.

Cheer, bustle, oohs and aahs at photos of Becca on Deborah's phone, the warmth of that room, the divine food—for the first hour Deborah could almost fool herself into thinking this was an ordinary visit with her favorite friends. As they ate the kringle, Liddie filled Richard in on the concept of "final finals" and their celebratory feast afterward. This was the first time Deborah could remember Liddie's making a casual reference to their life at Danforth.

Richard described his current list of "patients," including a horse about to deliver a couple miles away. "That's the life of a country doc," he said, patting his belly. "Always on call. I had a long talk with that mare yesterday, told her to hang on so I could have the day with you.

'Oh, sure,' she said. 'You're the boss.' But that little lady tends to have a mind of her own."

Deborah's fingers grew cold even with her hands wrapped around a mug of coffee. She suspected Richard knew today's news could impact Liddie and didn't want to leave her side.

"Let me see what else you've done with the place," Deborah said. She hadn't been here since the summer of 2008, when she flew in for Horace Golmboch's funeral. While Liddie scooped leftovers into jelly jars, Richard showed off the redone kitchen. There were no granite countertops, no restaurant-style refrigerator. Instead, the walls had been restored to their original wood, with huge beams spanning the ceiling. In the space between the counters and cupboards, Liddie had hand-installed tiles made by a local artist, ocean blues and melon colors, each one slightly different.

"I love it," Deborah said. "You know how they say some people come to look like their surroundings? You've done the opposite—it's like you've imprinted something essential about yourselves into everything around you."

The phone rang before Liddie finished stacking the pots and pans in soapy water on one side of the double sink. Richard held the receiver with both hands, giving the caller his full attention. "That's just what she's supposed to sound like," he said. "Don't you worry. I'll be right there."

Richard didn't waste time on expressions of regret—this was what he'd signed up for. He stroked Liddie's cheeks with both hands, then gave Deborah a bear hug. "Good to see you, friend. You be safe."

Charlie Brown let out a howl as soon as Richard tugged on his coat, whipping around in circles and threatening to topple the lamp with his tail. "You up for a walk?" Liddie asked Deborah. "This guy'll drive us bananas otherwise. Let me get you a warmer coat." From the back closet, Liddie drew out a down jacket and a luscious scarf of purples and browns with matching hat. "I had you in mind when I made that," she said. "Take it home." Deborah hugged the hat to her head and buried her nose in the scarf. It would go perfectly with her coat, a dark brown wool. Aaron had wanted her to buy one of those fake shearlings, but she'd pretended it looked too real—shearling was something she'd always associate with Will.

Liddie tucked Charlie's leash into her pocket and watched as he tore across the fields, searching for who knew what sorts of treasures. Deborah's muscle memory kicked in, the feel of her calves whipped by the wind on the way to the hearing thirty years earlier. Only this time Liddie's legs were strong and firm; it was Deborah who needed to stop to catch her breath.

A sharp whistle from Liddie brought Deborah back to the moment. "Stay here, boy," Liddie called to Charlie. They were close enough to Random Lake to see people ice skating, a jumble of colored hats and whirling bodies.

"Whatever it is, Deborah, just say it."

Deborah stopped to make sure her voice wouldn't carry. All she could hear from the lake was an occasional whoop of laughter. "Someone came to see me," she said. "A reporter, Gillean Mulvaney, most obnoxious. I know it's uncharitable and unfeminist to say so, but she reminded me of a troll. The kind of person I just can't stand, no regard for anyone or anything but her own ambition."

"She came to see you because . . . ?" Liddie knelt down to slip the leash over Charlie Brown's collar. The dog uttered a low growl as Liddie massaged his belly.

"It's Will."

Liddie stood still as a snow statue. Charlie pointed his snout at Deborah and began to growl in earnest.

"He's running for the open Senate seat in Delaware. Somewhere Gillean got a whiff of what happened in college and wants me to expose the guy." Deborah decided not to mention Aaron's relationship to the other candidate, or Gillean's showing up outside their house. Fortunately, there'd been no sign of her that morning.

Liddie got to her feet and laid her hand on Charlie Brown's head. "I assume your board knows. Are they on you to talk to her?"

"Only the executive committee is aware of it. I've made clear that you're my priority. Period, full stop."

"Got it." Liddie slipped a dog biscuit from her pocket and let Charlie Brown snatch it out of her glove. "You want me to confirm that I don't want you to speak to the reporter, that you're not making decisions for me without asking me first?"

"Yes." Deborah couldn't help but smile. She had tried once to describe this trait of Liddie's to Aaron—"unblinking objectivity," Deborah called it, "a perfect bullshit detector but with an absence of self-righteousness."

"All right, then. You're correct. I do not want the troll anywhere near me. If she somehow spirits herself out here, I'll find a way to disappear for a while."

The dog was banging his nose against Liddie's pocket in hopes of more treats. Liddie got a firm grip on the leash and restarted her vigorous stride across the meadow. Deborah had to jog to catch up.

"You probably know this, but there are different schools of thought about PTSD," Liddie said. "Some people say jump in and confront your demons. Others say stay clear of situations that set you off. It took me five years to get anywhere close to the right diagnosis, another year to find a therapist I trust. As you may have guessed, she's in the 'steer clear' school."

When Deborah first came to that Sheboygan hospital for a visit, she'd never heard of post-traumatic stress disorder. She had no language to talk about what was happening to Liddie, written off by the psychiatrist in charge as a "borderline personality disorder who failed to accept the reality of her behavior." Really, the doctor said, aside from getting her to eat, there was nothing they could do for her. They sent her home after ten days.

For Deborah, the treks to the hospital and later to the Golmbochs' home were as much to bolster herself as to provide support for her friend. Being at Danforth without Liddie was like living in a world stripped of color and scent. Even a sip of the Liddie she'd known was essential for Deborah to manage the hurdles in her department and her growing responsibilities with Stop It Now.

Deborah continued to visit—turning Hanukkah and birthday money into bus tickets—after Liddie went to the associate degree program at Sheboygan Area Technical College and after Deborah's own graduation and move to DC, when she had a salary and could afford to fly. Then, in October 1985, *Ms.* magazine carried an article summarizing a major study on something the author called "date rape." Claire Rawlings phoned Deborah the minute the issue arrived. "It's got a name!" she shrieked. "There are solid numbers! This is a game-changer!" Over a three-year period, the author had surveyed thirty-two campuses and found one in six women said they'd been assaulted, 84 percent by someone they knew.

By that time Liddie was working at the greenhouse in Saukville. Deborah didn't mention the article over the phone. She gift-wrapped it and sent it special delivery, along with the phone number Claire included for a rape crisis line in Sheboygan. "You've had enough misdiagnosis," Claire had written in her own note to Liddie. "This group should know counselors who get what date rape is. The center also has support groups. Hope it's not too far away."

When the article arrived, Liddie did try a support group in Sheboygan but wrote Deborah that the members turned out to be mainly incest survivors. "As soon as I sat down, a woman started talking about being torn between hating the man who raped her and loving the dad he'd been. I had to get out of the room." But a staff person at the rape crisis center there took an interest in Liddie and the following year connected her to a therapist named Sylvia Rosenbaum, who happened to be doing research on PTSD and rape. "She said she'd see me without charge for an initial visit," Liddie had written. "Lucky for me, she's looking for research subjects and she loves knitting. We set up a barter system. I make her this and that, and she saves my life." In addition to the therapeutic insights, Sylvia Rosenbaum knew a textile artist who saw Liddie's talent and took her on as an apprentice.

Standing there now in the meadow across from Random Lake, Deborah thought of all the women she'd met over the years whose pain had been compounded by so-called experts who didn't have a fucking clue about the aftermath of rape.

"If that reporter gets the story out," Liddie was saying, "Will Quincy would find a way to turn it against me. I won't give him that chance."

"I know, Lid."

"I admire what you do, Deborah. But not enough has changed."

"You don't have to justify anything to me, Liddie. I fucked up thirty years ago, and I'm not about to do it again."

Liddie stopped so abruptly, Charlie Brown got caught up in his leash and began to squeal. Deborah squatted down to lift his front haunches while Liddie untangled him. She kneeled and took off her sunglasses so she could look Deborah in the eye.

"That's a big load of guilt you've been hauling, Deborah, and for an awfully long time. I'd like to see you set it down—but I'm not sure you're carrying the right bag."

Deborah began talking before Liddie finished her sentence. "I've thought about it a million times, Lid, how I did things without talking to you first—ambushing Will on campus and giving away our plan, going back to see the dean and dropping hints about Stop It Now getting involved."

Liddie rocked back on her heels. "I was pretty much a mess. Not so easy to talk to. No, that wasn't the main thing."

Deborah felt the snow trickle into her shoe boots.

"It was telling me about the girl Will was hitting on that day you saw him on the quad."

The snow wedged in under Deborah's socks.

"I'd seen my dad deal with people like Will—Dad did carpentry work like an artist and was treated like a servant. I knew we were up against a whole clan, and I knew we couldn't beat them, not even if we'd had a video camera hidden in my bed."

Charlie Brown edged his snout into Liddie's pocket and emerged triumphant with another doggie biscuit.

"You told me, 'Make up your own mind,' Liddie said. "But then you pulled out your trump card. Instead of a choice, you made it a duty."

Despite the cold, Deborah felt her turtleneck grow sticky with sweat. For thirty years she'd been having variations of the same nightmare. A hideous blob, like a jellyfish with tentacles, was chasing Liddie, chortling as it galloped along. Typically Deborah would try to erect some kind of barrier to stop it, realizing too late that by doing so, she'd revealed the direction of Liddie's flight. Deborah would wake up gasping, pajamas pasted to her body with sweat, just as the blob whispered "thanks" and a tentacle whipped out to squeeze the life from her friend.

All this time she'd been berating herself for giving away the flight plan, when the real mistake had been forcing Liddie into the monster's territory in the first place. Deborah had to thrust her hand into the snow to keep from falling over.

"Don't look so freaked. I'm not stewing in this. You can let it go." Liddie held out her free hand and helped Deborah to her feet. "I appreciate you coming out here. I appreciate you not telling me how awful it would be to have a rapist in the Senate."

"Oh, Lid."

"The truth is, I'll hate it if he wins the election. But talking to the reporter would feel like being back in that hearing. I can't give him another chance to erase me."

Deborah and Liddie held on to each other while Charlie Brown ran in a circle and wrapped his leash around their boots. As she looked over Liddie's shoulder across the field, Deborah had an image of Gillean Mulvaney riding through the snow on an ATV with Aaron at the wheel, cape flung out behind her, heading right at these two women chained in place by a braying dog.

Eighteen

Washington, DC:
Tuesday-Wednesday,
May 17-18, 1988

Aaron's sigh, which started the instant he hung up his phone, was so deep, it riffled the thank-you list in Deborah's hand. Even though Mrs. Minkin had questioned why her son needed his own line, she always dialed that number to ensure Deborah wasn't the one to answer and couldn't listen in on an extension. As if you had to be a genius to follow this thread:

"Yes, Ma. I know it would mean a lot to Nancy. . . ."

"No, that's not going to happen. . . ."

"We've been through this a hundred times. Tomorrow is our day. We're going to do it our way." Aaron's voice remained level, but his face afterward mimicked the gaping scream in the Edvard Munch painting.

"Of course I called her. . . ."

"Trust me, she'll be there. . . ."

"Gotta go. . . ."

"Love you, too."

Deborah shoved three packages over to make space beside her on the couch. Every surface inch of the dining room table and chairs and most of the living room floor was filled with silver-wrapped boxes, all of them from Aaron's side of the family. Following instructions,

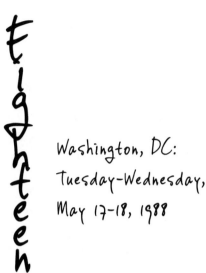

Deborah's relatives had sent money, mostly modest sums, for the couple's house fund. "You don't want a real wedding, fine," Aaron's mother had shouted, loudly enough for her voice to carry through Aaron's phone. "But this is the United States of America, and if my family and friends want to give you nice things, I'm not going to stand in their way." Deborah finally agreed to register at Macy's and scrambled to find suitable items. Aaron's promises to share this task morphed into head bobs at her suggestions of earthenware dishes, Bourgeat stainless steel pans, and towels thick enough to make love on.

"I promise, any crystal or silver, anything *not* on the list, we donate to charity," he told her. "And I'll make all the arrangements."

Now Aaron plopped down next to her, stumbling over the first box Deborah opened—a package from her mother containing a shawl that had belonged to Deborah's grandmother, white lace embroidered with flowers of violet and blue. "I don't know if you've cast out the 'something old/something new' ritual along with everything else," her mom had written, "but just in case, thought you might like this." Deborah held up the note for Aaron to read.

"I gotta say, passive-aggressive takes the cake over just plain aggressive," Deborah said. "But I do love this shawl. I might have to wear it for the wedding, even if it makes my mom happy."

Aaron put his arms around her. "Sorry, dear heart, on this front my family tops yours. Did Nancy ever tell you about her hope chest? Started it when she was *seven*. 'Here comes the bride' was her favorite game—she and her girlfriends battled over who had to be the groom. In her book, the only thing better than having a wedding is standing up in someone else's."

"She'll come, babe."

"I know." Aaron shifted his hips and pulled Deborah's head to his chest; she could feel his heart begin to slow down to its normal rate. "What about you? Did you do any of that stuff as a kid?"

"You mean, writing 'Mrs. Harvey Goldwasser' on yellow lined paper?"

"Exactly. Or did you spring from your mother's womb a full-blown feminist?"

Deborah's "Actually . . ." was drowned out by Aaron's phone. "Nancy," he mouthed. This time, he picked his way among the packages to slip into the bedroom.

While he was gone, Deborah wrapped herself in the shawl and thought back to all the times as a teenager she'd curled up like this with her grandmother, talking about the dilemma of how to be "a serious woman" and still be a wife and mother. Minnie Leavitt Borenstein should have been a union leader or a congresswoman. Instead, she laid aside her ambitions like toys you haven't really outgrown but everyone else says, "It's time." The woman raised four kids and kept the books for her husband's pharmacy, the same one Deborah's dad ran now. "It was what we did, *shana*," she said. "I had no choice. Your *mamele* thought she had no choice. You'll break the chain."

Still, Deborah never wanted a fancy wedding. As her grandma used to say, "So much *gelt* for one party? They should make a house instead." Then, her first year at Danforth, Deborah took a women's studies course and discovered feminism—finally, a way to make sense of her jumbled notions that women's lives should matter as much as men's. From then on, Deborah also rebelled at the idea of a wedding as a special day for the woman—as if the bride were completely transforming herself, while the groom was just getting an add-on, like a new sports car. And the engagement ring! "It's one man marking his territory," she told her grandmother over semester break, "like an animal does with his pee. He's warning the others, 'This is mine.' Yuck. I'll never be part of that." Once she'd broken off her semi-engagement to Brad, Deborah wondered whether marriage itself was something she'd be better off without.

That all changed when she finally met Aaron.

What clinched the deal for Deborah was something that happened early in their relationship. Aaron had invited her to watch a basketball game at a Boys and Girls Club near the Capitol where he tutored kids trying to pass the GED. Any Saturday he was in town, he also played basketball with the same group of kids. When Deborah and Aaron walked into the gym, a half dozen pint-size boys and two girls ran over and grabbed Aaron's knees, the back of his jacket—whatever they could reach. Aaron knelt down and gave every one of them a hug. He knew them each by name, listened as they lobbed tidbits at him "I got three gold stars on my chart this week!" "My cousin's coming for Thanksgiving!"

"Meet my girlfriend," he'd told them, sweeping his arm up to show off Deborah as if she were a movie star. "No more grumpy Aaron!"

The children turned out to be siblings of the kids he tutored. He brought them little treats, helped them with homework—and above all, he took them seriously. Deborah saw in a flash what kind of father this man would be.

There was no issue of Aaron needing to propose. Deborah was amazed when friends on the Hill tried to outdo each other with stories of romantic proposals and glittery diamonds. From their third date, she and Aaron knew they would marry—"I'm only interested if this is forever," Aaron had said. The question was simply when and how. They weren't in any rush. Aaron spent a lot of '86 working for a candidate in Pennsylvania's Seventeenth Congressional District. They decided to have a simple ceremony in the spring of '88, after the primaries and before the main push of the presidential race.

"Uh-oh," she said, as Aaron made his way back to the couch and interrupted her reverie.

"No worries, Nancy'll be there tomorrow. It just took a little doing."

"Did you have to give up our firstborn?"

Aaron lifted her chin with his thumb and index finger. "Not first kid—first toast. Turns out that's the role of the best man. Apparently, this elevates her in the eyes of those in the know."

Deborah lifted her lips to kiss him. "You're a good man, Aaron Minkin."

"I know you're disappointed that Liddie won't be there, honey, but truthfully, it turned out for the best. No bridesmaids is one thing, but only one who's not Nancy? She'd never have come."

Now it was Deborah's turn to sigh. If they were going to talk truthfully, she'd take Liddie over Nancy any day. But she didn't want to blow her wedding eve, or whatever the hell this day was called, so she kept her thoughts to herself. When Aaron's phone began to ring one more time, Deborah carefully removed her grandmother's shawl and crept off to the kitchen to make tea.

For some reason, Aaron had never understood Deborah's friendship with Liddie. He once joked that Liddie felt like a past lover who was still in Deborah's life. "I know you've been through a lot together," he told her a couple weeks earlier, "but you were just *kids*, for chrissakes. I don't quite get the attachment."

"Wait till you get to know her," Deborah had said. "She's the most perceptive person I've ever known, and the most genuine. Without her, I never would have survived the poli-sci department. She had a knack for turning tyrants into twerps. Plus, Liddie single-handedly opened my eyes to the world of beauty. And she's funny as hell, when she's—"

"Not a basket case?"

"Jesus, Aaron."

"Well, it *is* her best friend's wedding. You'd think she'd make an effort."

Standing over the kettle, Deborah reached up to massage her forehead and banish this memory. She would *not* fall prey to pre-wedding jitters. Aaron had stood up to his family and championed the kind of ceremony she wanted. He embraced the vows they would make tomorrow. He was a true partner. And when he did finally meet Liddie, he'd love her, too. Moving quickly, Deborah opened the bedroom door and stood there until Aaron sensed her presence. As soon as he turned to face her, she lifted her T-shirt over her head and swung her bra like a lasso until it landed at his feet. By the time she unzipped her jeans, Aaron was using his chin to end the call so both hands were free to remove his own jeans.

At 8:30 the next morning, Deborah's brother arrived to help Aaron attach Liddie's gift—an amazing ivory-colored quilt with entwined circles—to the narrow wooden poles he'd brought from Cleveland for constructing the chuppah. As Deborah watched them out the kitchen window, she dialed Liddie's number and described the scene to her.

"It's absolutely gorgeous, Lid. The whole ceremony we'll be standing under a canopy of your spirit. I can't tell you what it means to me."

"I wish I could be there."

"I know."

As soon as she and Aaron decided on a time frame for the wedding, Deborah had picked up the phone to invite Liddie. "We'll choose a date around when you can get here," Deborah said. "It'll be just like we talked about years ago. Aaron's boss has a house with a big yard in Silver Spring and has offered to let us have it there. I'll send you the vows I've been working on."

Besides the easy checklist of things *not* to do—no "man and wife," no "obey," no name change, no father "giving away" the bride—Deborah wanted her wedding to be an affirmative statement of equality. She hated people like Phyllis Schlafly who accused feminists of being against marriage and against love. "We're helping create a new model," Deborah told Aaron. They would each promise the other "to love and cherish your unique being, to celebrate and nurture your successes, to soften life's blows, to stand together for justice, to share fully the joys and responsibilities of creating a family and making a home."

They debated adding a section on maintaining individual interests—why should Aaron give up handball because it gave Deborah shin splints, or Deborah visit Liddie only when Aaron could join her? One of Deborah's pet peeves was people who equated falling in love with "becoming one." As her grandma had put it, "Believe you me, ninety-nine percent of the time, that 'one' is the husband. Don't let anyone swallow you up." After drafting and scrapping several versions of this idea, Aaron maintained that it was covered under the "unique being" clause, and Deborah agreed.

Liddie gave the vows a thumbs-up, but she wasn't ready to make the trip. "Crowds, parties, punch bowls, any music played at the frat house that night—they all trigger responses in me," she said. "The good news is, I know this. Bring the guy here. I'm dying to meet him."

She reiterated that invitation now. "I'll take you to Devil's Lake for a hike. And my mom will bake you a kringle. She wanted to send you a batch of them for the wedding, but she sprained her wrist playing a game."

"Cribbage?" The Golmbochs had taught Deborah how to play.

"Red Rover, Red Rover."

Six hours later, the wedding went off without a hitch. Both sets of parents walked the couple to the chuppah. There was no veil or rings; Deborah held no bouquet. She and Aaron each carried a matching silver bangle bracelet handcrafted by a friend, engraved with the date and the words "To my beloved," which they slipped on each other's wrist after exchanging their vows. Forty-eight guests danced on the grass to music spun by a DJ, dined on food catered by a local coop, drank wine and beer chilled in coolers, and listened to Aaron's sister toast "a future power couple of our nation's capitol."

Aaron and Deborah spent a lovely honeymoon weekend in Cape May, New Jersey. The following month, Deborah did try—as she'd arranged twice before—to bring Aaron to meet Liddie. Once again, he had to cancel because of demands at work. Deborah suspected there was more to it than scheduling. But she didn't push the issue.

"Enough trouble lurks around the house," her grandma used to say. "Why open the door and let more in?"

Nineteen

Washington, DC: Monday, February 1, 2010

After nearly three decades in DC, Deborah still wasn't used to living in an area that collapsed at the first sign of a snowflake. What she grew up calling "flurries" made District residents apoplectic. Plows, salt, sidewalk clearing—all foreign concepts, as exotic as spelunking or water polo.

But the evening of her visit with Liddie, it was Milwaukee, standout of snowed-upon cities, that let Deborah down. If Midwest Airlines had canceled the flight when she called from the road, Deborah would have held on to the rental car and driven back to Liddie and Richard's for a warm bed, an old blues album thrumming in the background, another piece of that apricot kringle. But no. "The plane will just be a little late," the airline staff said when she checked in, before they said it would be ninety minutes late, and then another forty-five, and then they piled all the passengers on board and kept everyone on the runway for two hours more "while our crew dot the 'i's and cross the t's," the pilot said, and then, golly gee, "So sorry, turned out the weather caused ice buildup on the wings, and ya wouldn't want us to take a chance with that, would ya?" By the time the passengers trudged back into the terminal, there were, of course, no other planes to take, just a long, crooked line with one remaining clerk. Deborah thought she'd outsmart them by calling the 800 number on her cell, only to be told when she finally got through to a human being that the airport clerk was the sole dispatcher of hotel vouchers. It was midnight before she trailed the other by-now-bedraggled travelers into the hotel, where she lost the battle with the plastic soap wrapping and had to use shampoo to wash her hands, brush her teeth with her finger, and sleep in her underwear for the few hours until the wake-up call for her 7:00 a.m. flight.

Becca had driven her mother to the airport Sunday morning, still sullen but glad to have wheels at her disposal. But it was Deborah's not-so-delighted husband in front of the terminal, honking, when she arrived. His brows were drawn together like a slash across his forehead.

"I told Becca I'd take a cab," Deborah said as she tucked herself into Aaron's Subaru. "I didn't want her to be late to school, but I didn't mean for her to bother you."

"Picking up my *wife* is not a bother." Aaron stuck his hand out the window to adjust the windshield wipers.

Deborah tried to remember to exhale. She'd hoped for a call from Aaron while she was gone, triggering expressions of regrets about Friday night's restaurant debacle and apologies all around, but her phone had remained silent—no text, no email, no voice mail. When she called her daughter about the flight delay, Deborah reached Becca on her cell. (Her friend Louisa answered: "See, Ms. B., Becca would never drive and talk on her cell at the same time. We didn't even know it was you!") Neither mother nor daughter mentioned Aaron.

"Good thing the temperature didn't fall, or we'd have been looking at real snow here," Deborah said to him now as he drew in his hand, the glove sopping wet. "Are they still warning about a blizzard this weekend? Watch, we'll get two to three inches and the whole place'll shut down."

"Can we skip the small talk?" The wiper on Aaron's side was working, but the windshield in front of Deborah looked like they were driving through a car wash. "What did she say?"

"Let's wait till we're home, Aaron." She swallowed several

platitudes about needing to concentrate on the road. Aside from the downpour, the only sound in the car was Diane Rehm on the radio, talking about how to manage your finances and save more money. *My life*, Deborah wanted to say. *Tell me how to manage my life and save my marriage.*

The rain, which had pockmarked Becca's snow family and drenched the snow father's red scarf, began to let up when Aaron took a hard turn into their driveway and pulled up next to the back door. Like most houses in this area, theirs had no garage.

The minute Deborah walked into the kitchen, she had déjà vu of Friday night. Without a word, she put on the kettle and spooned yogurt into a cereal bowl on the island; she would have something to eat, and she would not enter the living room. The clock read 11:14 a.m. "As soon as I grab a bite and do a quick freshening, I've got to head in to work," she told Aaron. "I already missed the staff meeting and my first appointment." So much for vanity—she should have let her hair stay flat on one side and taken the Metro straight to the office wearing yesterday's underwear.

"At this point, two minutes for the Liddie update won't matter a lick," he said. Deborah watched her husband reach into his jacket pocket for a cigarette—he quit smoking ten years ago yet still had the habit of fingering that pocket, as if searching for a phantom limb. "How'd she feel hearing her rapist wants to be a US senator?"

Deborah stirred blackberries into her yogurt and sprinkled some granola over the top. She would not be lured into this trap. "Liddie knows what's at stake, Aaron. She hates for Will to be in this position, but she won't allow herself to be exposed to him again. She does not want me speaking to a reporter. End of story."

"Did you tell her about me?"

Some granola got caught in Deborah's throat. She started coughing and threw her arms straight into the air. Other times she had done this, Aaron made jokes about performing the Heimlich maneuver. Today he just grabbed the Brita and poured a glass of water, which he set in front of her. "And the answer is . . . ?"

Deborah took a long drink. "No. The answer is no, I did not attempt to manipulate or influence Liddie in any way. I told her I would do whatever she wanted. What Liddie wanted unequivocally was to be left in peace."

Aaron pulled out a second chair so hard, it left a skid mark on the kitchen tile—a blemish he'd never notice, even if Deborah announced that something was amiss in the kitchen, like the hidden pictures page Becca used to love in some kid magazine. Maybe the men of the next generation who grew up doing chores wouldn't have these blind spots. Aaron turned the chair around and mounted it like a horse, holding on to the short backrest and splaying his long legs on either side. "She may call it peace," he said. "I call it betrayal."

"That's not fair, Aaron." Deborah kept her voice even, but she could feel the good intentions seeping out of her body.

"Oh, I think it's entirely fair. Let me count the ways." Aaron spread out the fingers on his left hand and used his right to fold down a finger for each point. "Betrayal of you and your organization and everything you stand for." Pinkie through middle finger. "Betrayal of other women who want to speak up against sexual violence." Index finger. "Betrayal of the American people, letting them be duped into voting for a guy they'd never accept if they knew who he really was." Thumb.

"Like *your* candidate is a friend of women!" Deborah heard her voice rise from reasonable to shrill. "Andrew Plale opposes abortion even if the woman's life is at stake. Twice in the name of 'fiscal responsibility,' he voted against more funding for the Violence Against Women Act—that means less money for shelters and crisis lines and treatment centers and, oh, organizations like mine. Shall I go on?"

"Well, Ms. Politically Correct, he may not pass all your litmus tests, but feminists will be screwed royally if Dems lose the Senate. That's the bottom line here, and none of us can afford to forget it, not for a second." Aaron plucked several blackberries off the yogurt dish that Deborah had pushed aside and swallowed them without chewing. "Not to mention the other bottom line—the mission of Breaking the Silence. Since when did that become expendable?"

"Jesus fucking Christ, how many times do I have to explain? Empowering women means *they* decide when, where, and how to speak up. Maybe they'll press charges or go public, maybe not—depends on a lot of factors. You act as if it's a moral necessity rather than an issue of empowerment." Deborah could still hear Claire Rawlings over the phone so many years ago making this same point.

Aaron straightened his legs and rose off the chair. "Don't you lecture me like I'm some male chauvinist asshole."

"Then stop talking like one!"

Deborah picked up a dish towel and brandished it to repeat the points she'd made the previous Friday about the impossibility of protecting Liddie from media frenzy and the damage that would cause her.

"When is she going to get over this already?" Aaron had stationed himself by the kitchen window, which was once again being pelted by raindrops. "Why are you encouraging her to be so weak?"

"Who the fuck do you think you are? Would you say that to an Iraq War veteran with PTSD?"

"Jesus, that's not even apples and oranges—it's apples and artichokes!" Aaron pushed both hands through his hair. "Let's get back to the real topic of this discussion—betrayal. Because you've got to add me to that list. Even if Liddie doesn't know I'm heading the campaign for Quincy's opponent, you do. What happened to that promise to 'celebrate and nurture each other's successes'? When are you going to support me and my career after all I've sacrificed for yours?"

Deborah could feel the pounding of the pulse in her temple. "Don't you dare lay that on me! If you could have gotten a gig like this sooner, you'd have been on it in a heartbeat and to hell with Becca, to hell with my life's work—and don't you ever call it a *career*! I don't care about rewards and laurels—that's what *you* want!"

Years ago, Deborah had promised herself she'd never challenge the fiction Aaron had created that his stalled career was in fact a conscious choice to take over care for Becca and support his wife's work. Never mind the errors in a key Senate race back in 1995, the firm denying him a partnership, his decision to freelance and refuse smaller jobs while he waited for the right break—at some point Aaron began characterizing himself as needing to work at home for Becca's sake, even though their daughter went to Bright Futures child care center every day and then started full-day kindergarten.

So much for internal promises.

Every muscle in Aaron's face contracted. As he took two giant steps across the kitchen floor, Deborah wheeled around to head upstairs—only to run into Becca in the hall, her hand covering her mouth and a lock of hair wet with tears stuck to her cheek. Shit—they'd both forgotten Becca went to her internship on Monday mornings and often stopped home to change before going back to school. Before Deborah could say anything, her daughter ran back out the door. A minute later, Aaron slammed the same door and revved the car engine.

Deborah skipped the shower and speed-walked to the Metro.

Marquita slipped into Deborah's office as soon as she arrived, shortly after one o'clock. "Liddie wants silence, Aaron furious, big mess," Deborah had texted her chief of staff just before getting on the train. Filling in the blanks didn't take long.

"I'm just going to say it." Marquita's dimple always stood out when she ground her teeth together. "His ego is all wrapped up in this shit—that's a bad sign. I know you're not asking for love advice. So talk to me. What's your biggest fear right this minute?"

Deborah pondered the question. She hadn't allowed herself to think this before, much less say it out loud. "Honestly, I'm scared he'll sic Gillean Mulvaney on Liddie. He's the only one besides me who knows where she lives."

"Sounds like Liddie's got her antenna up," Marquita said. Deborah took note of the fact that Marquita didn't rule out the possibility of such a move on Aaron's part. "You got a bigger headache to deal with first. The executive committee call starts in seventeen minutes. Catherine Snyder and Angela Treat both checked in to make sure it was on. Catherine sent a very long email reiterating her concerns about mission integrity and so on and so forth."

Deborah groaned. She'd completely forgotten about this call.

"Seems to me they agreed on a process and you carried it out. Your friend gave a clear answer. Case closed. If push comes to shove, let 'em push—you've still got Yomara and Della, and that gives you the majority. Why don't you take a minute to decompress before I have Shari set up the call?"

Deborah plugged in the automatic kettle she kept beside her desk and dug out a bag of ginger tea while she composed a text to Becca. She deleted three versions, each fairly convoluted, before settling on six words: "Tell me where 2 meet u."

Marquita kept tight control of the phone meeting. Angela sputtered, Catherine interrupted, and both insisted on a written record of the conversation, duly noting their objections to "squandering such an enormous media bonanza," as Catherine kept repeating. Marquita, who took notes during these calls, half rose out of her chair and raised her hands into fists at the suggestion that her account would not be accurate.

"I want this on the agenda at the full board meeting February thirteenth," Catherine said. "And be sure someone there is keeping a record of how many times Gillean Mulvaney has tried to follow up with Deborah."

Deborah and Marquita locked eyes over the phone console. Shari wrote out a pink message slip for each of those contacts—they were up to thirteen—and delivered them to Marquita, who filed them in one of the recycled tampon boxes she kept on hand for such purposes.

Before Catherine finished her sentence, Deborah's phone lit up with a text. She grabbed it, hoping Becca had replied. Instead she found a message from Yomara Vasquez. Deborah reached over the speakerphone and held up her BlackBerry for Marquita to see.

"Game on, sista! Phone me now."

As soon as they ended the conference call, Deborah dialed Yomara; Marquita went back to her own office and picked up the extension.

Yomara's voice had traces of her roots in Mayaguez, in Puerto Rico; she'd given both of them an open invitation to stay at her parents' home there anytime.

"Just want to be sure you're in on the game here," Yomara said. "All this drama over Gillean Mulvaney's an excuse. Catherine's getting ready to make her move. She's tired of these young sisters with attitude out here stirring up girl power among the colored folk and the poor. You know how she's been wanting to add a few 'women of influence' to the board."

Donors on the board had been a sticking point for a long time. Of the fifteen available seats, one was vacant and two more were coming open. The activists wanted to add people representing local groups and create a special Donors' Advisory Council. Catherine Snyder and Angela Treat wanted all the openings filled by high-end donors.

"Oh, yeah," Marquita said. "The only street they want making decisions is Wall Street."

"Well, listen up." Yomara's three-year-old twins must have been standing right behind her; Deborah could hear them in the background, telling each other to 'liss up.' "Catherine has been lobbying hard. She's sent out an agenda for the board meeting to a select group. I'm not at liberty to divulge names. Let's just say one of them has a favorite key on her iPhone called 'forward,' and Della and I happen to be on the other end."

Even though she knew Yomara's message was not good news, Deborah found herself smiling at the idea that someone in this polarized group would break ranks.

"Let me guess," Marquita said. "They want to modify the budget and move up the executive director's performance review."

"I knew it!" Yomara said. "You *are* a witch." Yes, Deborah thought, except for a few times, like when Marquita convinced them to set up an answering service on the side so they'd be less dependent on foundations. They were still paying off the lease on the equipment.

"They want to hire a big-name media team and transfer money out of grassroots organizing," Yomara was saying. "It doesn't take a genius to see the blueprint here: remake the mission, demand the ED wrap herself up in that mission . . ."

Or find someone else who will. Deborah thought the words, but it was Marquita who spoke them.

Twenty

Washington, DC: Thursday, March 8, 1990

Bringing a sheet cake to the task force meeting was Aaron's idea. Ever since Deborah had told him about International Women's Day, he made a point of ordering a little cake from their favorite bakery on March 8 each year to celebrate. "Someday, instead of sweets, we'll have mass protests on that date," he announced when he established the ritual. "And then one day we'll have parades."

Deborah had gushed to Liddie about the gesture and the perspective. "Hopefully we'll skip the stage that comes between those two events," Liddie replied.

"What's that?"

"The shopping day."

When Deborah mentioned that the task force on the Violence Against Women Act would be meeting on March 8, Aaron immediately ordered a special concoction. High-peaked red flowers rimmed the cream cheese frosting. Letters in the same color spelled out "Celebrate International Women's Day. Eliminate violence against women."

Deborah arrived early to the conference room in the Russell office building—they had to move to a larger space after so many advocates showed up for the first gathering at Senator Biden's office. Her own boss, with very little urging from her, had been one of the early sponsors of the bill in the House. Helping to staff this group was Deborah's favorite assignment.

"Here, let me get the door." Amanda Pruitt peered into the cardboard box containing the cake as she held the heavy door open. "Oh, my. I won't be able to resist that. What's International Women's Day?"

Amanda must have been in her early forties, a dozen years older than Deborah and part of the group who just missed the advent of women's studies classes on campus. Without Professor Davis at Danforth, Deborah wouldn't have known a thing about this holiday, either, not the fact that it was celebrated from Iceland to Thailand, certainly not that it was inspired by marches of women's garment workers in New York City in the US of A.

Deborah gave Amanda a brief overview while they arranged the cake on the side table and lined up the plates, forks, and napkins. The coffeemaker was already humming.

"Goodness." Amanda said. As the first vice president of Equality Unlimited, she was used to being the one to zip off facts and figures to congressional staff and reporters. "We don't know diddly-squat about women's history. Or I don't, in any event."

"Ditto," Deborah said. She used to be intimidated by Amanda, whose bearing signaled elbow-length white gloves and equestrian clubs—she had to have been a debutante back in Plano, Texas. Once, when Deborah made a comment on how delicious it was that "coming out" had taken on such a different meaning, Amanda actually flinched and quickly began talking about a *Washington Post* story on Title IX. But after sitting in numerous meetings with her, Deborah had come to appreciate this woman. Amanda seemed to be familiar with everyone, and kept track of who was seeing whom as much as who was sponsoring what bill. While she always aimed to be part of the news and sometimes elbowed into position to be the news breaker, Amanda Pruitt was generous with information—and, as she herself put it, "I never bullshit about what I don't know."

In her job, Deborah had to deal with all sorts of people—lobbyists and advocates and constituents vying for face time with her boss. Congressman Kaminofski gave her this insight early on: "The day you take this job is the last time you'll hear sincere praise. People will also go after me through you. Don't take it personally."

As the other meeting participants started filing in, Amanda turned away from them and drew closer to Deborah. "How about a glass of wine after the meeting?" she asked.

Deborah tried to wiggle her toes. She was wearing the pointy-toed heels she kept in the closet in her office, nestled there along with a pair of pumps, panty hose in beige and black, a charcoal-gray suit with narrow pin stripes, and two white blouses. Kaminofski's staff often wore turtleneck sweaters and pants. Deborah slipped on these look-like-you-belong-on-the-Hill clothes whenever she had to go to a meeting or onto the floor. Since she'd taken the job, she'd acquired two other suits: a navy classic and a deep teal, which she had on today. She'd also bought several actual dresses for fund-raisers. "Let them remember you for what you do," Aaron had advised her, "not what you wear. Blend in." He'd also encouraged her to add some makeup.

After long hours preparing for this meeting, Deborah had been looking forward to pulling on jeans and slippers and having a quiet dinner with Aaron at home. Still, he wasn't likely to arrive before eight o'clock. "Sure," she told Amanda, "but only for an hour. Aaron and I have our own IWD celebration planned."

"You sure did find you that one in a million," Amanda said. She'd been married for a decade to a high-powered lawyer with two sons from a previous marriage who stayed with them on alternate weekends and for a month in the summer. The couple solved household division-of-labor issues by having a full-time housekeeper, supervised entirely by Amanda. Deborah imagined her colleague eating alone at one end of a long dining room table. "I promise to get you home in time," Amanda said. "Think of this as my International Women's Day treat. We'll cab there, and I'll drop you off at your place."

The cake was a huge hit with the task force members—Deborah and Amanda were not the only ones to have seconds. In all, twenty-four people attended the meeting, mostly advocates and a handful of congressional staff. They spent two hours mapping potential sponsors for the bill, drawing up a detailed list of who best to approach and which arguments might move each of them. "Never assume this stuff hasn't affected someone they know," Amanda said. She'd spoken to two congressmen whose mothers had been battered women, and a senator whose daughter had survived a vicious rape. Deborah kept track of assignments and promised to get copies to everyone by the following Monday.

After packing up the remains of the cake and dropping off Deborah's files and heels at the Rayburn building, the two women made their way to an evening smelling fragrant with early spring. "My sister in Iowa said they had golf ball–size hail this morning," Amanda said as she commandeered a cab with a two-fingered salute. "I'm so glad to live in a city that doesn't get crazy winters." The cab dropped them off at Nora's on Florida Avenue, an elegant organic place Deborah had heard of but never been to before. She took in the cushioned seats and relatively quiet room, the walls draped with quilts and tapestries. Apparently, Amanda had more than gossip in mind. Deborah wondered what kind of favor she might have to consider.

"I'd like a taste of your best pinot noir," Amanda told the waiter, who appeared as soon as they sat down and brought the wine back immediately. Amanda's auburn hair, sculpted into a chin-length bob, moved in one smooth motion as she sniffed the wine, bent her head back for a drink, and nodded her approval. Deborah's knowledge of wines was still limited to zinfandel and merlot. This was one area where she was content to let Aaron take charge.

"Don't you just love that task force?" Amanda said, as the waiter brought back a bottle of the pinot noir and poured them each a glass. "Trundling along, even though the bill isn't going anywhere under this administration. If Bush vetoes abortion funding for girls impregnated by their daddies, he surely doesn't give a flying fiddler's fuck about a little rape or domestic violence." The waiter's face remained expressionless, as if they were talking about the weather or the NCAA tournament.

Deborah laughed. She still hadn't gotten used to Amanda's mixing of aristocratic diction with casual profanity. "I know. But I think we'll get some Republicans on board."

"But, honey, won't this bill just put taxpayer money into the hands of ball-breaking feminists?" Amanda did a passable imitation of Phyllis Schlafly's voice.

Deborah bared her teeth and snarled.

"Actually, we had several encouraging meetings yesterday." Equality Unlimited had just held a lobby day with scores of activists from around the country meeting with their elected officials. "The Wisconsin folks are especially hopeful about Gunderson."

Deborah raised her glass. "Here's to smoothing the way for passage when a friendlier administration comes to power. Let me rephrase that: when we *put* a friendly administration into power."

Amanda clinked Deborah's glass with her own. "I like the way you think. Which brings me to the real reason for this outing. I want you to apply for the policy director job at a new group called Breaking the Silence."

So prepared was she for a request for special access to her boss, Deborah had to concentrate to keep from gawking. "You're kidding," she said.

"As my daddy used to say, I'm serious as a heart attack. This is an exciting group. My friend Catherine Snyder is helping start it. They saw the need for an organization that focuses just on sexual assault. How many more girls have to be gang raped by football players before enough of us say, 'Stop it now'—like you did at Danforth?"

Deborah's wine sat untouched on the table. She felt as if she'd just discovered her phone was tapped. "How do you know about that?"

"The real question is, why did I have to hear about it from Catherine Snyder?" Amanda paused to refill her own glass and take a drink. "You're the only person in this town who doesn't shout her accomplishments from the Capitol steps. Most people will regale you about being recording secretary of their high school student council or a member of the college Dems. Here you started this model campus group, and you've never mentioned it."

"So how do people know I was involved?"

"We had an intern research all the campus groups that have been started since the rebirth of the women's movement. Also, a lot of us had dog-eared an article by Professor Margaret Davis about the work at Danforth."

Deborah had learned about Professor Davis's cancer only days before she died, in 1987. She remembered the exchange between Claire Rawlings and Professor Davis about whose expertise would get more recognition in Liddie's complaint hearing. Thankfully, the *Ms.* article on date rape had validated Margaret Davis's own pathbreaking research. It was heartbreaking that she hadn't lived to do more of it. The memorial service was the one time Deborah had been back to Otsego since graduation.

"I thought only academics read that article," Deborah said. "Besides, it didn't mention anybody by name."

"Our intern called to get more information." Amanda ran her hand along her pearls. "Anyway, this new group hopes to do just what its name suggests—break the silence about rape, make it easier for women to step forward and speak out, get some visibility for those who do, flip the shame onto the goddamn rapists."

The waiter had returned with the menus; he stood to the side and waited for a pause to present them. Amanda ordered a crab cake appetizer. "Nothing for me," Deborah said at the same moment that Amanda asked for him to be sure to bring two plates.

"It sounds very exciting," Deborah said. "But I don't have any experience with nonprofits. The people doing jobs at that level are much more seasoned than me."

"Much older, you mean. That's the problem. We need young blood. Besides, none of us biddies has the kind of on-the-ground experience you do. And no one has better connections with Hill staff—we need to make sure this legislation keeps the language you drafted on sexual assault."

"Can't I do that better on the inside?"

"We need someone out here talking to the press, keeping the heat on. Otherwise, the Dems will piss it all away in the so-called spirit of compromise."

The crab cakes arrived, golden brown and massive. Deborah picked at the one laid gently in front of her. Age and experience were only part of the reason for her hesitation. Although she had come up with some of the wording for the bill, especially on stopping the use of sexual history in rape cases, Deborah was reluctant to step into the spotlight. She felt like she was back at Professor Davis's claw-footed table, still looking to be held accountable for what happened to Liddie.

On the other hand, Liddie was significantly better since she'd found Sylvia Rosenbaum. She'd greatly expanded her knitting and taken up weaving. Last July, her mother had brought some of Liddie's creations to a craft fair in Spring Green—they'd sold out within an hour. The label read simply "E.V.," adopted in honor of Liddie's grade-school art teacher, Evelyn Wiener, the person who nurtured Liddie's talent as a kid and encouraged her sardonic view of the world. "When your name is Wiener," she'd told Liddie, "you're a little more appreciative of just how ridiculous the world around you is."

Liddie described this development with more gusto than she'd shown in all the years since she left Danforth. "I'm not keen on public events," she told Deborah. "But my mother was thrilled to death to do it. She believes I can make a living this way."

"She must be so happy to see people snatch up your work," Deborah said.

"I suppose. Mostly, she wants me to be normal. I told her, 'Sorry, Ma, that train left the station the day I entered Mrs. Hopfensberger's kindergarten class."

Amanda snapped her fingers. "Earth to Deborah!" she said.

"So sorry."

"I was just saying that I know you want to set the stage for having a kidlet. Well, this job'll pay a lot more than Kaminofski's giving you. Promise me you'll think it over." And with that same royal wave of the hand, she called for the check.

At home, between pounding thin strips of veal and chopping scallions for her dinner with Aaron, Deborah studied the job description Amanda thrust into her hand as they left the restaurant, especially the list of qualifications. The last one read, "Seeking someone whose passion matches his or her organizational skills." Whenever Deborah plunged herself into a project—the explorer club she started for kids in the neighborhood when she was seven, a newspaper she ran off on the school ditto machine in junior high, the thespian group—her mother would laugh and mutter, "There she goes again." And every time, her grandma would clap her hands and say, "Passion—just what this world needs."

When Aaron arrived, Deborah waited to raise the topic until after they consumed her feast and the leftover cake—enough for a large piece for him and a sliver for her. "You have catching up to do," she told him. "I downed two pieces at the meeting."

They climbed onto the sofa, where Aaron read the job description twice and asked a string of questions about how stable the funding was, how large the staff, and how soon the job would start. Amanda had said they had a significant start-up grant from two major funders, guaranteed for at least three years, and a core team of four, two already on board.

"It sounds like a great opportunity," he said, stroking her hair. "Lots of upsides."

Deborah curled up against him. "Thanks for the encouragement, sweetheart. It means a lot to me."

"Are you kidding? I love the fact that you'll get to work with women who are courageous enough to speak out and refuse to hand over power to the rapists."

Deborah felt as if the temperature had dropped to below freezing and the furnace had suddenly gone out.

Aaron sat up and looked into her eyes. "What, did I say something wrong?" He pulled her close. "C'mon, babe, you know what I mean. I'll learn the proper lingo." He nuzzled her neck, working his fingers under her sweater and running them lightly over her skin. Deborah's limbs began to loosen.

"Remember what we said about 'developing our unique beings'?" Aaron tipped her chin up. "This'll be a great vehicle for you. And I'll be right there to support you."

twenty one

Washington, DC: Wednesday, February 3, 2010

If someone had informed Deborah when she woke up this morning that she'd be in Will Quincy's hotel room before dinner, she'd have declared the person certifiably insane. But that was before she encountered the joint force of Amanda Pruitt and Marquita Reynolds.

Unlike a week ago, Amanda had bypassed all of Deborah's electronic devices and gone straight to Marquita. When Deborah opened the door to their offices at 7:52 a.m., Amanda was waiting in the reception area, a Persian lamb hat covering her sleek helmet of hair. Deborah remembered the time she saw animal rights activists confront Amanda about her fur collection. "My daddy started me hunting with a bow and arrow when I was five," she'd said. "If we're not superior to those critters, shoot me now."

Deborah was embarrassed to admit she'd simply forgotten about Amanda in the hurly-burly that passed for her life these days. The night before, Marquita sent a warning text. "Told AP you'd been swamped," it read. "She insisted on follow-up talk. Gird up."

Between then and Amanda's appearance this morning, Marquita must have decided the occasion called for more substantial support. She waited for Deborah to hang her trench coat in the closet and then ushered the two women to the corner of Deborah's office, easing into the chair across from them. The china tea service, kept in bubble wrap for special occasions, was already set out on the table. Amanda's perfectly arched eyebrow rose slightly. "I was thinking we'd have a private conversation," she said to Deborah.

"Oh, Marquita's my closest adviser." Deborah said, admiring the way Marquita crossed her legs and dangled one high-heeled boot in front of her knee. "We talk over everything. Please speak freely." Without Marquita's presence in the room, Deborah would be stammering like a teenager who just got caught holding a beer can, trying to explain why an entire week had gone by without her getting back to Amanda. Now the momentum had shifted.

"All righty," Amanda said. Her hat remained perched on her head. "I found out why you've been wavering on the Quincy endorsement—your husband's holding the reins in Plale's campaign, trying to keep that jackass on a particular path. Which is probably a smart one, I'll give Aaron that, but it doesn't mean a damn thing about how this guy will be in office. He'll just plop a lot of doo-doo for the rest of us to muck our way through."

Deborah inspected her own boots, chosen for warmth, rather than glamour, as if to ensure no horse shit was sticking to them. The toes were scuffed and still splattered with salt from last weekend's snow. "I haven't endorsed Andrew Plale, Amanda."

"Smart girl! I put my money on you, Deborah, and I want to win bragging rights. I'm confident when you meet this Quincy guy, you'll be convinced we should all give him our full support. There hasn't been a Republican with something hanging between his legs who's this good on choice since Bob Packwood. And with these Tea Party maniacs flapping their jaws everywhere you look, I don't have to tell you what's at stake." Amanda rolled her meticulously made-up eyes.

"As for Aaron's role in the other camp, why, so much the better. Legislators and funders will lap it up—the selflessness, putting the cause above personal considerations, blah-dee-blah. It's perfect. There's a reason that Carville-Maitlin road show is such a draw."

Deborah transferred her eyes to Marquita's boot, which swung in a slow pendulum.

"And I'll tell you what else, darlin'," Amanda said. "This will boost your chances of being selected as the Egalitarian Couple of the Year." Each Valentine's Day, Equality Unlimited honored three couples personifying new models of intimate relationships. Two received honorable mention, and one was heralded with a piece of artwork, specially commissioned from a local metalsmith. Last year the winners were men, one a judge and the other a therapist, who had adopted a child from Paraguay and taken sequential three-month leaves when she arrived. Deborah and Aaron were among the current nominees. "Fortunately, all the couples are hetero this year," Aaron had said. "They shouldn't be allowed to consider gay men. Those guys *have* to be more evolved, or they'd never survive." Deborah and Aaron had been thrilled to be nominated.

Amanda twisted on her seat cushion to take full measure of her colleague's expression. "That's why I've set up an appointment this afternoon at two thirty for you to meet William Harrison Quincy the Third in person," she said.

Deborah felt as if her scalp was burning; she wondered whether she was having a premature hot flash or a panic attack. Before she could conjure up an excuse to get out of the meeting, Marquita set her boot back on the ground. "Help yourself to sugar," she said, extending a teacup to Amanda, who promptly used the silver tongs to pluck two lumps of sugar from the matching bowl, all the pieces an ivory color decorated with delicate sprigs of bluebells. Deborah didn't trust her hands to hold a cup. Marquita didn't offer one.

"Sounds like a great opportunity, DB. I checked your schedule when I got in, and luckily you're available from two o'clock on."

"Well, who knew you were a mind reader?" Amanda looked Marquita in the eye for the first time that morning. "Smart girl, Deborah, to have her in the meeting."

When Deborah added up her accomplishments in life, not doing a double take or dropping her jaw at this turn of events would have to be among them. Marquita rose and steered their guest out of the room even as Amanda was prattling on about room numbers in the Capitol Hilton and the importance of getting there by at least two fifteen.

A few minutes later, when Marquita reappeared, Deborah hadn't moved an inch. "That woman is a trip and a half!" Marquita said, planting herself in front of Deborah. "Nice facial control there, DB."

Deborah felt her mouth moving, like Becca's goldfish used to do when she'd sprinkle fish food in the tank, but no words came out. Lucky, because all she wanted to do was scream at Marquita for daring to put her in this situation.

"Amanda almost lost her eggs Benedict when she saw I wasn't leaving that room," Marquita said. "And then to have me take over the meeting—well, no wonder she couldn't stop flapping her lips. I know what she wanted to say: *But you're the black sidekick! You can't make decisions!* Except that it was just the decision she wanted you to make."

Marquita's spot-on imitations of white people usually made Deborah laugh out loud. Today she barely noticed. Despite the "blind spot" reminder in her notebook, she hadn't thought about the sidekick issue once since Marquita raised it. A pulse in Deborah's temple was beating so hard, she covered it with her fingers. Truth be told, she hadn't loved Amanda seeing Marquita as the decider.

"Point well taken," Deborah said. "You saved my butt in that meeting. I . . . look, it's not just Amanda."

"Oh, yes, Kemo Sabe, we *will* come back to this. But right now, you've got to get ready."

Deborah took a deep breath. "Even if you have the right to make decisions, that doesn't mean you always make the right one. Please tell me how the fuck I'm going to be in a room with that man."

"So glad you asked." Marquita lowered herself back in the chair. "Here's how I see it. He's on one of those get-your-ass-to-DC-to-meet-the big-boys trips. His campaign staff will have put together a long day of meet and greets. They'll do a quickie 'who's this' just before each person walks in the room. To the extent that they're prepping ahead of time, Quincy'll be focused on the folk with deep pockets. You're probably one of several women called in. Unlikely staff will have briefed him on you until you get there."

"I may look older and wider, but I'm sure he'll remember me."

"That's the point. He'll remember, but he'll be off guard. You can use the power of that moment. Gillean Mulvaney's name doesn't have to pass your lips. Just let it hang in the air whether or not you'd go to the press."

"There's a piece you don't know." Deborah winced at the image of the oily-haired guy who'd served her the papers back at the dorm. Occasionally, the blob in her nightmares had an exaggerated version of that guy's long neck. "After the hearing, Will's legal team threatened Liddie and me with a slew of charges if we ever mentioned the case again." Claire Rawlings and Professor Davis had convinced Deborah to sign the gag order after Liddie left Danforth with her dad. They'd already agreed the organizing didn't require them to identify the parties involved. No one wanted to waste energy and resources on legal battles.

Marquita's dimple gleamed. "What's he going to do, sue you?"

Deborah allowed herself a little smile.

"Listen, I know this dude is evil. And I know it's not going to be easy to be in the same room without wanting to scratch his eyeballs out and feed 'em to a stray rat. But from what you told me, thirty years ago you felt like you let him in on your game plan. Well, this meeting could give you a glimpse of his. Right now you're thinking there's not a single damn thing you can do. That could be. At least you'll know what you're up against. Maybe you'll learn something useful."

As she was leaving the room, Marquita pointed her perfect red fingernail at Deborah's boots. "You know you're not wearing *those* to the Hilton." Marquita did a little karate kick with her right foot. "Mine will add a subliminal kick-ass message. I'll put some newspaper in the toes and drop them off an hour before you leave, so you can practice walking in his door without tripping."

"How do I practice not losing my lunch?"

Marquita leaned against the door. "Assume he's done his homework. He may not realize before you get there that you're on his dance card, but do not be surprised if he knows everything else about what you do and who you share your bed with."

As Deborah was telling the cab driver her destination, the beep on her BlackBerry announced a new text. "Back by 6 tomro," Aaron wrote. He'd been in Delaware the last two days. "Tlk then." Becca would still be on her road trip with Louisa and Louisa's mother to colleges in the northeast—excluding Tufts and Danforth. "I don't want to be considered as a legacy," she'd told her parents. "And don't tell me I can apply without mentioning it. The second they enter your name in a computer terminal, I bet every single factoid about you pops up, including what kind of toilet paper you use and whether you were ever on Ritalin."

After their blow-up Monday morning, Deborah and Aaron had declared a truce for their daughter's sake. Becca sat on her bed braiding and unbraiding her hair while the two of them stood in her room together that evening. "We have a disagreement related to this campaign," Aaron said. "Both of us are a little fried, and we overreacted. We're really sorry you had to see us behaving badly, Bec. Please don't worry." Deborah couldn't bring herself to say anything other than "If you like, I can do a French braid for you before you leave in the morning."

Now she pictured Becca, hair tamed in the French braid, nodding politely to admissions officers and arranging to visit classrooms. She'd find a way to hang out with students in the bathroom or some coffee shop afterward. "The students *not* assigned to the tour," Becca had told her as they packed her duffel bag before Louisa's mom arrived. "That's how I'm going to decide. I'll Skype you from the road."

Deborah had intended to use the cab ride to do deep breathing and steel herself for the sight of Will Quincy, but the driver arrived too quickly at the Capitol Hilton. Once inside, she had to concentrate on keeping her balance on Marquita's high heels while going up to the designated suite on the twelfth floor. By the time Deborah knocked on the door, sweat was pooling under her arms and around her breastbone.

"Thanks so much for coming." The aide who answered the door looked like he was too young to shave. "I'm Todd Jennings, Mr. Quincy's scheduling coordinator. And you must be . . . ?" He looked at a spreadsheet on a tortoiseshell clipboard.

"Deborah Borenstein." As she peeled off her coat, Deborah hoped the young aide wouldn't worry that she was having a heart attack. Fortunately, he didn't look closely enough to notice the sweat on her forehead and above her upper lip. Her suit jacket was too dark to show underarm stains.

"Great, our two thirty. You're a little early, and of course we're running a little behind. Do take a seat and help yourself to a cup of coffee. The candidate will be with you shortly." He ushered her into a room with what looked to be comfortable couches—the boots were killing her, but Deborah suspected her legs would be wobbly even if she were wearing Keds. In a corner, the TV was tuned at a low volume to CNN.

"Shortly" turned out to be forty-five minutes. Deborah busied herself trying to lower her body temperature, reviewing her notes, and observing the two people who went in before her, one of whom she knew, the head of a small environmental group, who got a whopping four minutes with Quincy, and the other a tall guy in an alpaca coat who stayed in the inner sanctum more than half an hour. Several other staff with cell phones wandered in and out from another suite across the hall.

"Okay, we're ready. Sorry about that." Todd Jennings took her by the elbow and led her toward the main room. Normally Deborah hated strange men touching her in that proprietary way, but this time she was grateful. A petite woman, hair in a neat twist and materials tucked in the crook of her elbow, met them at the threshold.

"This is Deb Bernstein," Jennings was saying. "Runs one of the key national women's groups. Deb, that's Will over there, and this is his campaign vice chair, Sonja Nielson."

At first glance, Will, who was motioning them in while talking on a cell phone, looked very much the same—trim, perhaps a little taller, hair still blond, the color fading into gray but in that elegant way that doesn't look like much different from the original. Every hair on his head fell into place—he must have had one of those $400 John Edwards haircuts. As soon as they entered the room, Will shrugged his shoulders, held out his nonphone hand in mock surrender, and turned it into an index finger promising to be only one more minute.

"So nice to meet you, Deb." Sonja looked to be in her midthirties. "I've prepared a packet for you on our positions on women's issues. I think you'll be very pleased. Frankly, there are a lot of women in our party who are thrilled to see Will Quincy with a real shot at the

Senate. All these years he's been immersed in business, not ideology. His sister helps run the place—he says she whipped him into shape." Sonja Nielson pressed the glossy packet of materials into Deborah's hands. "Look it over. I think you know there aren't many campaigns on either side that have women at my level. But if Will weren't the real deal, I wouldn't be here in any capacity."

Before Deborah could absorb this speech, which sounded practiced but sincere, Will walked over to greet her and took her right hand in both of his. The packet would have scattered to the floor had Sonja Nielson not latched onto it.

"How nice to meet you, Deb!" Will's voice sounded deeper, but Deborah would have recognized it anywhere. "I know Amanda Pruitt and her colleagues at Equality Unlimited are really excited about having someone on our side of the aisle who'll be in their corner. I hope you will be as well."

Marquita's advice echoed in Deborah's ears: *Keep swallowing. It'll clear out the bile, and it'll give you time to get your shit together when he shakes your hand. Which he will.* Deborah pressed down on the perilous heels of her boots as she extracted her hand and held it out to Sonja Nielson, who squeezed it and then refilled it with the folder.

"Here you go, Deb."

"Actually, it's Deborah. Deborah Bo-ren-stein. Danforth University class of 1982."

"What a coincidence!" Sonja exclaimed. "Will's class of eighty! Did you two ever run into each other up there?"

With a tiny intake of breath and two rapid blinks, Will slid his own hand into his pockets. "Tell you what, Sonja: Why don't you and Todd excuse us so we can catch up on the Otsego Ocelots? Deborah, is it? Here, please have a seat." Will pointed to a pair of chairs at a small table. When Deborah remained standing, so did Will. Both aides vanished from the room.

Deborah had practiced three opening lines, one involving small talk, a second referring to his fraternity. She had no trouble going straight to the third: "You've come a long way from that room at Goodman Parrish, Will."

"Most of my classes were in Frederick Hall, econ and business."

"Are you still in touch with Randall Peters? I hear he was appointed to the federal bench in 2001."

Will took a seat in his chair, opened a rectangular silver box with "WHQ" engraved on it, and lifted out a cigar. "Do you mind if I smoke?" he asked, as he snipped off the end of the cigar with some device that resembled a guillotine.

"Yes, I do."

Will grinned and pulled a lighter, also silver, from his pocket. Deborah felt her stomach churn as the flame shot up and surrounded the other end of the cigar. She swallowed again before she spoke. "So, I imagine reporters are digging for dirt in everybody's campaign. What's your plan?"

"I take it your hubby sent you," Will said, his eye on the flame.

Deborah might have remained standing, but her feet cried out for relief. She dropped into the other chair and sent silent thanks to Marquita for having predicted this. "We keep our professional lives entirely separate."

"I'll just bet you do." Will took a puff on the cigar and turned his head to blow out the smoke. "Look, I can see why you'd want to try to boost your hubby's career. And I can picture the fund-raising letter you'd fashion out of this. But I gotta tell you, rumors about college sexual dalliances are hardly fodder for prime-time news."

"I'm not the one spreading those rumors."

Will held the cigar pointed straight up and laughed, a deep, you-can't-touch-me-motherfucker belly laugh. "Should any slander emerge, the source will immediately be pegged to my opponent's campaign manager and his lovely wife, apparently an unreconstructed strident feminist hoping to raise money to pursue her radical agenda. My campaign will look into appropriate legal action. While the mainstream media will ignore the story, the *National Enquirer* and the like will camp out all over your girlfriend's land—Random Lake, Wisconsin, isn't it?—so hard to clean up after those folks. Facebook is a marvel, helps me stay in touch with my fraternity brothers, the ones who saw your friend slobber all over me. Some of them are bound to want their fifteen minutes of fame. Not a pretty prospect, but hey, whatever floats your boat."

Will stopped to draw on his cigar. Deborah searched for some water, but only one glass sat on the table. The thought of putting her lips on something his lips had touched made her want to collapse on the spot.

"Amanda Pruitt's a marvelous woman." Will's voice grew exuberant. "Very pragmatic, very shrewd. She's been doing a bang-up job lining up endorsements from women's organizations. Looks like she's sewn up most of the big-name groups. Like her, they're all focused on the big picture."

Will stubbed out his cigar in a heavy crystal ashtray and looked her in the eye. "I'm proud to be working with them, Deborah. And I'd be really glad to have you add your name to that list."

The iPhone sat next to the silver box. Will pressed one key. Sonja Nielson was at his side by the time Will set the phone back down.

"Todd's got your next appointment waiting, Will, and Adam's holding," she said as she handed him a different iPhone. "We're delighted you were able to make time to come over, Deb. Let me escort you out."

"Lovely to catch up with you, Deborah." Will remained in his chair and put the phone to his ear. "Adam, my good man. Yes, I'll be back home tonight."

Sonja Nielson steered Deborah right through the waiting room and out the door. The minute the elevator door closed, Deborah wedged herself into a corner and peeled off the boots, slipping into a pair of flats she'd tucked into her tote bag. "I needed to be able to run out of there," she told Marquita after the cab brought her back to the office and they made their way to the "girlfriends" couch.

"So, did you learn anything?"

Deborah kicked off her flats and rubbed her right ankle. "Oh, yes," she said. "Two things: Number one, trust my instincts. I was absolutely right that he'd go after Liddie if he has to." Deborah described the conversation in detail.

"And the second thing?"

The area above Deborah's right eye pounded in response. "I'm not paranoid. No matter which way I turn, someone is out to get me."

twenty two

Random Lake, Wisconsin: Thursday, July 20, 1995

Becca put both chubby hands on the backside of Liddie's German shepherd and tried to wiggle her way on board. She landed on her behind with a thump as the dog leaped up and let out a round of indignant barks.

"You're okay, sweet girl," Deborah told her daughter as Becca began to wail. "Grizzly's not a horsie—he's a doggie. You can't ride him, but you can pet him. Here." Deborah marveled at how big her hand looked as she covered Becca's tiny fingers with her own and guided the palm to Grizzly's flank. The dog folded himself onto his legs and made small woofs of contentment.

Liddie pushed the kitchen door open with her hip. She was carrying a wicker tray with a pitcher of lemonade, two glasses, one sippy cup, and a porcelain bowl holding the oatmeal raisin cookies her mother baked that morning, just before she left to pick up Deborah and her daughter at the Milwaukee airport. "I wouldn't hear of you renting a car," Mrs. Golmboch wrote Deborah as soon as the trip was arranged, "not with a toddler and all the contraptions you have to drag along. Besides, it means I'll have some time of my own with you." She'd spent the whole drive reassuring Deborah about Liddie's success. "She won't tell you the half of what she's done, and she hates for me to brag about it to her face."

The small house Liddie was renting in Random Lake had no air-conditioning, but the ceiling fan and cross-ventilation from the windows created a nice breeze, aided by the large elm tree off the front porch. "The owner's a friend of my dad's, just got a condo in the Dells," Liddie told them when they arrived. "He's letting me lease it dirt cheap. I think he knows he'll hate the Dells and want to move back, needs someone to look after it for him in the meantime." She'd set up her loom in the most spacious and sunny area, what would have been the dining room, and created an eating nook in the kitchen. Deborah felt at home the minute they walked in.

As soon as Liddie sat down in the rocking chair, she reached out her arms for Becca, tears vanquished by the treats. "There's room for you up here, Rebecca," Liddie said. Sippy cup in one hand and half a cookie in the other, Becca allowed herself to be lifted into the lap of her mother's best friend. Within five minutes she had nodded off, a bubble of lemonade blooming on her lips.

Deborah drank in the image of Liddie slipping off Becca's sandals. The girl was wearing a dress made by Liddie from pale yellow seersucker and presented as a belated birthday gift when they arrived. Becca clapped her hands when she saw the matching headband and immediately tugged off her shorts and held up her arms for the removal of her T-shirt.

"I can't believe she's already three years old," Liddie said. Deborah, perched on the braided rug next to the rocker, wrapped her arms around her knees as she contemplated the unspoken part of that sentence—*and I'm just now meeting her.* During Rebecca's first year, Aaron was insanely busy; traveling alone with an infant was more than Deborah wanted to manage. After that, two sets of grandparents demanded their fair share of whatever time the couple found to get away. Even worse was what else Liddie didn't mention—that she had yet to meet Aaron. Still, how could she complain, having turned down a steady stream of invitations and a frequent-flyer ticket from Deborah to come see them in DC? Liddie still stayed away from large groups of people, but she seemed to be doing well otherwise. She was making a living from her knitting and weaving, had years ago quit the greenhouse job. And although she wasn't dating, she'd made several friends in the local artisan community.

Deborah scooped her hair off her neck. "I can't believe it either. Every time I blink, Becca hits another milestone. And the energy level? It's like she's stoked on some internal steroid. You just witnessed it—she doesn't ever slow down, just goes and goes and goes and then, bam, she stops, as if her battery wears out. You'll see the recharge in about half an hour."

"Want another one?"

Deborah slipped an elastic band from her wrist and pushed her hair into a ponytail. "God, I'm so torn. And it feels like there's not much time to decide." Deborah regretted the words the second they left her mouth. Liddie was also thirty-five. If she'd asked, Deborah would have told her she had plenty of time left.

"So why not just do it? If this is the prototype"—Liddie used her pinkie to wipe away the drool from Rebecca's chin—"how can you go wrong?"

Deborah reached for her lemonade. She couldn't find a way to explain the scramble every morning to figure out who had to be where by when, whose can't-miss-it-no-matter-what appointment took precedence over the other's, and especially how to manage when Aaron was on the road. Even harder, how to explain his lack of travel in the past six months, since the firm had denied him partnership and he'd stormed out, declaring he'd take his talent elsewhere—a threat the partners made no move to stop. Yet somehow Aaron still had no time, insisting he had to spend every minute setting up one-on-one meetings to make sure he landed in just the right spot.

"Goddammit!" he'd said the other day when she'd begged him—really, there was no other word for it—to stay home with Becca, who was running a fever and thereby forbidden to come to day care, so that Deborah could speak at a press conference about the implementation of the Violence Against Women Act. "You think searching for a job isn't *working*?" Aaron was up and dressed by six thirty, even though the appointment wasn't until nine o'clock. "This is a very important meeting—they're just the right fit for me. I can hardly convince them what a committed and valuable asset I'd be if I have to cancel my interview because I can't manage my home life! Call Mrs. What's-her-name."

"Mrs. Smith, as I've told you repeatedly, was very clear: she can't take the risk of bringing home germs to her own kids."

"But they're in *school*!"

"You think Becca will stop getting sick when she's eight?"

"The babysitter can wash her *hands*!"

Deborah swallowed the last of her lemonade. No, she could not tell all this to Liddie without revealing why Aaron was denied partnership: the decision to have his well-educated Senate candidate in Indiana don hunting gear and not just brandish a rifle but shoot it. The kickback knocked the guy on his ass, a sight the media present made available to all the national outlets. What had begun as a close race ended in the biggest loss for any candidate in Indiana state history. In that world, a public misstep could wipe out years of the kind of thoughtful, behind-the-scenes brilliance Aaron provided.

"What can I say—it's a challenge even with one kid. We adore her, but the thought of adding a baby to the mix is a little more than we can handle right now. Things could change after Aaron gets situated again."

The rocking chair made a faint squeak with each forward motion. Deborah imagined Mr. Golmboch striding out to his truck to get his toolbox the next time he stopped by.

"Seems like your hard work is paying off, though. Did my mother tell you the whole family watched you on *Donahue*? Dad taped it on the VCR, and Mom made a big feast."

And a big fuss today in the car about seeing their daughter's best friend on TV. "Did you laugh at all the gunk they put on my face?" Deborah asked Liddie. "My brother wanted to know why they let a mortician do the makeup. It was, shall we say, a humbling experience. I don't know if you watched the other segment, but that woman got her makeup done first—we were in the room together. She's not that much younger than me. The makeup artist puts a little blush on her, a little mascara. Then it's my turn. This time the makeup artist brings out a whole tray of tubes and creams and sponges. Argh!" Deborah reached up to touch Becca's bare foot. "Thank you, darling, for the lovely bags under Mommy's eyes."

"You looked glamorous." Liddie batted her eyes. "Everybody thought so."

"Who's 'everybody'?"

"We invited Evelyn Wiener and her husband, and my dad's youngest sister, Mary, who's always been my favorite. It was my parents' idea to make it a party. So picture the scene: My dad worried all day about how I'd react. Mom knew I'd be fine, but she was worried about him, so she was fussing with this and that the whole time. Mr. Wiener has dementia—he kept asking when the newsreel would be over and the movie would start. Only Mrs. Wiener and my aunt Mary were cool. Every time you spoke, Mrs. Wiener would clap and Mary would yell, 'Amen!'"

God, Deborah missed having Liddie around all the time.

"I liked all the things you said, DB. Mrs. Wiener commented on how smart you are. Aunt Mary thought you were passionate."

"What did your dad think?"

"He kept saying, 'How's she remember all those things without any notes?'"

"Actually, I had a crib sheet in my pocket that I dragged out every time they had a commercial break." On a scrap of paper that fit in her palm, filled with the tiniest handwriting she could muster, Deborah had written key concepts she wanted to be sure to include: "no triv," for the need to stop trivializing rape; "PTSD," to remind herself to talk about the new research and therapy methods; "protocols," to explain the recommendations they were making to college campuses; "injury," the long-term impact of rape on a survivor—a conversation targeted at Aaron.

Liddie moved Becca slightly to remove a hand trapped under the girl's shoulder. "I have to say, my favorite moment was when Donahue made that comment about PTSD."

"Me, too," Deborah said. She'd loved the indignation and also the sentiment: "It's too bad you needed to find something that happens to men to compare the experience of rape to before people began to take it seriously," Donahue had said. "It's like calling childbirth a disability."

"So, how nervous were you?"

The director of Breaking the Silence was visiting friends in Barcelona when the call from the *Donahue* show came in. Deborah had two days to prepare. Nervous didn't come close to describing how she'd felt—more like terrified.

"Just what you'd imagine. But that friend I was telling you about, Marquita Reynolds? She did a great job prepping me. That helped a lot. That and the crib note." Marquita had offered to play the part of Donahue in practice sessions—she even ran around the room with a pretend mic and kept reminding Deborah that the host was basically giving her a forum to talk about their work. But Marquita also assumed the persona of various obnoxious audience members, demanding to know why Deborah was letting college women off the hook, with their "loose morals and binge drinking." Thank God none of the real audience members had been nearly as obnoxious.

Grizzly, who had joined Becca in an afternoon nap, made little yipping noises in his sleep. Deborah moved closer and circled her hand on the dog's back.

"Anyway," Liddie said, her face still relaxed, forehead smooth, "I want you to know how glad I am you're doing this work."

"You have no idea how much that means to me. It'll take time, but we're making it harder for the Wills of this world." Even a year ago, Deborah wouldn't have uttered Will's name in front of Liddie. Silently, she sent thanks to the universe.

"I'd like to meet Marquita." Liddie stopped the rocker. "And I wish you could meet Sylvia Rosenbaum. I feel like she's given me a raft of gifts."

"Can you tell me some?" Deborah asked.

"For one thing, Sylvia described leaving Danforth as 'banishment.' Really, that's what it was. And she helped me see how many things Will took from me, including my image of myself as someone who stands up for herself and others."

"Oh, Lid."

"There was a time in high school—I'd completely forgotten this, like a whole part of my brain got shut off and she had to figure out how to reopen it—I had this teacher for history, Mr. Luther, who always had it in for a kid who stuttered. His name was Jerome Jasper, poor guy—'j' was one of the letters he had a hard time with. Jerome wasn't the only student this teacher went after—I remember a boy from Laos, and a girl from what might have been the only Jewish family in Saukville. Luther was always asking her how the bank was doing, even though her father was dead and her mother taught at the elementary school." Liddie's cheeks grew pinker as she told this story.

"Good God."

"Anyway, one day he started making fun of Jerome. 'Je-je-je-rome, would you please tell the class how many peasants they had in the poorest parts of Peru?' because of course the letter 'p' was also a doozy for Jerome. I stood up—it was as if someone was pulling me up—and read from those school slogans they tack up on the walls: 'Saukville students are a team!' and, next to it, a mimeographed flyer about 'if someone goes against school standards, speak up.'"

"I love it! What did the teacher say?"

Liddie put her free hand out in the air, pointing her index finger. "'What on earth do you think you're doing, Elizabeth?' he said. You'd have thought I'd brought in my tape player and turned it on full blast. 'Why, I'm honoring my school motto and refusing to allow a student to be insulted,'" I replied.

Deborah imagined Liddie looking just like she did that first day at Danforth, short hair framing her face, wearing a white shirt and a denim skirt. "So, what did the other students do?"

Liddie shifted Becca so the girl's weight was more evenly distributed and started up the rocker again.

"We can put her down on the rug," Deborah said.

"Not on your life." Liddie gave Becca a little hug. "Well, a couple kids in the back started reading the same slogans. Then a few others, then most of the class."

"Wow, the students in my high school class would have gone crazy laughing at the kid who stuttered."

"Oh, trust me, most of these kids were that bad or worse. But they all hated Mr. Luther. And this was a lot more fun than the regurgitation drill he was about to make us do."

Deborah got up on her knees and took Liddie's hand. "I've always known this about you, Lid. You were the one who inspired me to stand up to Professor McIlhern, the grandmaster of assholes."

Just then, Liddie's phone started ringing. "I'll get it," Deborah said. "It might be Aaron. I left the number just in case."

The only phone in the house sat in the dining room on a small wooden stand within reach of the loom. The cord wasn't long enough to stretch into the kitchen.

"Hey, sweetheart, I thought it might be you. Becca's conked out; wait'll you see the—"

"Where'd you put my blue shirt with the thin white stripe? I can't find it anywhere."

Deborah held her mouth as close as possible to the receiver. "It might still be in the hamper."

"Are you kidding me? You know that's my lucky shirt. And you know how important this meeting is today."

"Really sorry about that. Too much going on."

"For fuck's sake, Deborah, I did every single thing on my side of the list and then some. I can't believe this."

Deborah tried to will Becca or Grizzly to wake up, start a commotion that would require all hands on deck, anything to get her off this call. But the house was completely silent, making the click of the phone on the other end sound like a clash of thunder in her ear.

"We miss you already," Deborah said. "Yes, Liddie's terrific. We're having a great time. Wish so much you could have gotten out of that meeting and been with us. . . . Yes, I'll give her a big hug and kiss for you."

Hanging up the phone felt like being onstage back in high school. Deborah could still remember the drama coach, Mrs. Jackson, reminding them to hear the pretend person's response in order to gauge how long to pause before the next bit of dialogue. She turned back to the living room and tried to paste a little smile on her face.

"You okay?" Liddie asked.

Deborak pushed down the fluttering against her ribs. "Sure. Aaron's got a meeting with this big prospect, tends to get a little nervous beforehand. No biggie."

Becca stretched in her sleep and dropped her sippy cup, which hit Grizzly in the back of the head. The hubbub Deborah had been looking for broke out in full force. The dog's barking woke Becca, whose shrieks sent Grizzly into a frenzy. Wordlessly, Liddie and Deborah worked out the division of labor—mother tend to daughter, Liddie take the dog out for a quick jog around the block. By the time they got back inside, there was dinner to prepare and Chutes and Ladders to play, songs to sing, and Liddie's reading of *Goodnight Moon* to listen to.

Only after Becca was down for the night in the small guest room did Liddie return to the afternoon phone call.

"You've been a good friend to me, DB. If you need one, I'm always here."

"I know, Lid. Once he finds the right position, everything will be fine."

"And if he doesn't find the right position?"

Deborah, the high priestess of plan B, turned up her empty palms.

Twenty three

Washington, DC:
Thursday,
February 4, 2010

When Deborah left the office after the Will Quincy meeting, her head ached even more than her feet. Two doses of ibuprofen and a week's worth of TiVo'ed *Jeopardy* episodes hadn't made a dent. No matter, this morning she had to haul herself to the grocery store and then in to work. All the newscasters were predicting a blizzard of epic proportions starting tomorrow—even Deborah was beginning to believe them. She had long to-do lists to get through before the storm hit, starting with a confidential talk with Amanda Pruitt at nine fifteen.

The get-together was one of several suggestions from Marquita after she'd listened without interruption to Deborah's account of the meeting at the Capitol Hilton. "First, go to your empty home and do whatever it is you do to unwind," Marquita advised. "I'd go for a little drumming, a little wine, and a lotta vibrator, but your combo might be different."

Deborah remembered the slow foot massages she and Aaron used to give each other. When had they stopped doing that?

"Then schedule a tell-all with Amanda, the whole deal, including how Quincy acted this afternoon. Maybe you can't go public, but you can still do some damage if you peel away supporters like her."

"Okay." Deborah tried to picture Amanda's face listening to the story but drew a blank. "It's worth a shot."

"Depending on how that goes, you might be able to sit down with some of the other women she got to jump on his bandwagon."

Deborah would love to diminish feminist support for Will. But Marquita could be naive. If the women's groups stopped short of making their opposition public, the loss of their endorsements wouldn't swing the election. And it sure as hell wouldn't satisfy Aaron.

"There's that lip-pull thing you do," Marquita had said. "You're thinking about Aaron. Clearly, he does not need to know about your secret mission to the enemy camp."

Deborah couldn't have agreed more.

Getting hold of Amanda was easy enough—she'd sent two texts while Deborah was stuck at the Hilton: "Still there?" the first one read. The second: "Call me INSTANT you walk out hotel door." Deborah waited until after the debrief with Marquita, then texted Amanda, asking if she was free for breakfast Thursday at Deborah's office. "In person better," she wrote. "Guarantee treats." That required a call to the organization's accountant, whose mother made homemade rugelach. Last fall Deborah had sent this woman weekly emails encouraging her to go into business and linking her with various resources, including a local nonprofit for women entrepreneurs. "It's entirely selfish," Deborah told Marquita. "If it's a business, she'll have to make the stuff all the time."

When Deborah arrived at the office, staff members were dashing in and out of the small kitchen, buzzing about the upcoming storm. Marquita convened an impromptu meeting in the conference room to clarify policy: "They've already announced schools are closed tomorrow," she told everyone. 'If you have kids in the schools and no one to watch them, you may take a snow day, with pay. If the roads are clogged and public transit isn't working, you may take a snow day.'"

"With pay?" The question came from Belinda Mortgensen, a young staffer without kids who was wary of favoritism toward parents.

"Am I not speaking clearly? Yes, with pay. If our building is closed, same deal. You get my drift—no pun intended. However, everyone who can work from home, obviously, we encourage you to do so. We'll all be able to plug into the network and access files. Please check with your supervisor about ongoing projects and who needs to take home actual pieces of paper. Let's try to be clear about what's possible, what's priority, what can wait till the heavens clear."

Deborah had to stifle a you-gotta-be-kidding-me head shake. Everyone was talking as if the city were going to close down for a week. It was just a blizzard, not a flood! Still, Deborah was delighted to have Marquita in charge and slipped away to her office to prepare the tea and set out the rugelach.

Ten minutes later, Shari announced Amanda's arrival. "I heard about the Egalitarian Couple of the Year nomination," Shari said. "That's so cool. I want you to know your marriage is an inspiration to me."

Deborah's lungs seemed to be drawing in only a sliver of oxygen. She hated that Aaron had had to leave town before they could work things out. But before she could dwell on her home life, Amanda swept in, wearing a long white fur coat with matching hat—rabbit? ermine? Deborah couldn't guess and hoped not to find out.

"I know you, Deborah Borenstein," Amanda said, hurling her coat on the chair and settling in on the couch. "When you're this mysterious, you're sitting on something big. Spill it."

"I will, but I have to ask for confidentiality, Amanda." Twice before, Deborah had experienced conversations with Amanda dealing with sensitive matters. The woman had proven herself willing to keep a confidence—but she needed the clarification in advance.

Amanda raised her teacup in Deborah's direction and wrinkled her little upturned nose. "Done, darlin'. Go."

According to the digital clock on the wall, it took Deborah twenty-two minutes to lay out the whole story, starting with the sight of Will Quincy's arm across her roommate's throat and ending with his confirmation that he kept tabs on her and Liddie and knew where Liddie lived. Amanda helped herself to several rugelach halves and refilled her cup at least once during the telling.

"That's why I can't go public, Amanda. Will couldn't have been clearer that he'd go after my friend. She's got way too many scars already. But if I can at least convince you and some of the other women's leaders to withdraw your endorsement. . . ."

Amanda's teacup made no noise as she set it back on the saucer. "I didn't fall off the turnip truck, darlin'. That was a horrid story, despicable man, but it doesn't surprise me at all. Congress is filled with abusers and liars of every stripe. If we went with character, Equality Unlimited would never endorse a single individual. We have to go with the candidate who's best on our issues."

"But—"

"William Quincy may have fucked your roommate, but Andrew Plale would fuck over the majority of women in this country. Excuse my French."

Deborah was thankful she'd eaten one of the rugelach before her guest arrived. She doubted she'd be able to consume anything else the rest of the day. "No one's asking you to support Plale, Amanda. Just don't endorse Will. You've done that before, stayed out of a race."

"Only when we had two Tweedle Don'ts."

"Is that final?"

Amanda spread her fingers on her neck and nodded. "No one said playing with the big boys would be pretty. But we've got to stay in the game."

Few of the other feminist leaders were likely to break ranks with Amanda. Deborah pressed her hands on the cushions and pushed herself up to standing. Thrusting her arm under Amanda's coat, Deborah lifted it from the chair and passed it over. The fur tickled her wrist. "I hope the storm doesn't cause too much trouble for you," she said.

"Ditto to you—this one or the blizzard that's on its way."

The rest of the day was a blur. Deborah met with the organizing staff to plan what they could do from home. Much of their work was designing materials and talking on the phone with local leaders like Yomara in New York and Della in Chicago—the Keep Your Hands to Yourself! campaign had expanded to a dozen cities. Two staff were crafting a media plan for a Detroit protest against a professor who described enslaved black women raped by their owners as "mistresses." Deborah had a separate meeting with Ben Gleason, who oversaw the Men Stopping Rape chapters. Deborah and Ben were exploring a campus tour in the fall, titled "Only Yes Means Yes"; most of that planning could be done through phone and email. "It's not likely we'll be without power," Deborah told him. "And by Monday the worst should be over."

The majority of staff decided to stay late at the office, but Deborah packed up just before four thirty. "I need to be settled in before Aaron walks through the door," she told Marquita.

"Don't waste time cooking," Marquita said. "Dunk yourself in a bubble bath and order takeout."

The Metro was so full, Deborah didn't get a seat until the Brookland stop. All conversation centered on the upcoming storm and how long it would take area plows to dig out. A guy in his early sixties, wearing a gray hat with plaid earflaps, made gloomy predictions to the woman hanging on to a strap next to him. "We really gotta stock up," he said. "I say no one gets out of their house again till Tuesday."

"I'll bet you fourteen thousand dollars that you're wrong," the woman said, reaching over to pull on one of the flaps. In spite of her funk, Deborah smiled at the thought of how much money these two might have wagered over the course of their marriage.

As soon as she got home, Deborah went straight to the upstairs bathroom and filled the tub with bubbles of some lavender concoction, a gift from Aaron. He had a great sense of smell and was partial to soothing aromas, whether in bubble baths or candles or food. One of Deborah's favorite memories was of Aaron hoisting Becca up in her red footie pajamas and burying his nose in her slightly damp hair after her bath. Becca used to squeal with pleasure at the ride, but Aaron would often have tears in his eyes. "We're so lucky," he'd say. In the tub now, Deborah's heart clutched at the image. How on earth had everything gotten so out of whack?

She left her BlackBerry perched on the towel stand right next to the tub. Two minutes into her soak, the phone shook and lit up for two beats before Becca's ringtone—"Tie Your Mother Down" by Queen—started to play.

"Hey, daughter!" Deborah pressed the speaker button and

practically shouted with joy at the thought of hearing about Becca's trip. "I miss you so! Tell me everything!"

Becca snorted. "Tie my mother down, indeed. How 'bout headlines?"

"I'll take whatever I can get." Deborah rested her head on a purple foam pillow and luxuriated in her daughter's voice.

"I can't Skype now—Louisa totally drained the battery on my laptop watching some slasher flick. Don't ask."

Deborah would have loved to see Becca's face, even if it meant getting out of the tub. Unlike Deborah, her daughter felt completely at home with the technology and grew more animated using it. "That's okay, Bec. Just talk."

"Okay, NYU's definitely out. Omigod, you can't believe how much time people spend just dealing with logistics—where to find a place to live they can afford, how to get from there to school, how to find roommates who won't drive them insane. There may be tons of stuff to do in New York, but fuggetaboutit—I don't want the hassle."

"Sounds right. What about Bard? Did you get to stay with Louisa's cousin?"

"Oh, yeah. She so turned out not to be the best advertisement for the place—way too obsessed with herself, so were her buddies, and they kind of monopolized us. But, Mom, Wesleyan—I just loved it. I already made two friends. Everywhere I went, I could see myself."

"Mmm, Bec, that makes me very happy."

Becca chattered for a few more minutes about the classes she'd attended at Wesleyan, including one on education and social justice that spent most of its time teaching and learning from inmates at a nearby prison.

"Check out the YouTube video I made about the visit—I sent you a link. Okay, gotta go. Louisa's mom is honking. She's worried about the storm and wants to head out now, take it slow. Promise you won't worry and you won't wait up."

Deborah smiled. The kid knew her too well. "I'll do my very best, okay?"

Following Marquita's advice, Deborah stayed in the tub for a delicious twenty minutes, keeping the water as hot as she could stand it and picturing tension and toxins seeping from her limbs. Wrapping herself in jeans and a purple sweater Aaron said made her look sexy, Deborah drifted down to the kitchen. She didn't even glance at the items she'd tossed into the fridge that morning but instead pulled out the file folder of takeout menus and called in an order of tilapia curry and a rice noodle dish from Mandalay.

It was almost seven o'clock when the front bell rang. As a rail-thin young man handed over the bag of food, Deborah heard Aaron pull into the drive and enter the back door. She ran to the archway between the kitchen and the dining room, where she'd already set the table with the earthenware dishes, lit a pair of long red candles, and stood on a chair to reach the wine rack and pull down a bottle of Aaron's favorite cabernet.

"Hey, you, look what I got!" she said, waving the Mandalay bag. "You're home. I'm so glad you're home."

She could see Aaron's duffel deposited in the back hallway, right under the herringbone coat he'd hung on one of the hooks. He was leaning against the island in the kitchen, undoing his tie and kicking off his shoes.

Deborah moved into the kitchen, close enough to face him. "Really glad, Aaron." Her voice was barely more than a whisper. "Not let's-keep-the-truce glad—want-to-start-fresh glad. I'm so sorry about what I said the other day. What can I do to make things right?"

Aaron laid his tie on the tall back of one of the island chairs. "How 'bout you give me a heads-up before going to chat with my opponent?"

Deborah's body lost all the warmth from her long bath. When Gillean Mulvaney came to see her, Deborah had worried about bugs and hidden mics. She'd never given a moment's thought to someone physically spying on her.

"Good God, do you have someone following me?"

"Of course not. When Quincy's in town, we always have a staffer watching who comes in and out of his suite. It's standard operating procedure."

Deborah didn't want to know how they staged that. "This is me, Aaron. You know how I feel about the guy. I hated every second of it. Amanda Pruitt set it up without asking me first, and Marquita convinced me to go, see what I could find out."

"Really? When my staff brings it up, can I tell them you were doing reconnaissance for us and just forgot to mention it to me?"

Deborah heard a moan and realized it came from her mouth. The Mandalay bag started to slip from her grasp. She stuck her hand underneath and turned back to the dining room. As she was scooping food from the paper containers into two serving dishes, Aaron came up behind her and wrapped his arms around her midsection.

"That was a stupid thing to say. Please forgive me." He leaned over and laid his head against hers. "It must have been awful to see him."

Deborah stood perfectly still. "He shook my hand."

"I'm so sorry, babe." He turned her around and planted little kisses all over her face. "I've missed you, too. I want to find a way to work this out."

Deborah's knees felt too weak to stand on. "It doesn't go away. That's all I've wanted you to hear. Thirty years and the revulsion, the sweats, the pain in the pit of my stomach—it's still there."

"I hear you. I do." Aaron maneuvered them onto the chair in the corner of the dining room. He settled Deborah on the chair cushion and sat, both of her hands in his, on the ottoman. "I hate that guy for what he did to you and to Liddie."

"I didn't mean to put you in a tough spot with your staff, Aaron. You can imagine how much I resisted going at all." She described the meeting with Amanda and Marquita's rationale. "What she said made sense. I needed to know how far he'd go—and oh God, Aaron, he confirmed all my worst fears. Tabloids, frat brothers, the whole shebang—including the fact that he already knew where Liddie lives. It just creeped me out."

Aaron released one of his hands so he could lift her chin with his thumb and index finger. "It's why I believe we have to stop him."

Deborah felt her jaw stiffen.

"Listen to me, Deb. I'm not going to bullshit you. The win is important to me. Maybe it shouldn't be, I should be big enough not to need this, blah blah, but I'm not—I want to reestablish myself. So there's that. But this is about much more than my ego. Every fiber of my being tells me Will Quincy shouldn't get away with what he did. Whenever I think of Becca going to college and running into someone like that . . . Jesus, you don't even want to know."

No need to. Deborah had her own fantasies involving items she'd only read about, Glocks and .38s and even M16s. She looked up at Aaron, whose teeth were clenched so tight, he'd complain about them the next day.

"I know, babe—Liddie," he said finally. "But what if there were a way to do this without involving her?"

"Ever since I saw Will, I've been racking my brain to find one," she told him. "The problem is, I'd have to be the one who blows the whistle. And I have validity only because it happened to my roommate. Someone didn't tell me about that rape—I walked in on it. The second I say that, I out Liddie. If I don't say it, I play right into Will's hands. He'll dismiss me as a radical feminist with a huge conflict of interest—namely, you. I become the story." Deborah's voice buckled. "*We* become the story."

Aaron wiped away the tears that were trickling down Deborah's cheeks. "What if Liddie went away somewhere for a while, just avoided the media? We could raise the money, figure out a place. You speak out, have a notarized statement from her saying, 'I confirm these details. Out of respect for my privacy, I ask that the media not try to locate me. I have nothing further to add.' There's a big donor to our campaign who has an amazing spread in Bozeman, Montana. Liddie might love it there."

Deborah tried to imagine Liddie away from her lovely home, her loom. Richard couldn't just pick up and leave. "She'd have to be willing to be gone all the way to November," Deborah said. "I don't see how she'd agree to that."

"No reason to think it would last that long. She'd have made it clear she's not talking, you'll have provided the details. If Quincy goes apeshit, you use it—take advantage of the publicity to call attention to all the work you're doing on campuses, the street-harassment stuff."

"I can ask." Deborah brought Aaron's hand to her lips. "It's a lot to digest. She's going to need time to think about it."

Aaron caressed Deborah's mouth for a moment, but his eyes kept darting to his phone. "Listen, I told Spacey I'd text him someone's number. It'll take just a second, I promise."

"Go ahead. I'll check on the food."

"You sure?"

"Yes, my sweet. Do your thing."

Aaron's thumbs looked gigantic poised above the tiny keyboard. Deborah headed into the dining room and heard only brief clicking as she tasted the curry and decided it needed to be warmed up. When she came back from the kitchen, she was holding Becca's winter hat by its straps.

"It's been a long time since we had a BlackBerry-free evening," she said, dangling the hat in front of him. "I'll toss in mine if you'll toss in yours. If Becca can't reach us, she'll use the landline. Everyone else can wait." With her free hand, Deborah silenced the volume on her phone and placed it at the bottom of the hat. Aaron followed her lead, then grabbed onto her as if they were in the midst of a tornado and in danger of being torn apart.

"I'm not going anywhere," Deborah told him. They stayed in that embrace until the oven timer began to chime.

Two hours later, after a lovely meal and another bath, this time together, Deborah left Aaron asleep in their bed and shuffled down to the back door to check on the weather. She stopped at Aaron's office, where she'd stowed the hat, to grab her phone in case Becca called and to plug Aaron's into its charger. A few minutes later, her BlackBerry did ring, but it was not Becca's tune; the screen read UNKNOWN NUMBER.

"I'm calling from the road."

"Richard?"

"The troll—she showed up."

Deborah had assumed Liddie would tell him about their talk.

"I'd been keeping close. She must have been watching the house, waited to pounce till I left to tend a new colt and Liddie walked outside with Charlie. From what Liddie managed to tell me, the woman started out businesslike. Liddie recognized her right off from your description and headed straight back to the house. That's when the yelling started."

"No, no, no." Deborah sank to the kitchen floor. She could hear Gillean Mulvaney hissing at Liddie: did she really want to be responsible for letting a rapist into the Senate, how could she live with herself, on and on.

"Charlie went nuts. Sounds like my wife came this close to letting him tear that reporter to shreds."

"Oh, Richard."

"She locked herself in the basement till I came home. We're going to Evelyn Wiener's for a few days. If you find out who sicced that reporter on my wife, tell them my shotgun's loaded and I will not hesitate to use it."

Deborah hung up the phone, numb everywhere but her temples, which were pounding again. She couldn't erase the image of Liddie huddling with Charlie Brown on the basement steps. Maybe Gillean Mulvaney was just a dogged investigator who would have found Liddie no matter what. Not that hard to track down her parents, follow one of them to Random Lake. Perfectly plausible.

But how much easier to tap into the anger of someone who happened to have that information.

After ten minutes of arguing with herself, Deborah crept back to Aaron's office. The room was entirely dark except for the blinking yellow light on his phone charger and the red dots signaling new email and text messages. Deborah hit the text icon and scrolled down past a dozen unread messages to the last one Aaron wrote, at 7:46. The phone number was unfamiliar, and no name appeared, but the message was unmistakable: "Change of plans. Back off."

It didn't take long to spot the number again. It appeared a minute later, right after Deborah had confiscated their phones. "Already here," it read. "She won't talk."

Twenty Four

Random Lake, Wisconsin: Sunday, October 15, 2000

"How much longer till they get here, Mom?"

"The time it takes a crow to fly across the lake and back."

"Mom!" Becca rolled her eyes and poked Richard's niece, Carly, also age eight, who was seated on her other side. Both girls wore frilly dresses and shoes with raised heels.

"Any minute now."

"Do you think Liddie'll wear a long veil or a short one?"

Deborah adjusted one of the butterfly clips holding Becca's wavy hair off her face. "More likely she'll have a garland of rosebuds in her braid, sweetheart. Liddie's not really into veils and fancy gowns." Becca's best friend had recently gotten a Barbie bride doll for her birthday. While Becca hadn't outright asked for one herself, given her parents' aversion to all things Barbie, she hadn't hidden the fact that she played with the thing every time she was at Louisa's house. Becca had even saved her allowance to buy pink velvet ribbon to fashion matching bracelets for herself, Louisa, and Barbie. Deborah hated to think about the teen years, which would be here before she could catch her breath.

For now at least, thank God, Becca still liked hanging out with her parents and their friends. Yesterday, after they'd arrived, she'd been giddy when Richard invited her to accompany him on his rounds to visit two horses and a golden retriever that had just produced a litter of puppies. Becca talked about the animals nonstop through dinner and until she went to bed. "She all but got down on her knees begging me to let her take one of those pups home," Richard told Deborah and Liddie later that night. "I have to admit, they were pretty irresistible." Fortunately, he'd convinced Becca the flight would be too hard on the puppy and that she was welcome to come back and visit anytime.

Becca had been extremely fond of Grizzly, Liddie's German shepherd. From the time they visited when Becca was only three years old, Liddie sent the girl a note every month from Grizzly, sharing news about the seasons, his favorite walks and sticks and places to pee, as well as his pet peeves—cars that drove too fast down their lane, expressions like "sick as a dog" and "doggone shame." Two years ago, when he had to be put down, Deborah had gathered Becca in her arms to tell her what happened.

"It's sad news about Grizzly, Bec. You know that he had gotten very old."

Aaron had a T-shirt with a dog skeleton on the front and the words IN DOG YEARS I'M DEAD. So sensitive was Becca about the life span of dogs, she'd made her father stop wearing the shirt.

"Did something happen to him?" Fear twisted Becca's features. "Was he squished by a speeding car?"

"No, sweetheart. He just got too old to move around anymore, and then he died." Liddie would know how to explain "put to sleep" to a six-year-old, but Deborah had to go with the euphemism. "Liddie wanted you to know that Grizzly had a great life, and that you were one of his dear friends."

Becca sobbed on her mother's shoulder. "Poor Liddie," she said, getting right to the heart of the matter.

"Yes, Liddie misses Grizzly very much, and she always will. But listen to this, love—something kinda magical happened."

Becca sat up, tears dripping off her chin. "What?"

"Well, Liddie had to take Grizzly to a vet. Her mom offered to do it, but Liddie insisted on being there. And the vet turned out to be this wonderful man named Richard. He was very gentle and very kind. It's like Grizzly knew Liddie would be lonely, and so he led her to this amazing new friend."

When Liddie called with the news, she described how much time Richard had spent with Grizzly, soothing the dog, rather than tricking him, so that Grizzly seemed ready and at peace. Afterward, Richard offered to help Liddie with the burial and actually wept with her at the gravesite. "He followed me to make sure I got home all right," Liddie said. "I didn't want him to leave."

Richard had a dog as well, a beagle named Beagle, who greeted Deborah and Becca when they arrived yesterday in Random Lake. Becca thought the name was hilarious, but she hadn't warmed up to him like she had to Grizzly. "He runs away when I try to pet him," she complained to her mom. "He thumps me with his tail, and it's *hard*. So is his nose. Liddie needs to get her own dog."

Beagle may have failed to pass muster, but Richard was a huge hit. "He's crazy for you," Becca told Liddie before she went to sleep Friday night. "Talked about you the whole time we were out."

That morning, when Richard asked for helpers "to decorate the hall where I'm going to wed my love," Becca jumped out of her chair to volunteer. She and Deborah spent the morning with Richard's brother, Mike, a paramedic, and his family—Carly had identical twin brothers who must have been ten and a mom who helped run her parents' dairy farm. First the crew pinned balloons and silver bells to loops of crepe paper that crisscrossed the room, some of which had to be replaced after the twins decided to see who could jump high enough to thwack the balloons. "Mom!" Becca had cried. "They're ruining *everything*." She easily convinced Carly to start a sit-down strike until the boys were banned from the room. Becca and Carly skipped to a corner table that was brimming with craft supplies and worked with Mike's wife to repair the damage while the boys took their slam dunks into the hallway.

"I think you and me can cover the rest," Mike told Deborah. They set out trivets and warming dishes for the feast Mrs. Golmboch was preparing and uncrated the place settings for the four tables in the back.

"He saved my life, you know," Mike said. "Richard. Wasn't for him, I'd be in jail or in a ditch somewhere, stoned out of my mind on crystal meth." Deborah knew from Liddie that Richard's mom got ovarian cancer when Mike was still in high school and that the younger brother had been a handful, but she didn't know the details.

"When our mom got so sick, Dad just fell apart. I was already in trouble. Richard, he came back from college and took charge. That's why he never married before. I know how close you are to Liddie, and I didn't want you to think . . . I mean, he had girlfriends before and all, but he was so busy helping us, and then saving money for vet school and such, he just didn't have time for all that. Plus, I believe he was meant to wait for Liddie. I've never seen him this happy."

Deborah squeezed Mike's hand. She tried not to think about whether Aaron would have made sacrifices like that.

The girls finished the last task, placing cushions on each of the two dozen folding chairs after Mike arranged them into a horseshoe facing the glass wall. That way all the guests could watch the sun set on Random Lake. "Mid-October is a tricky time in Wisconsin," Richard said when he and Liddie called to invite Deborah's family to the wedding. "Could be in the seventies, could be snowing. But fall is our favorite season because it makes you feel the most alive—the air and the colors are all sharper." They'd chosen the community center because the lake would be beautiful no matter what the weather. In fact, this was a day right out of a fairy tale, sun sparkling on the water, trees decked out in copper and gold. Deborah wouldn't have been surprised to see bluebirds darting out from the branches.

"Okay, darling daughter," she told Becca, who, like Carly, was speckled with glitter from the silver bells. "Let's go wash that stuff outta your hair so we can come back here and see a wedding!"

Two hours later, they watched the pastor stride to the front of the group, his fingers wrapped around the handle of a large wicker basket. A boom box waited on a table to his side. Although Deborah and Becca had been part of the preparations, details of the ceremony remained a surprise.

"What's in the basket, Mom?" Becca asked.

"Flower petals," Carly whispered. "Least I hope so."

The pastor handed the basket to Richard's father, an older version of his son with a lot more hair, who bit back a smile as he slipped something out and passed the basket along. "Mom, look! Kazoos!" Whatever disappointment Becca felt at the lack of bridal tradition quickly gave way to delight as she grabbed one of the metal instruments. The pastor pressed the button on the CD player. A minute later, Richard and Liddie glided into the room while the Dixie Cups, accompanied by twenty-four kazoos, belted out "Going to the Chapel."

Carly joined Becca in a shriek of approval when the song ended. Her brothers, tucked between their parents, continued to play an extra chorus. Mike and his wife held hands behind the boys' shoulders as they shushed them; no one besides Becca and Carly seemed to mind the commotion.

Deborah gazed around the horseshoe. Aside from Richard's dad and Liddie's parents, the older guests included Evelyn Wiener and her husband and two other couples. Richard's best friend and his wife were there. In the middle sat Sylvia Rosenbaum, a tall woman in her fifties whose graying hair was thrown into a topknot and whose shawl—obviously an E.V. creation in crimsons and purples—was tossed over her shoulder, as if she'd encountered a wind tunnel on the way in. Sylvia had approached Deborah as they were taking their seats to introduce herself and two friends Liddie had made in her support group. "I'd have recognized you even if we hadn't seen you on *Donahue*," Sylvia said. "Not a lot of Borensteins in Random Lake."

Deborah grabbed the therapist and held her close. "I've so wanted to meet Liddie's exorcist," she whispered.

"My dad restored antiques," Sylvia said. "He'd strip all the gunk off till the original wood shone through. That's kinda what I do, too." She thrust a bunch of Kleenex into Deborah's hand.

Becca and Carly beamed throughout the short ceremony, but Deborah dipped into the Kleenex stash the moment she saw Liddie, who did have a garland of white rosebuds in her hair. She was wearing a lavender dress she'd made from some silky material that skimmed over her hips and fluttered around her calves. The vows left Deborah breathless: "I will tend to you and flourish," Richard said. "And I you," was Liddie's reply.

Oh, Liddie, Deborah thought, *this is just the guy you talked about back in college*. "I want someone steeped in decency," Liddie had said, sitting back-to-back with Deborah on the floor, hands clasped over their shoulders. "I don't care what he looks like, but he has to be solid. Someone who says hi to people on the bike path, who always knows the name of his server, someone quick to laugh and slow to yell. A guy whose idea of success is waking up beside me every day."

Deborah reminded Liddie of this conversation the previous day. They'd taken Beagle on a long walk by the lake while Richard was introducing Becca to his flock. "I can't think of a single person who deserves this more than you do, Lid. I'm so happy for you."

The wind had picked up a little, and Liddie, one foot on Beagle's leash, stopped to pull her hoodie up over her ears. "Yeah, he's that guy, all right. I was telling Sylvia he makes me feel *grounded*—protected and strong at the same time. If I hit a bad patch, he doesn't coddle me and he doesn't freak out. Treats it like an asthma attack, something that needs care but with proper treatment will pass."

"Your parents must be thrilled," Deborah said. She imagined the prayers of gratitude the Golmbochs uttered at their dinner table every night.

"The other day I overheard them talking about us. 'He gets her sense of humor,' my mother said. 'Oh, Ethel,' my dad told her, 'that man brought her sense of humor back to life.'" Liddie picked up the leash and wrapped it around her palm.

Deborah looped her arm through Liddie's. "Becca's over the moon about Richard, and she's not easy to please. You saw how tough she was on Beagle."

"Can't really blame her on that score," Liddie said. "But hey, if the guy were perfect, he wouldn't be real, eh?" Wisps of hair surrounded her face, which was flush with joy.

At thirty-seven, Richard was three years younger than his bride. Deborah knew from calls with Liddie that they'd stopped using birth control, but so far, no luck. Such a shame. Deborah would never say this out loud, but these were genes that should be passed on.

"So what about you, DB? Aside from not having time to take baths or visit me more often, are you living the life you wanted?"

"It's a little crazy, but I love the work." Breaking the Silence had just completed a model sexual assault prevention program; Deborah was working with activists at half a dozen colleges who were in various stages of getting the program adopted. A funder had already promised money for evaluation.

"And home?" Liddie asked. "Becca's a prize—anyone can see that. But you haven't said a lot about Aaron."

"Oh, he's good, great, doing great." And really, aside from his angst over his career and the occasional flare-up as a result, Aaron was . . . maybe "happy" wouldn't be the right word, but certainly still vibrant. Deborah felt a pang of guilt for not gushing over him more.

"You should see how fabulous he is with Becca," she told Liddie. "He turned the dining room into a dance area for her and researched the best place for her to take classes—you saw how she loves to move around. Last month Aaron took her to see a real ballet as a surprise. He told her they were going to run errands, but he'd hidden her fancy dress in his gym bag. When they drove up in front of the theater and she saw the marquee, he parked the car and pulled the dress out. 'You might want to throw this on,' he told her. You should have seen her leaping around the house, describing it to me, when they got home."

Liddie pulled Deborah closer. "I wish I had."

"Right now he's on a polling project for a big firm, hoping to get an offer." Deborah had already explained that this was why Aaron was missing the wedding.

"And if he does get the offer, what would it mean for all of you?"

"Oh, we'd manage. There's an after-school program, and I'd scale back a little. I have to admit, I've been spoiled these past few years having him work from home. But we can swing the hustle-bustle. It's just . . ."

Before she could say more, Beagle started barking wildly. Richard and Becca were waving from the other end of the field. "I saw a horse, Mom!" Becca shouted. "And puppies!" Deborah and Liddie, still arm in arm, turned back to meet them.

Only now, during the ceremony, did Deborah work out what was bothering her. Before, she'd been preoccupied with whether Aaron looked vain or petty for being hung up on the status of which political firm to work for. But after witnessing Liddie and Richard, she realized her disappointment went much deeper.

If only Aaron would wake up in the morning, wrap her in his arms, and say, "Wow, am I a lucky guy."

Twenty-five

Washington, DC:
Friday,
February 5, 2010

Aaron had been the early riser for so long, Deborah felt as if she'd never seen him sleeping before. Surely there were times he slept with his mouth open, letting loose snores and farts, his hair greasy and sticking up on one side. But not this night, when she would have rejoiced to see him coarse and unattractive. Instead, he lay on his side in a deep slumber, knees drawn up and hands in prayer position. His hair was curled into tendrils from the long bath they'd shared.

When she'd discovered the texts, Deborah's first instinct had been to charge up the stairs and rip off the covers, brandish a flashlight in his face, and interrogate him until he had just the tiniest glimmer of recognition of what Liddie must have felt like when Gillean Mulvaney accosted her. But in the rush, Deborah tripped over the throw rug in the hallway and would surely have broken her wrist had she not landed on Aaron's duffel bag. She crouched in the dark, rubbing her arm, tears of fury and frustration streaming down her face, and decided to wait until morning to confront her husband. An hour later, she pulled herself up the stairs and fell into the armchair next to the bed, where she nodded off until the gray light of morning slid through the crack between the curtains.

When Aaron first opened his eyes half an hour later, his features remained soft and youthful. "Hey, beautiful," he said, rolling on his back. "Climb back in here and let me warm you up. My arms feel unbearably empty."

Without a word, Deborah held up her husband's BlackBerry. Like a creature about to pounce, she leaned forward and thrust the screen as close to his face as possible without smashing it into his cheek. Aaron jerked upright in the bed.

"What the f . . . ?" He grabbed the phone, face scrunched as he read the return message from Gillean Mulvaney.

"Richard called from the road a few hours later." Deborah pushed herself back in the chair, gripping the cushion to keep her hands from shaking. "He left a message for you—well, for, how did he put it, 'the animal who sicced Gillean on his wife.' Said to be sure you knew he had his shotgun loaded and will use it if anyone tries to find out where they went."

The BlackBerry bounced on the mattress. Aaron's hand was clutching his ribs, and his eyes were filled with tears. "Oh, baby, I'm so sorry. This was not supposed to happen."

"Which part—you fucking over Liddie or me finding out about it?"

Aaron scooted to the side of the bed and reached out with both hands. Deborah recoiled as if they held hot coals. "It was a freak overlap of events," Aaron said. "You've got to understand. I'd come up with that alternate plan, worked on it the whole time I was in Delaware. I wanted to do something that was sensitive to Liddie without letting Quincy off the hook. Oh, God, I was so excited to tell you. All I wanted was to get us back to a loving place. And we did, sweetheart. Last night was incredible: That's what we're capable of. Please don't let this get in the way."

Aaron got to his feet, but before he could reach her she'd rushed to the opposite side of the bed and was tearing off the sheets, yanking her pillow out of its cover as if it were contaminated with an infectious disease and had to be washed immediately.

"Deb, please, can we just . . ."

She jammed the sheets into one pillowcase and took the steps two at a time down to the basement. Aaron followed close behind and stood by the folding table as she tossed the load into the washing machine and turned the water dial to HOT/HOT. If she hadn't been so enraged, Deborah would have laughed at the sight of him, shivering in his boxer shorts and T-shirt, feet bare on the concrete basement floor, struggling to keep some semblance of dignity while his arms and legs pimpled up like turkey skin. He didn't dare touch her, but he did use the low and caressing voice of last night.

"Don't you see what happened, love? When Spacey told me you'd been at Will's office, I felt as if I'd been body-slammed into a wall. I couldn't feel my fingers or my toes, like the blood had stopped circulating. I actually thought I might be having a stroke. It was obvious to everyone that I knew nothing about that meeting. Truthfully, it was like I'd found out you were sleeping with someone else—that's how much it hurt." Aaron wrapped his arms around his shoulders as if he were trying to console himself, as well as to warm up. "Think about how that felt—like you didn't trust me enough to ask my opinion, or have enough regard even to give me a heads-up. I was a mess."

The washing machine jolted into action. Deborah kept one hand on the top and let the vibrations flow through her. "How did this become about you?" she asked.

Aaron grabbed a sweatshirt from the laundry basket at his feet and pulled it on, oblivious to the pesto sauce crusted on the right sleeve. "I just want you to see where my head was at. Gillean had been pestering me for days. She called for the umpteenth time right after I got this news from my staff. I gave her only the name of the town. She had to go through all kinds of hoops to figure out the rest. As soon as I came home and realized you hadn't known in advance about that meeting . . ."

"Jesus, Aaron. This is like a batterer saying, 'If only you'd straightened up the kitchen or made the steak the way I like it, I wouldn't have beat the shit out of you.'"

"C'mon, Deborah. That's not fair." He was holding his ribs again, as if warding off blows.

"Do you know me at all, Aaron?" Deborah looked him in the eye for the first time. "Is there anything I've talked about more than not wanting the media to harass Liddie?"

Aaron had pulled some sweatpants and socks from the basket of dirty laundry and was holding them in front of himself like an offering. "You saw my text, Deb. All I wanted was to call it off. I had no idea that woman could move so fast."

"Never underestimate the media—isn't that your mantra?" Deborah pushed off from the washing machine and charged around the other side of the table to the stairs. Aaron followed a minute later, fully clothed in last week's castoffs.

Oh, the pleas he could offer: Forgiveness! Compassion! A cooling-off period! All the while, she was filling the kettle and rinsing the berries and assembling the teapot and vitamins and yogurt supplies, Aaron begged for time. Finally, he planted himself in front of her station at the island. "Please listen. I know what I did was despicable, but don't let it be insurmountable. I love you with all my heart. I have to go in to work now. I'm going to take the Metro. They're saying the worst of the storm won't hit till this afternoon." Out the kitchen window, the sky had filled with a raft of clouds, dark and hunched over, but the snow hadn't started yet. "Can we talk when I get back? I'll do whatever it takes to make this right—you have to know that."

Exhaustion hung on Deborah's shoulders like a wet woolen overcoat. She watched the blueberries fall from the palm of her hand into the bowl. "We'll play it by ear," she said. "That's all I've got right now."

Aaron's head bobbed in gratitude. He moved to the counter to grind coffee beans while Deborah refilled the kettle and returned containers to the fridge. The howling of the wind surrounded their silence.

"Hey, did Becca ever make it home last night?" Aaron's hung jaw made him look like a cartoon figure who'd just remembered he left his baby on the Metro.

"Louisa's mother decided to stop at a motel off the highway. Thank God! I couldn't bear for Becca to witness this, this . . ." Deborah flapped her hands in a futile search for the right word. "Anyway, the snow had already hit the area they were driving through. Plan was to stay ahead of the storm. Should be home early afternoon."

Aaron took a step closer, but it was as if Deborah's body were surrounded by a force field that knocked him back. A moment later she heard his footsteps on the stairs and then the drumbeat of the shower.

Except for the berries and the tea, Deborah's breakfast wound up in the garbage disposal. As soon as the thud of the back door announced Aaron's departure, Deborah made her way to the second floor to take a quick shower and retrieve her laptop and tote bag. Her study was too small for the pacing she'd be doing today. By the time she'd set up a workstation at the dining room table and logged on to her email, Deborah had made up her mind: at least for the next few days, Aaron would have to sleep on the futon in his office. They'd been meaning to replace the mattress. The last guest who'd slept there, Aaron's sister Nancy, insisted it had thrown her back out. Not Deborah's problem. If Aaron didn't like it, he could make a nest on the floor or sleep on the living room couch. As for Becca, well, maybe it was time Deborah told her daughter the truth.

All morning Deborah worked on the campus tour, emailing back and forth with Ben Gleason and turning out drafts of a flyer for their host groups to adapt. In the background, the newscasters on NPR kept up a steady stream of storm predictions. Already someone had nicknamed this one Snowmageddon. Becca called every hour to let her know their progress. "The highway's fine, Ma. KC and DP." ("Keep calm and don't panic"—advice the AP English teacher wrote on the chalkboard before every exam.)

A little after noon, Deborah's cell phone began playing, "Sisters Are Doing It for Themselves"—Marquita's ringtone. "I may still be in my pajamas," Marquita said, "but I've been one very productive lady. Met with Biden's people by phone—they're optimistic about keeping the increase in VAWA funding in the budget. I put the highlights into an email message for all the task force members, with a cc to you—about to hit SEND. To top it off, I bring you one urgent message and one brilliant idea."

"Urgent first."

"Someone named Marilyn Kettleman's trying to reach you. She left a voice mail—'urgent' was her word. Says she knows you from Danforth. Here, I'm emailing you her number."

The name didn't ring a bell; Deborah had talked with scores of female students at dorms and classes. "Thanks, Marquita."

"And the brilliant idea—aren't you dying to know?"

"I'm all ears."

"Not even going to go there, DB." Once, before some gala, Marquita had brought Deborah a photo of an updo, but Deborah had refused to consider it because she thought her ears were too big. "I've been thinking about that West Virginia case where the judge wouldn't let the rapee use the word 'rape' because it might prejudice the jury. Yomara and Della have been talking about a national day of action. We could have all our folk organize events outside their local courthouse where everyone shows up with tape over their mouths. Great visual for the media. The bloggers could do a blog carnival on the subject of naming and silencing."

"Yeah, good."

Marquita cleared her throat. "When Deborah Borenstein says, 'Yeah, good,' either she's secretly watching *Jeopardy* or something is sitting on her chest. Talk to me."

Deborah chewed a place on her lip that she discovered was already raw. "Gillean tracked down Liddie. Aaron was responsible. He found out about me going to Will's. Later he tried to stop Gillean, but not in time."

Marquita's pause was a beat too long. Deborah remembered when she'd raised this fear a few days ago, Marquita hadn't tried to talk her down. "I am really sorry to hear that, DB," her friend said now. "What do you need?"

"Sorry, I just can't . . . I have to stay focused on the fifty projects on my plate, or else I'll . . ."

"Got it," Marquita said. "Call that Marilyn Kettleman."

Outside, the wind riled tree branches until they scratched against the house. Deborah didn't recognize the 515 area code she dialed for Marilyn, who answered immediately. "Thank you for getting back to me so quickly." The woman sounded like she was getting over a cold or had been doing a lot of crying.

"Of course. Glad to talk to you." Deborah turned away from her laptop, where Google had just informed her that 515 was the code for Des Moines, Iowa. She reached for a pen and pad of paper.

"You won't remember me, but I was a year ahead of you at Danforth. I heard you speak in a soc class once when I was a senior. All these years later, I can still hear what you said. 'No one asks to be raped. Ever.'" Deborah waited as Marilyn gulped in some air. "I've always wanted to thank you."

"I'm really glad to hear that, Marilyn. And today—did something happen that made you want to call?"

"Yes." Marilyn's breathing was shallow and ragged. "A guy who raped me when we were at Danforth. Spring of 1978. At his fraternity. On a date. Back then, I was a caricature of the girls they went after—young, naive. Stupid is what I would have said until I heard you talk three years later—flattered to have been asked out by the cool guy, the whole ball of wax. I never reported it, only told one person, spent my whole life trying to get over it."

"Marilyn, I'm so sorry this happened to you." Deborah's notes read, "Danforth fraternity. Date rape. Rapist's name: ___________." She breathed deeply.

"I had big plans to study economics and go on to law school," Marilyn said. "But that's where I met him, World Economics 290. I couldn't run the risk of being in the same class again. So I switched to library science. It's not where I pictured myself, but, you know, it's okay, my life was okay. And then I heard on the car radio yesterday that this same guy is running for Senate. It was like someone reached into an old wound and dug out scar tissue. I had to pull onto the shoulder of road and stay there almost an hour."

Deborah's pen filled in the long underline.

"I can't bear to think that this man could become a national leader. I didn't know who to call, but someone else—there's another woman Will Quincy (that's his name) raped, Helen Dimitriou—I'm in touch with her. She's still in Binghamton, and she remembered that counselor Claire Rawlings and called her, and Claire mentioned you, and she had your number."

"SECOND WOMAN," and Deborah added Helen's name to her page.

"I hope you can understand this." Marilyn was now openly weeping. "I never told my husband. We have kids, girls, they're teenagers,

I can't think of how I'd tell them now. But Helen, she's livid about this, she's willing to speak to a reporter. And if she did, I could corroborate her story and tell my own, if they'd let me be an 'unnamed source.'"

"Helen Dimitriou—you knew her at Danforth? Knew her at the time Will raped her?"

Deborah heard the muffled sounds of Marilyn blowing her nose. "Helen lived on the same floor at Dorothy Beckett Hall. One day someone at lunch mentioned Will's name and Helen bolted from the table. That night I went to her room and we figured it out. It never occurred to either of us to report it—we were both drinking, our parents would have died, you know the drill. By the time I heard you speak, he'd graduated."

Snow, heavy and wet, had begun to dot the branch by the dining room window.

Deborah and Marilyn agreed to set up a three-way call the next day at two Eastern time with Helen Dimitriou, who taught middle-school math and was away on a field trip. "I want you to be honest about the prospects," Marilyn said. "Whether anyone will listen. What Will is likely to do."

"Yes, I promise. And I have a dear friend who's in this as well. I need to talk to her."

"Please do. Whatever happens, thanks for being there and for staying the course."

On the notepad, Deborah drew a box around the name of a sympathetic reporter at the *Washington Post*. Fuck Gillean—if the story came out, her byline would not be on it. Just below, Deborah created a second box and labeled it "Will's response." She felt as if the pen listed the bullet points of its own accord:

Make public Liddie's married name.

Argue he was "proven innocent" a long time ago.

Accuse Deborah of manufacturing the charges and coaxing women to make false accusations for her own and her husband's personal gain.

By the time Becca burst through the back door, Deborah had not found a way to alter that list.

"Mom, we made it! We're alive!"

Deborah ran to the kitchen to welcome her. In just the time she'd spent getting from Louisa's mother's car to the back door, Becca was engulfed in snow. It clung to her hair and eyebrows, dripped from her coat. Deborah gave her daughter air hugs and kisses and threw her a dish towel. Before either of them could mop up the puddle at Becca's feet, the house phone started ringing.

"Hi, Pa!" Becca said. "No, I just walked in. What's your twenty?" Aaron and Becca had an old CB radio when she was little, and they'd memorized all the lingo.

While she caught her father up on the campus scene, Becca darted between the fridge and the cupboard, laying out sandwich ingredients and foraging for chips. Deborah leaned against the wall and drank in the sight of this sparkling creature, wondering how she'd navigate the Safeway chips aisle once Becca left for college.

"Roger that; love you, too." Becca hung up the phone and bit into her towering creation. "Dad's battery is low. Looks like he's going to camp in his office. They're predicting four-hour Metro rides. Woo-hoo! We're gonna have a winter wonderland. I'm going to take you snowshoeing and—"

Deborah's cell phone interrupted Becca's declaration. "Save me a bite," Deborah said. "Be right back."

The screen showed the caller to be Amanda Pruitt. "Congratulations, darlin'. You did it!" Amanda said. "I'm popping a cork in your honor right now."

"Because . . . ?"

"Because Deborah Borenstein and Aaron Minkin have just been selected as Egalitarian Couple of the Year."

Twenty Six

Devil's Lake, Wisconsin: Friday, August 1, 2003

"Ninety-three degrees? How is that possible?" Deborah pointed to the thermometer on the side of the Devil's Lake visitors' station, where the ranger acknowledged the sticker on Richard's van and waved them into the parking lot. "In DC, we'd be melting, even in the parks. This place feels divine."

"Combination of the pines and the height," Richard said. "We get humidity in Wisconsin, but not up here." They saw clusters of people in all directions, but Richard had no trouble finding a parking spot. He climbed out of the van and dragged the cooler—"Look," Becca had said when they packed it, "it has *wheels*!"—to a spot on the grass where Liddie promptly lined up five lightweight backpacks. Each of them would carry a thermos of water or iced tea or Gatorade, two sandwiches, a PowerBar, and a bag of dried fruit or trail mix. Deborah saw Richard slip a rectangular-shaped packet—hopefully a Mrs. Golmboch kringle!—and two beers into the side compartment of his own pack.

Becca leaped from the van, flung out her arms, and began to twirl. "Yay, we're here! I can't wait to see Balanced Rock and Devil's Doorway!" She'd been studying guidebooks the entire ride from Random Lake.

"Guess what else you'll get to see tomorrow or Sunday?" Liddie's floppy hat hid most of her face, but not the big grin. "Circus elephants! They're down by the lakefront in Milwaukee, and Richard's offered to take you. Those creatures are so excellent—as long as you avoid the puddles."

"I love puddles!" Becca's wardrobe had included rain boots ever since she was a toddler. Some kids loved to leap over puddles; Becca preferred to leap into them—a phenomenon Aaron had documented over the years with photos. One held an honored place on Liddie and Richard's mantel.

Richard shaded his eyes and looked up at her from a squat position. His hat had a flap that covered his ears and neck, as well as his head. "As I found out one really hot day when I took off my shoes and rushed through them, the water is not cool, it's warm. And it's warm because it's not water. Those puddles are actually—"

"Elephant pee?" Becca stopped spinning. "Yuck!"

"Okay, Miss Rebecca." Richard held up the smallest pack. "Yours is ready."

Deborah watched as her daughter drew in her taut dancer's body and did two forward flips on the grass to reach Richard. Her nipples, just starting to bud, poked the Xena: Warrior Princess T-shirt she'd insisted on wearing again, even though last night she'd spilled homemade strawberry ice cream on top of the lightning bolt.

"This stuff looks great, Richard." Aaron was helping Richard divide up the first-aid kit between their two packs. "Bugs can zap us, the sun can burn us, the trail can trip us—you've got it all covered!"

"Just wear your hat and watch your footing. We should be dandy," Richard said, closing his own pack and hoisting it onto his shoulders. "All righty, I think we're ready. If no one has an objection, I propose that I lead the way and that Miss Rebecca here be my deputy. You have to be at least eleven to take on that post." He bowed his head in her direction and handed her the trail map.

"Halt—sunscreen first," Liddie said. She squirted lotion in everybody's hands and, after covering all the places they could reach themselves, had them form a circle in order of height to coat each other's shoulders and necks. Becca stood on the cooler to reach her mother while being tended to by her dad. As they lathered up, they watched a party of rock climbers emerge from two vans and amass a heap of ropes and loops and harnesses.

“I won’t have what they’re having,” Deborah said.

Aaron laughed and leaned over to wipe some excess lotion from his wife’s nose. He finished rubbing Rebecca’s shoulders and turned her around to face him. “So, darling daughter, which way are we going?”

Becca unfolded her map. “Actually, from the name, I thought Devil’s Doorway would be the hardest. But it turns out it’s an easy path. We can get there from the Balanced Rock trail, which is much steeper and trickier. Richard said it goes straight up the rocks, but it’s steps and we can all make it. Except for Beagle, which is why we didn’t bring him. And then Richard said we can take a break and go on the East Bluff trail.” Since they’d arrived yesterday, Becca’s sentences had been strewn with “Richard says . . .” Deborah glanced at Aaron, who simply smiled and adjusted his Yankees cap.

When they stopped at Devil’s Doorway to admire the view of the lake and the stupendous rock formations, Richard told stories of coming here as a kid. “My parents had an old camper we used to set up for a week every summer,” he said. “For years I crossed days off the calendar until that week came.”

“I can see why you loved it,” Deborah said. “I’ve never been anywhere like this. It’s so powerful and yet so serene.”

“Why do they call it Devil’s Lake?” Becca asked.

“The Ho-Chunk Indians named it Spirit Lake—Da-wa-kah-char-gra.” Richard said the syllables slowly and waited while Becca repeated them. “They said they often heard the voices of spirits during their celebrations here.”

“And white settlers changed the name to Devil’s Lake?” Aaron had been reading a book Richard lent him about Native American tribes in Wisconsin.

“Yep,” Richard said. “It’s so deep, they thought it led straight to the devil.”

“I wish it were still called Spirit.” Becca untied her sneaker and poured out some pebbles. “That’s how I’m going to write about it in my diary.”

"I believe the spirits saved my brother's life, actually. By the time Mike and I were teenagers, our parents let us go hiking on our own. I was a little reckless, but mostly I had my wits about me. Mike . . . well, that's when he was starting to use drugs. One day he went off the path and started jumping down the rocks. Scared me half to death."

"Oh my God!" Becca said. They'd just passed an older man whose arms and legs were badly scraped from tripping on the trail. "What did you do?"

Richard put his arm around Becca. "To be perfectly honest, I made myself watch and I held my breath and tried to imagine those spirits holding up giant hands to keep him from falling."

Aaron lifted his thermos. "From what I've heard, Richard, you're the one who provided a net for your brother. He was lucky to have you."

Deborah leaned against the boulder behind her and massaged her temples. Aaron had been a mensch the whole day. He'd been a good sport about taking direction from Richard, genuine in his praise, loving and fun with Becca, generally affectionate.

So why was Deborah obsessed with thoughts of leaving him?

While they gathered their supplies and resumed the single-file hiking formation, she replayed scenes from yesterday, the day Aaron and Liddie finally met.

Becca had been bouncing in her seat on the drive from the Milwaukee airport to Random Lake. Usually she nudged them to play Twenty Questions or make up stories about passengers in other cars, but on this ride, she babbled nonstop about things she remembered from earlier visits to Liddie and Richard's. "Wait'll you see the garden, Dad. They have, like, four different kinds of squash and humongous tomatoes, ten times bigger than ours. Oh, and Liddie's loom! It's like the old-fashioned kind you see in the history museum, only it's way faster. And the kitchen always smells so good, like they just baked a pie. I can't believe you've never been there!"

Deborah could scarcely believe he was going to be there at all. Seven months ago Aaron had announced he was taking a break from political consulting and embarking on a novel. "This'll be an insider's view of a campaign," he'd told her, his eyes lit up as if his candidate had just won. "Like *Primary Colors*, only the campaign is just the backdrop to a thriller about bribes from lobbyists and how that rewrites the whole energy industry." At the time, she'd had mixed feelings. On the one hand, she was glad to see an end to roller-coaster interviews with top consulting firms—those just led to bursts of activity followed by dry spells. And she was curious to see what he'd come up with. Still, Deborah would have preferred that Aaron accept a job with a smaller, less prestigious outfit and have steady work and income. She dreaded the round of rejections that were sure to accompany the agent queries he kept saying were just around the corner. Aaron, who'd gotten multiple rejection letters from consultant firms, referred to them as FOADs, short for "fuck off and die." As for the actual draft of the novel, that was top secret. She hadn't even been allowed to see the outline.

But at least Aaron no longer had an excuse for missing the trip to Liddie's. "Everyone needs a break," Deborah told him when he argued that he should probably stay home and use the quiet to focus on his novel. Never mind the giant chunks of time he had each day when Deborah and Becca were out of the house.

Deborah could have gone along with the aspiring-novelist persona. She could have handled the boasts from Aaron to Liddie and Richard about how "this allows me to be the primary parent, something I really think more men should experience," despite the fact that twice during this interlude, when asked to run a series of focus groups, he'd had no compunction about leaving Deborah with total responsibility for Becca's schedule, just as he did anytime he had a gig. It all would have been bearable, if only Aaron hadn't been such an asshole about Liddie.

"She's really come a long way!" he'd told Deborah the night before when they were getting ready for bed. He'd just found a Milwaukee radio station playing Bob Dylan and was sprawled out on the guest bed, tapping his fingers to "Masters of War."

"I beg your pardon?" Deborah had vowed not to start anything on this trip. She tried to focus her attention on getting her and Becca's hiking things ready for Friday's excursion to Devil's Lake. Becca had dumped her suitcase in their room and rushed out to sleep in the pup tent Richard set up in the backyard.

"I mean, Liddie seems to be on top of all the details about this hike. She got all the gear ready, and the maps, and made those instructions on how not to get separated from each other but what to do if we did. I'm really impressed."

"For God's sake, Aaron, she was assaulted, not lobotomized."

Aaron swung his legs over the side of the bed and furrowed his brow. "What the hell is that supposed to mean?"

"Exactly what it says. An injury can be crippling, but it isn't tantamount to incompetence."

"Oh, that's just fucking great." He sprang to his feet and jabbed his finger in her direction. "No matter what I say about Liddie, I can't please you. For twenty-three years you've been coddling this woman, and now you're going to get on my case for complimenting her?"

The throbbing behind Deborah's right temple spread to the bridge of her nose. "Coddling?"

"Why don't you let me have all of it at one time?" Aaron said. "What else did I do wrong?"

Deborah turned up the volume on the radio. "I should have a fucking notebook where I keep track of every time we've had this conversation. You never get it, and then you make me out to be a strident, PC hard-ass for bringing it up! This is my life's work we're talking about, Aaron."

He stuck a pretend violin on his shoulder and pretended to play.

Deborah dug her nails into her hand. "Okay, you want to know what else? Try speaking to Liddie in a normal voice. You don't have to talk soft and slow."

Aaron responded by grabbing his laptop and slamming the door behind him.

Earlier, during dinner, when Liddie proposed a toast to Deborah's promotion to executive director of Breaking the Silence, Aaron had excused himself after getting a text on his BlackBerry. "So sorry—it's an agent someone referred me to," he said. "These guys are insanely hard to get hold of."

They were well into their grilled walleye when Aaron came back to the table. "Sorry you had to miss Liddie's toast to your lovely wife," Richard said. "You would have burst with pride."

Aaron picked up his wineglass. "Yes, absolutely. To Deborah, whose light shines brightly enough to illuminate the path for us all."

Deborah ducked her head toward her own glass and avoided eye contact with Liddie. Few men, especially those immersed in the guy world of the political elite, had an easy time watching their wife advance while their own career stagnated. She held this awareness like a protective shield to keep disappointment from rattling the cage around her heart. Mostly it worked—except for the times she spent with Richard and Liddie.

Because Richard wouldn't mind.

Deborah was asleep by the time Aaron came back to bed. This morning he'd busied himself getting ready for the hike. As she was about to go check on Becca, Aaron grabbed her hand. "We were both a little prickly last night," he said. "I know Becca's crazy excited for today. Let's be our best selves for her, okay?"

Now, at their stopping place on the trail, she watched as Aaron flung himself on a patch of grass and began to devour his sandwiches. Richard produced the secret packet, which did indeed contain a homemade apricot kringle, and tossed Aaron one of the beers.

"Hey, look!" Becca pointed at the climbers across the way, arms and legs spread wide as they inched up the rocks. "Are those the same guys we saw in the parking lot? That's way cool. I'd love to try."

"Ask again in ten years," Aaron said.

"By then I'll be twenty-one and can do whatever I want," Becca reminded him. "But don't sweat it. I wouldn't risk my dancing legs."

Richard passed around his binoculars and pointed to his favorite vistas. "You know how the rocks look gray and rose?" he said. "Try 'em with these things."

"Wow." Becca planted her feet as she held on to his glasses. "You're right. I see rust and yellows. It's like you have to learn how to look."

They kept watch for red-shouldered hawks until Richard leaped to his feet and pointed due north. "There," he whispered, as if the pair of majestic birds could hear him. First one, then the other, swooped down to perch on a ledge fifty feet away.

"I had no idea their wings were so huge!" Becca said. "And look at that one's head—it's like it's turning around! That's so excellent!"

Deborah laughed. "You're turning her into a little Wisconsinite," she said.

Soon Becca announced she was ready to explore more of the East Bluff. Richard and Aaron jumped up to join her. "Why don't you ladies stay here and relax?" Richard said. "You haven't had any time alone yet. We'll return with the mastodon." He bent over to kiss Liddie under the privacy of her large brim.

Liddie handed Deborah a slice of her mother's kringle as they watched the others disappear. "Pinch me—are we really here? I've been wanting to bring you for so long."

Deborah moved closer until she and Liddie sat back-to-back, something they used to do at Danforth. She inhaled the sharp scent of evergreens. "It's amazing, Lid. Such a gift. Thank you so much."

After a few minutes of silence, Liddie reached her hand over her shoulder until she and Deborah locked fingers. "So tell me how you're really doing, DB. Your career taking off while Aaron's remains stuck, the whole novel thing . . . I don't know much about publishing, but everything I've read says it's a bear. Last night the two of you seemed pretty tense."

Deborah felt a loosening in her chest at the luxury of unburdening herself. "Oh, Lid. The truth is, I feel all this rage and disappointment and I can't figure out what to do with it. I think the real purpose of this trip is to decide whether or not I should leave him. And that makes me totally crazy, because you see how great he can be, and how much Becca adores him."

"Part of this is how he feels about me, isn't it?"

Deborah leaned her head back on Liddie's shoulder.

"The last few times you've been here, something's kept you from talking to me about what's really going on."

The hawks flew right over their heads. "You seemed to have enough on your plate," Deborah said.

"I think there may be another reason." Liddie squeezed Deborah's hand. "I think you haven't wanted to own how unhappy you are because you want to hold on to the image of you and Aaron as role models for an equal partnership."

The instant she heard the words, Deborah knew they hurt too much to be off the mark. She let out a deep sigh. "Maybe so. But I don't know how to separate that from my feelings about Rebecca. It's really important to me that she grow up believing in the possibility of love and equality, whether she loves a man or a woman. I can't bear to think of her becoming one of those girls who avoids attachment because she's lost faith that she can find what she wants. And the idea of her schlepping back and forth between two houses—ugh, I can't stand it."

"She's really smart, DB. I don't think you have to worry about her."

"Mom, Liddie!" Becca ran back to their site and plopped down beside them. "We saw a nest with a baby hawk! Like a little fuzz ball! It was so awesome! And look at these leaves!" She held out a stalk with three scarlet ovals on it. "Richard says it's sumac."

The trip down went a lot quicker. Back in the grassy parking lot, as Liddie and Richard finished loading the van, Becca celebrated completing the hike by practicing flips over her father's arm. "Next year we all have to come back here to camp!" Becca declared. "For a whole week. Okay, MaPa?"

Becca had invented "MaPa" as a toddler, when she wanted both her parents' attention at the same time. "Sit, MaPa," she'd say when she wanted them to play a game or look at a drawing. Deborah used to dread that her daughter would grow out of the expression. Now the word was like a net that fluttered over her until it tightened and turned into a vise.

twenty seven

Washington, DC:
Saturday,
February 6, 2010

"Fear not, Mamele." Becca seized the broom handle and thrust it in front of her like a pretend javelin. "I, the young maiden, will rescue us both while Sir Aaron is kept captive by the elements. Behold my armor! I have suited up and am heading forth to battle the storm."

Deborah, who'd been padding around the kitchen in her pajamas and robe, looked up from the mixing bowl and curtsied before her daughter. Becca was outfitted in the shiny blue ski pants she used for snowshoeing.

"Give me a minute to get dressed, and I'll help," Deborah said. "But first take a peek out the door and see if the world is still standing."

Becca ran down the three stairs and opened the inside door. "Omigod, there's at least two feet of snow smack up against the glass. You've gotta see this."

Deborah pulled her robe tighter around her and, still sore from her Thursday-night tumble, walked slowly down the stairs as Becca leaned her well-muscled shoulder into the storm door. It wouldn't budge.

"I hate to burst your fantasy, dear one, but no one—Sir Aaron included—could get to that shed and unbury the shovels." Becca's mini–snow family had disappeared amid the new drifts; not even the red scarf was visible. The bushes sagged under the weight. "Wow. In Cleveland everyone in a neighborhood like this would have a snow blower. Some neighbor would dig a path for us—but here, I do believe we are, you should pardon the pun, royally screwed."

"I'm calling Louisa." Becca was already peeling off her outer garments. "Her uncle has some kind of plow. It's one thing to be snowed out of school, but snowed *into* the house—it's so not happening!"

Deborah returned to the stove and spooned pancake batter into the skillet. Memories washed over her of Sunday mornings when Becca was five, the three of them hunkered down on the living room couch, eating blueberry pancakes with pecans and a few chocolate chips, listening to tales of Hogwarts. When they came to the end of a tape, Aaron would say, "Go on with the story" while they carried dirty dishes into the kitchen and made up snippets of conversation between various Muggles. Deborah let go of the wooden spoon so she could massage the ache in her chest.

"Drag out the Scrabble, Ma," Becca called from the dining room. "Apparently, plows can't get through. The front door won't budge either. Why couldn't this happen on a school day? Do you think the roads will be clear by Monday?" Deborah swallowed several times and struggled to compose herself as Becca's voice came closer.

"I wouldn't mind an extra day to work on my paper on Susan B. Anthony. Did I tell you Marquita and Malcolm sent me these racist quotes she said? My teacher's a big Susan B. fan—no gold star for me." Becca came up behind Deborah. "Anyway, I guess you're stuck with me."

Deborah tried to answer but had to choke back a sob.

"Hey, what's up?" Becca turned Deborah around and used her hands to dry her mother's face. "You're not crying because we're prisoners together, are you?"

Deborah turned off the pancakes and hugged her daughter close. She would tell Becca the whole story, really, as soon as the right words presented themselves. "Just a Hallmark moment. I was remembering times we ate pancakes and listened to *Harry Potter* when you were little. Now you're going off to college."

"Oh, puh-leeze. I haven't gotten accepted anywhere yet." Becca grabbed a spatula and lifted the three finished pancakes onto a plate. "For all you know, I'll be living at home, attending GW. So don't go all weepy yet."

"Okay," Deborah said, breathing deeply. She filled the skillet with the rest of the batter and hoped the sizzle covered up what felt like gasps for air. "Syrup's in the microwave."

"The stuff Liddie's mother sent at Christmas?" Becca grabbed the syrup with one hand and dribbled it over her pancakes, then glided to the radio on the windowsill and turned on 94.7, which entertained them with snow totals around the area. "Frostberg County in Maryland—I'm not making this up, folks—looks like the big winner!" the newscaster said in a lively baritone. "By the time Snowmageddon is over, the town of Allegany over there may get more than three feet of snow. And how many of you had trouble opening your doors this morning? Hear my words—stay inside and chill. Well, you know what I mean."

Many areas of the city had also lost power. "I'm going to make us an emergency pack," Becca said, piling her dishes in the sink. "Remember I had to memorize this once for Girl Scouts? Batteries, blankets, candles, first-aid kit, flashlight, water bottles." She ticked them off on her fingers. "We can deal with the fridge when and if, but I'll go get the coolers and have them ready just in case. And I'm going to go put pails of water in the tub—we'll be like prairie women!"

A rush of gratitude flooded Deborah's body for the sheer capableness and spirit of this daughter. Maybe Deborah, too, could muster the resources to handle whatever lay ahead.

The ringing of the landline in the kitchen interrupted her thank-you to the universe.

"I'm really sorry I left you two there alone," Aaron said. "There's no hope of getting out of here today. Looks like the snow's going to come down till nightfall."

Deborah snuck into the back hall and tried to keep her voice low. "Actually, it's a good thing. Not the snow. The separation. I need some time to think." Outside it was eerily silent—no plows scraping, no motors turning over, no horns blaring, not a single sign of life.

"Oh, come on, Deborah—please don't make this into a capital crime." She imagined Aaron digging through his pockets for phantom cigarettes. "You know how bad I feel."

"Jesus, Aaron, it's not like you forgot to put the pot roast in the oven."

"The whole fuckin' campaign is on the line here. I explained this a dozen times. You know what the stakes are! Why can't you ever once take my side?"

"Don't even go there." Deborah could hear the hiss in her own voice. "There's no justification for what you did. I haven't got the energy to make nice in front of Becca."

"What are you guys *talking* about?" Becca's voice on the upstairs extension was high and squeaky. "*This* is the Egalitarian Couple of the Year? Who are you kidding?" The bang of the phone in its cradle reverberated in the surrounding silence.

"I've got to go," Deborah said. As soon as she hung up, she heard Becca's cell phone ringing upstairs, but when she ran up to the bedroom door, the only sound was Becca sobbing. Deborah knocked just loudly enough to be heard.

"You have every right to be angry with us, Bec."

"Leave me alone!" Deborah's knees buckled at the fury in that scream. She backed away from the door and crept downstairs, setting the alarm on her phone to vibrate in exactly thirty minutes. Until then Deborah lay on the living room floor, staring out the window at the chaos of the storm.

When the phone went off, Deborah made a cup of tea and carried it upstairs, along with a box of Kleenex. She knocked again and pressed her mouth against the door. "I brought you some tea, Bec." Nothing. "If it's okay, I'm going to open the door now."

Becca was curled up on her bed, face buried in her pillow. Deborah placed the tea and tissues on the nightstand. At first when she climbed onto the mattress and scooped her daughter into her arms, Becca kept her body rigid and refused to hug back. "I love you, baby. And so does Daddy. Whatever happens, that will never, ever change."

Becca pulled away from her mother and hurled the pillow onto the floor. "What am I, six? You going to pull out the divorce book now and show me that Mommy and Daddy may kill each other but don't worry, it's not my fault?"

"Oh, Bec, I'm so sorry." The room smelled of patchouli incense, burning in a slender holder on the dresser. On the floor sat the beginnings of the emergency kit –a Whole Foods tote bag with three yellow flashlights sticking out. A pile of afghans lay scattered nearby; Becca must have been folding them when the phone rang. "Tell me what would help."

"Besides seeing me as an adult and telling me the truth?" Becca's face was mottled with rage and fear. Tears had drenched the top of her turtleneck.

The realization struck Deborah like a sharp jab to the ribs. She'd been treating Becca exactly the way she hated seeing Aaron treat Liddie—like someone weak and incompetent. Deborah pulled two of the afghans onto the bed and draped one around both of them, tossing the other over their laps. She waited while Becca sipped some tea and blew her nose.

"This story started a long time ago, when Liddie and I were sophomores at Danforth." Deborah grabbed a tissue and balled it up in her hand. "We thought it was all in the past, but there's someone at the center of it who's pretty vicious. Turns out he's none other than Will Quincy—"

"The guy running against Dad's candidate?"

Deborah nodded several times. "So it's become all tangled up with our family's lives. Have some more tea, and I'll start at the beginning."

Becca wept again as she learned about Will's assault on her beloved Liddie. She pounded the bed when Deborah described the hearing, sniffled softly at the story of Liddie's lost years and then her recovery. Not until Deborah came to the part about Gillean Mulvaney's barging into the office did Becca speak. "What did Liddie want you to do?" she whispered, and nodded as Deborah shared the conversation just last week in Random Lake.

"I think I get it," Becca said. "Dad must be really torn."

Deborah decided on the spot not to tell Becca about Aaron's communication with Gillean. The girl had a right to know this, but Aaron should be the one to tell her.

"So how is Liddie doing?" Becca asked. "Man, will it suck if this asshole gets to be in the US Senate."

"Well, there's a new twist—I just found out yesterday. Marquita called to say someone had left a message at the office, a woman named Marilyn from Cedar Rapids, Iowa. I called her back. Turns out she was also raped by Will at Danforth. Exact same pattern as what he did to Liddie, a year and a half earlier."

"Holy shit." Becca twisted the afghan between her fingers. "I swear I will never take a drink at a frat house, ever."

Snow had drifted so much that Becca's window was completely covered. It looked as if the snow were actually piled up to the second story.

"Marilyn isn't in a position to come forward, but there's a third woman, also assaulted by Will around the same time, and she's agreed to talk to the media. Marilyn could corroborate that story and tell her own as an 'unnamed source.'"

Becca seized Deborah by the shoulders. "That's great news, isn't it? It would mean Liddie could stay out of it, they could go after this prick, Dad's guy would win?"

Deborah remained silent.

"What?"

With a shudder, Deborah laid out the visit to Will and what she'd learned of his game plan. "He made it quite clear that he'd go after Liddie. He knows where she lives." Deborah held up her empty palms. "I'm back to feeling completely stuck."

Becca rolled onto her side on the bed and propped her head on her hand. "What would you tell me to do in a situation like this, Mom? 'Talk to Liddie,' you'd say. 'Let her decide.'"

"I know."

Becca tugged on Deborah's arm until they lay facing each other side by side. "It's still fucked up how you treated me." Becca knit her brow and bit her lip, the same expression she'd used since she was two to express disapproval.

Deborah longed to stay next to Becca, listening to the wind wrapping itself around their house. But she needed to get through to Marquita and their allies on the board while the power was still on, and then she needed to call Liddie. "Go to sleep for a while," she whispered to her daughter, tucking the afghan snugly around her.

Fortunately, Marquita responded right away to Deborah's text. Yes, her electricity was still on. She offered to arrange a conference call as soon as possible with Yomara and Della. Half an hour later, with warmed-up pancakes and coffee before her, Deborah joined the call and filled in her closest colleagues on the two new women ready to expose Will Quincy.

"Ay," Yomara said. "I feel like we have one foot headed for the finish line and the other glued to square one. We have what we need to go to the media, but that'd be just the kick in the balls that would send him after your friend."

Deborah dragged her fingers through her hair. "I keep reliving that conversation in his office, like a mini–Groundhog Day. Damn, this is when we need someone out of the movies—you know, the terminally ill person who volunteers to take him out."

"If anyone's listening in on this conversation," Marquita said, "she's only kidding."

"What if the women confronted him directly?" Della was usually the first to jump in, but she'd been quiet until now. "Maybe by *threatening* to go public, they could extract some demands."

"Like what?" Yomara asked.

"Let's go with this for a moment, ladies," Marquita said. "If they do this, they'd have to demand more than a vote or a donation or some crumb like that."

"Something about his behavior in college." Della was snapping her fingers as she spoke. "Not the whole deal, because he'd never do that. But a video directed at male students, acknowledging that he and a lot of other guys . . . I don't know, weren't that clued in when they were in college, talking about the importance of 'no means no,' 'what if it were your sister,' that kinda thing."

The pancakes sat untouched in front of Deborah.

"I hate to say it," Marquita said, "but that's like offering to let Father I Had Divinely Ordained Contact with Forty-Two Boys make a PSA on the importance of respecting young children. Sorry, this motherfucker doesn't get to play the hero."

"I hear you," Yomara said. "If we're going to make Quincy an offer, let the women go for it all: they'll go public unless he drops out of the race."

Deborah's jaw was open and her brain was whirring.

"But won't he just threaten to do what he told Deborah he'd do?" Della asked. "The whole 'I'll show the media you're a bunch of crazy, man-hating, vengeful bitches' thing—with the emphasis on this particular crazy bitch whose husband just happens to run the campaign of his opponent?"

"He'd probably threaten that spin," Marquita said. "But we got the goods here and he's going to know it: if this shit goes public, enough people—"

"Say the magic words!" Yomara added. "Key *de-mo-graphics*, like unmarried female voters. . . ."

"Amen. Enough voters would believe these women to make a serious dent in his support. And a lot of his financial backers would not be too wild about this, either. He can threaten all he wants, but his political consultants will know we're talkin' truth to power. The man's back in town, by the way. I heard him on the radio this morning, talking about a round of meetings over the next few days."

Static took over the line. When Deborah was able to hear again, Yomara was talking. "Can you hear me now? Okay, it's true, he could call their bluff. This plan only works if they're willing to go public five minutes later, have a reporter waiting in the wings."

They agreed that Deborah would raise the idea to Marilyn Kettleman and Helen Dimitriou on the two o'clock call. Still, Deborah shared Della's doubts—she'd seen Will in action. He *would* go after them—and what would be the impact on Liddie? On Marilyn, who surely would also be outed? Even on Helen, when she heard that Will would threaten legal action? Deborah would have to lay out all the risks.

The four of them brainstormed the details of a meeting with Will, if the women chose that route. "They're predicting the airport here is gonna be shut for several days," Marquita said. "We got one woman in upstate New York, the other over in Iowa—too far for the train. How about Skype?"

"Yes," Deborah said. "Not to mention how much easier it would be for them not to be in the same actual space as Will Quincy."

"And Liddie?" Della asked.

Deborah carried the pancakes to the garbage pail. "She's my next call."

Twenty-eight

Washington, DC: Saturday, February 6, 2010

Richard wasn't answering his cell phone, and Deborah could not remember Evelyn Wiener's husband's first name to save her life. Although she'd met the man more than once, she'd never have called him by his first name. In fact, as she cringed to remember, she never addressed him at all, since she couldn't bring herself to call him Mr. Wiener. Fortunately, the Saukville, Wisconsin, White Pages listed Evelyn Wiener along with . . . yes, Louis, who'd been deceased for six years but still held his place in the phone book.

It was Mrs. Golmboch who picked up. Her voice sounded frail, although she sent regular letters commenting on a long list of activities, including volunteering at the local Humane Society and at St. Ignatius Head Start. Her own husband had died three years earlier, but she refused to sell their house. "I don't want you to think he was a saint, now," she'd told Deborah at the funeral. "He had his ways, believe me. But I was lucky to share all those years with him, and I'm not going to one of those little boxes where there's not a trace of Horace anywhere."

Mrs. Golmboch recognized Deborah's voice right away. "You want to talk to Liddie, dear. She's just in the next room. No one's bothered her—Richard made sure of that. And I took care no one followed me. First I walked to the store and I dallied in there for a while; then I went out the back door and took the bus around the corner." Deborah didn't know whether to smile or weep at the image of Mrs. Golmboch watching out for spies.

"I'm so sorry this happened," she said when Liddie came to the phone. "Are you all right?"

"As fine as I can be with two senior citizens hovering and Charlie Brown glued to my side. No need to apologize. You weren't the one who called that witch." Deborah felt her stomach cramp. Since the talk with Becca, she'd been trying hard not to think about Aaron.

"I wish I were there, leaning against your bony back and inhaling that lemon oil you use on the loom," Deborah said as she started to pace. "There's a new development, Lid—two other women who were also Will's prey. One's willing to go to the press." Without commentary, completing seven laps around the dining room table, Deborah filled Liddie in on her conversation with Marilyn Kettleman and on Yomara's proposal.

During the pause that followed, Deborah could hear Charlie Brown scampering in the background. "I knew there had to be others," Liddie said finally.

Deborah tried not to imagine the alternate universe where these women found each other thirty years ago, before the hearing with Randall Peters.

"I've actually thought about how to locate them, but it's not like being an adoptee. I mean, where's the registry?"

One of Deborah's favorite movies involved three high school students who drew on the door of a bathroom stall the names of date rapists and teachers to watch out for. In the days that followed, other girls added to the list. Back at Danforth, Deborah had longed to use some gesture like that against Will, but she'd had those goddamn legal papers ordering her to keep her mouth shut.

"I bet he never for one minute worried about us making trouble." Liddie spoke softly, but Deborah could hear the rage in her voice.

"I'm sure of it." Aaron had told Deborah about the kind of internal background checks a political party conducted for candidates—scouring records on taxes and finances and firings, asking about nannies and pool guys. Sex scandals were definitely on the list. But questions about college date rape? The whole area was no doubt invisible. Most likely Will sailed through on his blue-blooded, long-married pedigree.

"Tell me their names again."

Deborah repeated the names.

"Marilyn Kettleman. Helen Dimitriou." Liddie drew out each syllable as if she were memorizing new lifesaving medications. "This is a gift, DB. I want to speak with them."

Deborah pumped one fist in the air. "I've already arranged a conference call at two o'clock my time—they'd love to have you join. I'll email you the number."

"And you'll be on, too?"

"Alas, I'm the one who gets to lay out all the things Will threatened, so everyone knows what we're dealing with."

No comment from Liddie. Deborah closed her eyes and exhaled. "And then I'll get off and let you all talk to each other. However you want to proceed, that's what we'll do."

"A lot to chew on," Liddie said. Before she could say anything else, Charlie Brown began barking to go outside.

Marquita was less restrained when Deborah called to report. "Thank you, Jesus!" she hollered. "You know what Malcolm says: One person speaks up, and it's blown off as a fantasy. Two's a conspiracy. But three—three's a trend. It would be much harder for him to bullshit his way out of it. And if the story broke, who knows how many others might come out of the woodwork?"

"Don't count your chickens . . ."

"I know, I know, or you'll just be left with chicken shit. If you weren't so superstitious, I'd tell you I got a good feeling about these ladies."

Deborah invoked her grandmother's spirit as she muttered, "*Kinahora*" to ward off the evil eye.

While she waited for two o'clock to dial in to the conference line, Deborah thought about the other women who carried Will Quincy's scars. She pictured Marilyn Kettleman on the floor of her den, head bent over Valentine's decorations with her teenagers, heart pounding every time she anticipated this call. As for Helen Dimitriou, Deborah imagined a straight-backed woman with a unexpectedly deep voice, walking into a frame house in Binghamton. She'd lay an NPR tote bag on the hall table, remove a yellow folder stuffed with students' math sheets, and then brew tea or maybe Greek coffee and carry it to an insulated sun porch, where she'd watch deer feeding in the woods behind her home.

By the time Deborah phoned in at 1:59, the three women were already on the line and Liddie was introducing herself. Helen, who did have a wonderful low voice, jumped in next. "I've been waiting thirty years for this moment," she said. "Now *here's* a reunion they should write about in the Danforth alumni magazine!"

Who would have thought the conversation would start with laughter?

Marilyn thanked Deborah for arranging the call. "Helen and I have sent each other Christmas cards every year since college, but we never talked about this again, not once, not until yesterday when I heard Will Quincy on the radio. Saying the words out loud—I can't tell you what it feels like."

"Thank *you*, Marilyn, for bringing us together," Liddie said. "That changes everything, no matter what else happens."

Deborah decided to sit down for her portion of the agenda, hoping that would keep her voice steady. "I feel like the storm-watch person on the news, the one who has to warn about sleet and hail and perilous lightning strikes. You three will be the ones who decide what to do about Will. But you need to be aware what he's capable of."

"It's okay, Deborah," Helen said. "Just say it."

"I'm sorry to tell you that I had a recent encounter with him, and, oh God, he's just as calculating, just as vicious, probably even more dangerous than he was back then." Deborah recited everything that happened that day in Will's hotel headquarters, the extent of his intel on Liddie and on Deborah and her husband, the threats of media and legal retaliation.

"I can't promise it won't get nasty if you do talk to a reporter. I'm talking really nasty, Will's minions digging for any sign that your lives have been less than perfect—marital, financial, psychological, youthful escapades, you name it—and then exploiting every single chance to broadcast it to the world."

Deborah paused to let that information sink in. "There is another option out there. One of my colleagues proposed that Helen—maybe all of you—confront Will and *threaten* to go to the press, but give him a chance to drop out of the race instead."

"We're talking about a United States Senate seat," Marilyn said. "You think he'd buy that?"

"We'd have to have a reporter all lined up, right?" Helen said. "I've played poker, and he's the kind of player who would call our bluff in a heartbeat."

"Exactly. Look, I want to be clear, this option doesn't prevent retaliation by Will. It also means you have to see him and hear him. Although, because of the snow here, if you want to do it right away, you'd be doing it by Skype."

"That sounds like something you do on an airplane," Liddie said.

Deborah's shoulders relaxed for the first time. "I'll get my daughter to explain it to you. It's a free program you download to a computer. Whoever does it needs a PC or a laptop with a camera—but you can position yourself so he doesn't see your face, if you'd prefer."

Helen Dimitriou spoke quietly. "I watched every minute of the Clarence Thomas hearings where they eviscerated Anita Hill. I'm not naive. You should know I'm an out lesbian. My partner and I have been around this block many times. I am ready to go public, especially knowing that all of you would have my back. Marilyn said she'd corroborate my story with her own, if she could do it without using her name. But Liddie, please hear me: if this would jeopardize you in any way, I want you to know you're much more important to me than getting this story out."

"I finally told my husband," Marilyn said. "Last night. We were walking the dog, and I just said it. Larry's not a big talker, but he reached over and grabbed me and said, 'Maybe it's a good thing you didn't tell me before, or I'da wound up in jail for shooting the asshole.' And now we're planning to tell the kids together. So, yes, I want to be a second source if it'll work. But I'm with Helen. This is for Liddie to decide."

"I don't know the media world like you do, Deborah," Helen said. "Will an unnamed second source fly?"

"There's a reporter at the *Washington Post*, Kirsten Dawes. We've worked with her before on situations just like this, and she's scrupulous about protecting sources. But I can't promise you that Will won't find some way to figure it out and go after you, too, Marilyn—or loop Liddie in." With her left hand, Deborah massaged her temples. "Imagine the worst-case scenario, each of you, and then let me know. We'll support whatever you decide." The three women thanked Deborah, who quietly clicked off.

Becca had slipped into the kitchen and prepared bulging egg salad sandwiches for both of them. "They're a little thick," she said, "but we can cut off the crusts, cut them in thirds, and call it high tea." Deborah, who realized she was ravenous, grabbed her sandwich and started to dig in even before she fell into her chair at the place setting Becca arranged at the kitchen island, a rose-colored cloth napkin swirling from the glass, tea steeping in a china pot.

"I couldn't help overhearing the last part of your conversation, Ma."

"Funny how that happens when you eavesdrop."

"Touché. Have to say, I like the weather-girl image. I'm going to buy you a slicker and a pair of those rain boots from Target."

"Then you better make the snow melt," Deborah said. And with that, she put down the egg salad and burst into tears.

Becca slid her chair right up next to Deborah's and patted her mother's shoulder. "You're allowed, ya know. Take your time."

Deborah had no idea how long she wept, stopping occasionally to blow her nose into the lovely rose napkin. "These women were amazing, Bec. They're willing to take Will on, look him in the eye—and they're also ready to back off, if that's what Liddie needs. They've never even seen her in person, but this horrid bond they share made them like sisters. Each of them already feels, I don't know . . . validated, just from having survived long enough to find each other. So I have to trust them and do what I promised. . . ."

"Which is?"

"Back their decision, whatever it is."

Becca listened and held Deborah's hand and supplied a new napkin. When the crying stopped, Becca plugged in her iPod and filled the kitchen with the righteous sound of Nina Simone.

The snow was still coming down when Liddie finally called around seven thirty. "It took a few back-and-forths, but we've figured it out, DB. We want the virtual meeting with Will, and we want to do it together. The three of us are meeting tomorrow night in Milwaukee. Helen has a laptop, and she's getting Skype."

Deborah had been making a fire when the phone rang. She dropped the poker and hung on to the receiver with both hands. "How did you . . . wow!"

"Marilyn and her husband will drive there—she has a sister in Milwaukee they can stay with. And Helen and her wife will fly. We're splitting the cost of their flights."

"Breaking the Silence can cover that," Deborah said. She rolled the poker around with her slipper.

"Actually, we want to do this—it's a small way of regaining control." Liddie went on to say that she'd talked to Sylvia Rosenbaum. Sylvia had a friend in Milwaukee who was visiting relatives in Colombia. The woman had given Sylvia use of her house and Sylvia insisted that whoever needed to could stay there Sunday night. They would do the meeting from there.

"One more thing. I'm going to do the same as Marilyn. I'll be another unnamed source."

The poker flew out from under Deborah's foot onto the rug. "Oh, Lid."

"I'm not sure I ever told you this. Sylvia had us do an exercise once where we talked back to our rapist. You were supposed to picture him in the middle of the room, stuck in a chair—he could be tied up if you wanted it, duct tape or straitjacket, chains, your pick. And you could say anything—how much he hurt you at the time, what happened afterward. That's what the other women in the group did. But when it was my turn, all I could say was, 'Are you going to warn your daughter before she goes to college? What will you say when she asks you how you know so much?'"

Deborah knelt down to pull in the poker and to bite back her amazement. "What if Will refuses to drop out, Helen speaks to the press, he sics reporters on you—are you ready for that?"

"I don't know about 'ready,'" Liddie said. "But here's what I do know. I'm not the same person I was thirty years ago, and I am not going to let him bully me again. Over the past two days, I've relived that moment with Gillean Mulvaney a hundred times. Each time I wish I'd made a sign that said 'NO FUCKING COMMENT'—all capital letters—handed it to her, and walked back inside."

"And Richard? What does he think?" The fire began making crackling noises.

"He's on his way to Shopko for magic markers and poster board—and fresh ammo for his shotgun, in case that doesn't work."

Twenty-nine

Washington, DC: Monday, February 8, 2010

The snowshoes were Becca's idea. No plow had ventured anywhere near their street, but on Sunday Mr. Symanski next door donned his waders and, with the help of three Boy Scouts, shoveled paths for everyone on their side of the block. The crew even made a dent in the snow on the steps and unblocked each house's front door; Becca took care of the rest of the porch. Then she lined up two pair of snowshoes in the front hall. "If you want to get to the Metro tomorrow morning and then to your destination," Becca told her mother, "these babies will make all the difference—I promise. We'll spend the afternoon practicing."

By Monday morning, Deborah still felt ridiculous and nearly toppled twice on the way to the Metro station, where she and Becca had to unbuckle the contraptions on their feet, wait forty minutes for a train, then strap the things back on again to walk down the middle of K Street to the Capital Hilton. But Becca was right there each time, and the snowshoes really did make it easier to cut through the enormous drifts and even the parts that a plow had reached. Deborah felt elated, as if she'd just mastered rock climbing. The snow may have shut down the government, but it would not deter her.

All the way to the hotel, Deborah thanked the universe for

unleashing this storm and keeping Aaron away from the house. She needed every cylinder engaged solely for the meeting with Will. "I know wherever I've stuffed these feelings, they'll jump out at me soon like some jack-in-the-box," Deborah told Marquita Sunday, while Becca was out shoveling the front steps. "But for now, the lid's on tight."

Together Marquita and Deborah mapped out each piece of the plan. Step one involved Deborah's tracking down Kirsten Dawes, the *Washington Post* reporter, who was checking her work messages and returned the call within half an hour.

"I need to ask you for maximum flexibility, Kirsten," Deborah said. "We may have an exposé about a powerful person. I can't tell you any more detail; plus, events may take a different turn, and this may not become a news story at all. What I can do is offer you an exclusive, with two provisions: that you can be available on short notice tomorrow morning, and that you won't ask any questions if it doesn't happen, because nobody will be talking."

"That's tantalizing," the reporter said. She'd been typing as Deborah spoke; the keys fell silent. "I like you, Deborah. You don't grandstand, and what you deliver has always been solid. I'll go with it." And with no further nosing around, Kirsten Dawes gave Deborah the number to her cell phone and promised to keep the next day open just in case.

Marquita took care of the second step: getting confirmation that Will Quincy's DC office was still at the Capitol Hilton and that his first appointment on Monday wouldn't start until late morning. "I used Malcolm's phone," Marquita said. "Told them I was a reporter at *Black Press Week*, asked what times Mr. Quincy would be available tomorrow for a profile."

"And they went for it?"

"I might have said something about 'black folk are tired of being taken for granted by the Democratic Party,'" Marquita said. "They assured me the whole morning was free until eleven thirty."

Next, the two of them plotted the heart-pounding details of how Deborah would get in once she arrived at the hotel suite. "You should be doing this," Deborah told Marquita.

"Because?"

"Because you can squash someone with your stare and pulverize them every time you open your mouth. I probably won't get past the gatekeeper boy."

"You just have to channel your inner fang-lady, DB. If that doesn't work, channel mine. And remember what we always tell women in our trainings: rehearse it till you own it, and—"

"I know: imagine all your friends are right behind the person you're talking to—"

"Right behind the *asshole* you're talking to, hooting and hollering because you're so magnificent."

On the snowshoe run, Deborah practiced her lines over and over with Becca, who promised to accompany her the next morning and wait in the lobby with the snowshoes, "in case my knees turn to jelly and you have to tie all four of these things together and drag me back home."

And now Deborah was standing in front of Will's hotel door. Her knock surely wasn't any louder than the clatter her heart was making in her chest. When Todd Jennings showed his smooth-cheeked face at the door and struggled to place her, Deborah bounded right in.

"I'm sorry, Ms. . . ."

"Get Sonja Neilson," she said. "Now. Tell her a gigantic and most unfavorable story will break in seven minutes unless she arranges a face-to-face meeting with Will immediately." Todd, who was a good foot taller than Deborah, gawked at her for ten seconds until she pointed to her watch. "Six minutes, forty-five seconds, and counting."

Todd pivoted and left Deborah alone in the thick-carpeted antechamber. She stared at her watch until Sonja Nielson stood in front of her. *Someone really should tell the woman that scrunching up her eyes like that will lead to big-time crow's-feet*, Deborah thought.

"I don't know what you think you're trying to prove here, Ms.—"

"Borenstein. Deborah Borenstein. Let Will know that it's no longer one person's story; there are now three. They're ready to go to the media, but they're willing to talk to him first to see if they can work it out. You have six more minutes to decide."

"You can't barge in here—"

"Actually, I just did. Five minutes and forty seconds." During rehearsal, this was Becca's favorite part.

Sonja backed out of the room, as if Deborah might follow otherwise. Todd apparently had been charged with guarding Deborah. He watched her silently, twirling a pencil between his fingers. Today he did not offer her coffee or invite her to take a seat.

With just under a minute remaining, Will and Sonja marched into the room. His hands were stuffed into the pockets of his tan Burberry sports coat, but his face remained expressionless. "I don't know what you think you're going to accomplish here, Deborah," Will said. "I'm not keen on blackmail and I don't take to ultimatums. If you and your girlfriend Liddie want to peddle slanderous tales to some hack, you go right ahead. Just be sure you have enough assets for the legal fees."

"I have my laptop." Deborah opened the lid and showed them the screen. "It's already on Skype. Because of the snow, the meeting will have to take place via remote. Helen Dimitriou is waiting to speak to you, along with two other women. I suggest you sit down right there." The chair Deborah pointed to was next to a small conference table, where she set up the laptop on top of a pile of magazines.

"This is not the way we do business, Ms. Borenstein," Sonja said.

Helen's deep voice emerged from the computer. "You can debate the fine points, Will, and my colleagues and I shall simply keep our appointment with the press. Or you can take a minute and listen. Where's the harm?"

Will, who was still wearing slippers, clamped his jaws together and spun on the ball of his foot to return to his inner sanctum. Sonja Nielson put her hand lightly on his elbow. "Remember, you can walk out at any time," she said quietly, guiding him to the table. With her other hand she quickly maneuvered a second chair next to the one designated for Will and pulled his out. He lowered his body into the chair as if he were trying to avoid sitting on dog turds.

Before taking a seat on the closest couch, where she could watch Sonja's expression, as well as Will's, Deborah pulled the seven-hundred-page *Brothers Karamazov* from her tote—placed there by

Becca—and positioned it to elevate the laptop so that Will's full face would appear on-screen. Yesterday with Marquita, Deborah had weighed the pros and cons of Skype versus a conference call.

"I hate that these women have to see Will's mouth and those icy blue eyes. Ugh."

"You're wrong on this one, DB," Marquita told her. "Watching him trash-talk will make them furious. And watching him fold—"

"*If* he folds—"

"Will be a high point of their lives."

On camera now, a woman who had to be Helen Dimitriou sat in front of a large banner. Just above her head in bold letters floated a two-line quote from Audre Lorde:

> WHEN I DARE TO BE POWERFUL, TO USE MY STRENGTH IN THE SERVICE OF MY VISION,
> THEN IT BECOMES LESS AND LESS IMPORTANT WHETHER I AM AFRAID.

Helen did have good posture, but she was smaller than Deborah had imagined, black hair laced with silver, prominent eyebrows, sharp features. "Why, hello, Will. Helen Dimitriou here. Tuesday-Thursday calculus class—the one you had to hire a fancy tutor to pass. I'm sure you know how flattered I was that a big man on campus would ask me out. I couldn't believe you'd noticed me. I certainly never dreamed you'd rape me."

Will folded one hand over the other on the table; only the slight pulsing of a vein beneath his eye indicated that anything in his world was amiss. "I assume you're aware that the person orchestrating this is the wife of my opponent's campaign strategist. I regret that she has manipulated you into participating in this pitiful endeavor. I warned her last week that I would take legal action. My lawyers are very smart, very swift, and very successful."

Deborah kept her gaze on Sonja Nielson, who sat frozen in her seat. She looked like she was holding her breath.

Helen's face remained on-screen, but Marilyn's voice came next. There were no tears today. "It's interesting you threaten my life savings, Will, since you already robbed me of thirty-two years of normal life. After you raped me, it took me a decade to trust another man. What we want is simple—we won't go public if you drop out of the race and promise never to run again for public office."

Will's fingers were now tightly entwined. "The legal terms are 'slander,' 'libel,' 'defamation,' 'extortion.'" He spoke each word with slow, exaggerated movements of his mouth and tongue as if he were addressing lip readers. "You might want to write them down so you remember them later."

Another voice entered the room, Liddie's, clear and sharp and surprisingly loud. Two seconds later, her face appeared as well. "I'm glad to hear you like documentation, Will Quincy. I still have the Polaroids of those bruises you left all over my body—especially the one from the stranglehold across my neck."

Deborah had to press her feet to the floor to keep from shouting out. Where on earth had Liddie gotten those photos? As far as Deborah could remember, Randall Peters kept all the evidence. At the time, it hadn't occurred to her to ask for anything back.

Sonja rose and once again slid her hand under Will's elbow. This time, her fingers were tensed. "We'll return in a moment," she announced, firmly and loudly enough for the women to hear. Will began to follow her into the other room but doubled back almost immediately, pulling the chair out so fast, it nearly tipped over. He started speaking even before he sat down.

"Listen carefully. You're all free, white, and over twenty-one, and you can do whatever you like." His hands gripped the edge of the table. "But be advised that if you go to the press with these lies, my lawyers will be serving notice before you've dialed the goddamn number."

Liddie moved her eyes so she was looking directly at the camera. "Here's a question I imagine reporters are going to ask you and your daughter, Will: When she left for college, how did you prepare her to avoid date rape?"

Will, who was already halfway out of his chair, flung himself back down. His jaws were shut so tight, he practically hissed his response. "My daughter happens to be drop-dead gorgeous. From the day she got to campus, she's been hugely popular. And everyone knows who her daddy is. She'd never be one of those *nobody* girls who'd be targeted . . ."

Sonja turned the laptop away from Will and closed the lid with both hands. "We're done here."

Deborah leaped to her feet and reopened the laptop. Liddie's beautiful face still filled the screen.

"Allow me to finish that sentence, Will." Liddie spoke in a voice that was almost a whisper, but steely in a way Deborah had never heard from her: "'targeted by frat boys cruising for girls who'd be too frightened and confused and alone to press charges.' That's what you were going to say, isn't it? How ironic that it was your Senate campaign that allowed us to find each other." Liddie's voice was growing stronger. "We're not alone anymore. You've made your decision. We've made ours. You might want to check out YouTube, Mr. Quincy—people will see this conversation again and again. We've also made a Facebook page—'Contact us if William Quincy raped you when you were a student at Danforth.' It will launch as soon as we call in."

Deborah was dying to see the expression on Will's face—she pictured those fine cheekbones purple with rage, veins in his throat popping—but she knew enough to grab her laptop before he hurled it through the window and to haul herself out of that room as fast as she could. On the way, she almost tripped over Todd Jennings, who'd fallen into the other couch with his legs spread out, hands clasped over his eyes. Only in the elevator did Deborah remember the Dostoyevsky.

When the elevator door opened, Becca was standing there, holding her own laptop in front of her like a trophy. On it were Will's folded hands and calm face, saying, "'Slander,' 'libel,' 'defamation,' 'extortion.'"

Right in the lobby, Deborah let out a whoop of joy. "How on earth did Liddie do this? She's the least tech-savvy person I know."

"Oh, I might have had a hand in that."

"How? When?"

Becca guided Deborah to the corner where their coats and snowshoes were heaped next to a red leather couch. "After you told me what happened, I wanted to talk to Liddie myself . . . I don't know . . . to let her know she was in my heart. Helen had just sent her the Audre

Lorde quote. Liddie loved that—she said she was ready to do the meeting and actually wished she knew a way to capture the conversation. So I gave her a quick tutorial on how to use Skype Recorder."

"I didn't even know there was such a thing!" Deborah clasped her hands to her chest. "And the Facebook page?"

"That was totally Liddie's idea. I just helped set it up."

Before Deborah could ask any more questions, her cell phone rang. The number was Richard's, the voice Liddie's.

"Oh my God, Lid, you were stupendous! I almost slid off the couch when you mentioned the Polaroids. How did you get your hands on them?"

Liddie's laugh was loud enough for Becca to hear. "I figure the guy's told enough lies. It couldn't hurt to throw in one of my own."

thirty

Washington, DC:
February 9–14, 2010

YouTube Video Could Affect Which Party Controls the Senate in 2011

Exclusive to the *Washington Post*, by Kirsten Dawes, February 9, 2010

A YouTube video that went viral yesterday afternoon may alter the outcome of the US Senate race in the state of Delaware—and could affect which party holds the majority after November's election. The video showed a confrontation between three women and William Quincy III, Republican Senate candidate from Delaware. The women all allege Quincy date-raped them while a student at Danforth University.

The number of comments posted on the video itself as of 10:00 p.m. last night: 17,489.

The number of comments from William Quincy III or his campaign staff regarding the video: zero.

The Background

Mr. Quincy, in DC to raise funds and gather endorsements for his race against Andrew Plale, had been staying in a suite at the Capitol Hilton. The women spoke to him from Milwaukee via Skype on a laptop brought to the hotel room by Deborah Borenstein, executive director of Breaking the Silence, a national organization dedicated to ending sexual violence against women.

"We weren't on his calendar," explained Helen Dimitriou, who led the exchange with Mr. Quincy.

Ms. Dimitriou, a middle-school math teacher from Binghamton, New York, told a reporter that she and one of the other two women, who asked not to be named at this time, had known each other at Danforth and were shocked to discover one day in 1980, their sophomore year, that they'd had identical experiences as first-year students with Mr. Quincy.

"We realized it was like a mathematical formula used by certain fraternity boys," Dimitriou said. "Identify the target—a naive girl who would be flattered by the attention. Invite her to a party at the frat house. Mix every kind of liquor into a potent concoction camouflaged with fruit punch. Get her to drink as much as possible as quickly as possible. Dance and kiss her in public. Find a way to get her up to a room. Subdue any resistance and force her to have sex. Leave the room right afterward."

"I wouldn't be surprised if the formula was actually written out somewhere, to be memorized by pledges," Dimitriou added.

When asked the typical response by such women, Dimitriou said, "Everyone had seen her drinking and making out with the guy—what could she possibly do? None of us had ever heard the words 'date rape.'"

Dimitriou and her friend kept in touch after Danforth but never mentioned the incident again—until the friend heard a radio report about William Quincy's Senate campaign. She informed Dimitriou, who remembered the name of Claire Rawlings, then a rape counselor who had visited Danforth, now a professor of women's studies at the University of Rochester.

Dr. Rawlings put them in touch with Deborah Borenstein, who had also been a student at Danforth—and who, in December 1979, says she walked in on her roommate being raped by Quincy. Borenstein then contacted her former roommate, who asked to join a call with the others.

"Hearing these women back each other up and create a plan was awe-inspiring," Borenstein said.

The Encounter

The former roommate decided to participate anonymously in a conversation the women would have by Skype with Mr. Quincy. What happened during that seven-minute encounter convinced this woman to go public with her story.

"As those who've watched the video know, our goal was to ask him to drop out," said Liddie Golmboch Blankenship. "We said we were prepared to go public otherwise, but we really wanted him to take that option."

It was a question from Ms. Blankenship that triggered the now-infamous outburst from Mr. Quincy.

"Here's a question I imagine reporters are going to ask you and your daughter, Will," Ms. Blankenship said. "When she left for college, how did you prepare her to avoid date rape?"

Mr. Quincy's response: "My daughter happens to be drop-dead gorgeous. From the day she got to campus, she's been hugely popular. And everyone knows who her daddy is. She'd never be one of those nobody girls who'd be targeted . . ."

Unbeknownst to Mr. Quincy—or to Deborah Borenstein—the women had decided to use Skype Recorder to tape the conversation and to release it if Mr. Quincy behaved inappropriately. "We expected he would make threats," Ms. Dimitriou said. "We wanted to be prepared."

The three also arranged for a Facebook page with a secure system saying, "Contact us if William Quincy raped you when you were a student at Danforth."

The Aftermath

Since the Quincy video went viral, Breaking the Silence has been deluged with press calls, not only national but international. Within the first hour, the three-and-a-half-minute clip had nearly 200,000 hits; it reached 1 million before the end of the day. Breaking the Silence immediately set up a team to verify and follow up on any replies to the Facebook page.

"What really got me was this man's utter lack of remorse," Ms. Dimitriou said. "I don't know whether it was arrogance, thinking a person of his wealth and stature couldn't be touched, or whether he

is just clueless about what was wrong with what he and his fraternity brothers did. He had no idea how badly he had damaged each of us."

The women shared what they described as the range of injuries they had experienced as a result of being date-raped: from changing majors or dropping out of college in order to avoid seeing the rapist, to difficulty sustaining relationships, to the unexpected and uncontrollable shaking, nightmares, and isolation of long-standing post-traumatic stress disorder.

Political Motive?

As William Quincy pointed out during the February 9 meeting, Deborah Borenstein's husband, Aaron Minkin, is the campaign manager for Quincy's opponent, Andrew Plale. Congressman Plale and the Democratic Party stand to gain should Mr. Quincy drop out of the race. The Delaware contest was seen as one of the pivotal races to determine which party emerges as the majority after November's elections.

When asked about Mr. Quincy's allegation that the women had been manipulated by those with a political agenda, Borenstein replied, "Women really need a moderate Republican ally in the Senate. It would have been great to be able to support such a candidate, regardless of who my husband represents.

"But politics doesn't trump principles," she said. "This wasn't a case of a sexual indiscretion. Thanks to the courage of these three women and many like them who are standing up to sexual assault, we will one day be a nation where people are held accountable for sexual violence. Only then will we see it eliminated."

"Date rape now has a name," added Ms. Dimitriou. "Groups like Breaking the Silence have helped a lot. But this is still a huge problem on college campuses and elsewhere. Hopefully our speaking out will help make a difference."

For more information on date rape, go to www.washingtonpost.com/daterape.

William Quincy III Expected to Drop Out of the Race

By Kirsten Dawes, February 10

An unnamed source in the Republican Party says Mr. William Quincy III, Republican candidate for the US Senate seat from Delaware, will hold a press conference on Wednesday to announce his plans. Mr. Quincy was the subject of a YouTube video that went viral yesterday, showing him in conversation with three women who alleged that he had raped each of them on a date in 1979 or 1980, while all were students at Danforth University.

Speculation among a wide variety of sources is that Mr. Quincy will step aside. Republican Party chairman Michael Steele said it would be "premature" to comment on who might replace Quincy in the race against Democrat Andrew Plale.

In a related development, the organization Breaking the Silence has already confirmed the likely legitimacy of seventeen replies to its Facebook outreach asking for others who may have been date-raped at Danforth by Mr. Quincy. "They were from women raped by someone in that same fraternity," said Marquita Reynolds, the organization's chief of staff. "The majority of these incidents happened before 1985. Six women identified themselves as Quincy targets; the others named different members of the fraternity." A team of national and local staff is following up with each of the women.

According to Ms. Reynolds, a generous donation from an anonymous donor has enabled the group to work on a linked page for women who had been date-raped at a college anywhere in the country.

CNN transcript, February 10, 12:00 p.m.

Wolf Blitzer: "William Quincy III and his wife, Kathryn, have called this press conference to make what he described as a 'brief' statement. Mr. Quincy said he will not take any questions from reporters and is expected to leave immediately after concluding his remarks."

William Quincy III: "I deeply regret the travesty wrought by my political enemies and the pain it has brought my family.

"Polls had been showing me with a substantial lead over my

opponent in the Senate race for the great state of Delaware. Clearly, their campaign was desperate for some quick-fix solution to pull them out of their doldrums.

"It is well known in political circles that Congressman Plale's campaign manager, Aaron Minkin, has been scrounging for a winning campaign since the fiasco he suffered in 1995, when his candidate in the Indiana Senate race was ridiculed for firing a gun he'd obviously never touched before and landing on his derriere. Mr. Minkin is married to Deborah Borenstein, a strident radical feminist who has used her political agenda to further her husband's career and her own organization's fund-raising goals.

"It is deeply disappointing—but hardly surprising—that the Democratic Party would stoop to such shenanigans in its zeal to win a Senate seat. If I were the only one involved, I would call their bluff and expose the lies and dirty tricks behind this effort to smear my good name.

"However, I am not the only one involved. I love my family too much to put them through this. As of today, February 10, 2012, I am withdrawing from the Senate race.

"I did not enter politics by choice but was tapped by my party to run for this seat. As business leaders—the real job creators—know, politics is hardly the only avenue to effect change. I look forward to returning to the company my family built through hard work and ingenuity, and continuing to have a major impact on Delaware and the country through my business operations.

"To the many people who have offered powerful words of support to me and my family in this difficult time, I humbly thank you and urge your support for the person the party will name as my successor for this nomination.

"God bless you, and God bless the United States of America."

Politico, February 11, 2010

There's plenty of buzz about the person named to replace Will Quincy as Republican candidate for Senate from Delaware. Those in the know peg Robert Sanders, a Delaware state senator, as inexperienced and a hard-line conservative. His biggest claim to fame is introducing a bill in the state legislature to lessen the penalty for violence directed against abortion providers. He is also a leading proponent of drug testing for anyone receiving public assistance.

Tea Party activists were Sanders' biggest boosters, but other Republicans believe he hasn't got a chance against Plale.

You'd expect feminists to be happy, given the attention this flap has given to date rape and violence against women in general. But Amanda Pruitt, executive director of Equality Unlimited, was overheard complaining loudly about having one more Dem in the Senate who'll put women's issues on the back burner.

Democrats, on the other hand, are rejoicing. "There's no question we'll hold on to the Senate," said longtime political consultant James Carville.

Washington Post Readers' Forum, Sunday, February 14, 2010

"Clearly we need more care in the candidate recruitment process. Who knows how many rapists are walking the halls of Congress?"

—Dina Barrett, Ann Arbor, Michigan

"This is one more example of political correctness run amok. What we're seeing is a group of women who slept around in college and got buyer's remorse three decades later, when their chins and other body parts began to sag and they needed some kind of pick-me-up. Along comes some femiNazis, and presto-chango! The sluts turn into victims."

—Roy Plowers, Arlington, Virginia

"'Free, white and twenty-one?' Yes, he really said that. Let me bear witness to at least one time William Quincy decided to cross the racial divide – the night he raped me in his fraternity house."

—LaDonna Baker, Atlanta, GA

"The real moral of this story? Any public figure should assume that you're always on duty. Whether you're on TV or having a burger at the corner bar, remember that anything you say could be online in 30 seconds. Imagine a permanent microphone on your lapel. If you can't take the scrutiny, step aside."

—Samuel Aronowitz, New York City

"Twenty years ago, I was raped by a professor. I gave up the field of study I loved because he would always have been able to influence my chances of getting financial aid or recommendations or research assignments. Last month I learned he'd been given a MacArthur genius award. Thank you to the women who spoke out about William Quincy, and thank you to groups like Breaking the Silence. I wish I'd known you two decades ago."

—Name withheld upon request

Thirty-One

Random Lake, Wisconsin: Saturday, February 13, 2010

"Why is it that the snow here feels welcoming?" Deborah linked her arm through Liddie's as they walked on the path next to Random Lake. "Blizzards in Wisconsin seem like opportunities to slow down and breathe. In DC, all hell broke loose."

"It's about *ex-pec-ta-tions*," Liddie said, lowering her head in imitation of the idiot provost who'd conducted their freshman orientation at Danforth. "Up here, everyone knows you need nonskid tires and warm mittens. But don't romanticize, DB. If you can't afford your heating bills and your kids are sharing winter coats, white stuff is still a bear."

Deborah stretched her fingers the width of her own warm mittens. "Good point."

Liddie freed her arm to unleash Charlie Brown, who immediately took off in pursuit of a squirrel.

"Turns out I have a lot of unromanticizing to do," Deborah said, "I bet Marquita a blowout dinner at our favorite restaurant that Mrs. Quincy would *not* be standing by her man."

"Guess you're not always the sharpest knife in the drawer—money buys a lot of allegiance." With their parka hoods up, Deborah couldn't see Liddie's face, but she knew the expression behind that voice: nostrils wide open, lips drawn tight. "It also can bend your brain in a certain direction. I bet Quincy's wife agrees with the party line: the frat boys were just having their fun; we're nothing but gold-digging girls gone wild, manipulated by—"

"A hard-core feminist whose agenda conveniently fills her husband's wallet." Deborah could almost see the wind lift her sigh and carry it clear across the lake. "Wait till they hear about me and Aaron."

Liddie reinserted her arm through Deborah's and drew her close. They watched Charlie Brown skitter through the snowdrifts.

"You don't worry he'll run off?" Deborah asked.

"He knows his way."

It had taken until Saturday, a full five days, for Deborah to make her way to Liddie's. The airport didn't open until Thursday, and all the stranded travelers had priority. "I'll get there," Deborah told Liddie over the phone the day after the YouTube video turned everything on its head. "I just don't know when. Hard to tell whether the chaos in nature is mirroring the upheaval in my life or the other way around. But it will subside. One way or another, I'll be with you soon."

Aaron finally made it home on Monday afternoon, an hour after Deborah's triumphant return from the Capitol Hilton. He burst into the kitchen without stopping to take off his overcoat or galoshes, tramping in snow everywhere. Later, Deborah found trickles of water under the island and the old corner couch.

"Wow, Ms. Borenstein, you really did it." With two strides, Aaron was at the sink, where Deborah had just finished spraying the plants. She felt him swoop her up from behind and swing her around, burying his mouth in her hair, until he set her on one of the tall chairs at the island and tipped her chin up with his thumb and index finger. "That was amazing, the most brilliant feat you've ever pulled off. God, I was so wrong about Liddie—she was really courageous, totally kicked ass. It's all anybody's talking about—this changes the political landscape, not just for one lousy race but for the long haul. And you masterminded it! Listen, any trash Quincy says about how you did this for me is bullshit—you know it, I know it. All that matters is we're on the same page again and—"

Deborah gently pulled her chin away from his hand. "Please listen to me, Aaron. We don't have a lot of time. Becca kept her snowshoes on to run to the store; she'll be back soon. I'm not hiding things from her, not ever again, but I want us to be clear with each other by the time she arrives."

Aaron yanked off his wool cap. The lines in his forehead seemed to have deepened since she'd seen him just a few days earlier. "What's that supposed to mean?"

"It means a lot's happened." Deborah pulled on the hem of her sweatshirt; she'd been thinking Aaron would be tied up at the office with the wild aftermath of the video and she'd have more time to prepare.

"And?"

"And I don't think we *are* on the same page."

"Because?"

"Well, for one thing, because you're still wrong about Liddie."

From his coat pocket, Aaron's cell phone beeped to announce a new text. He ignored the sound; when the phone began to ring, his fingers dug it out and turned it off. "C'mon, Deborah. I'm really glad to be home. I'm exhausted. Let's not quibble over words."

A late-afternoon sunburst snuck in through the kitchen window, as if to put Aaron in a spotlight. Motes spun around his head.

"Don't you see, Aaron? Liddie was always courageous. She stood up to the dean, she wrote that amazing statement, she challenged the psychiatric establishment, she refused to be numbed, she found a way to survive, and when she finally stopped being fucked around, she found a way to thrive. It's not that she suddenly found courage. What changed is that she no longer had to be out there on her own."

"Unbelievable!" Aaron shed his coat and kicked off his boots. "I come here to exalt you, to hold you and celebrate with you and go back to the way things were, and all you can do is lecture me? Are you fuckin' kidding me?"

Deborah wrapped the dish towel she was holding around her fingers, to keep herself from picking up Aaron's coat and heaving it at him. "Look, I need to get away for a while. I thought I'd go to Liddie's, turn my phone off, clear my brain."

"What are you talking about? This is the biggest win the organization's ever gotten—you can't leave now."

"Actually, Marquita was the one in charge of this operation. She's got it covered."

"But there's another storm on the way. They're saying it could drop more snow than the first one. Airport'll probably be closed for days, everyone'll be stuck at home—it's the perfect time for us to work things out."

Deborah tightened her abdominal muscles. "It's just . . . I need to get my bearings first."

Aaron's eyes filled with tears as he unwound the dish towel from Deborah's knuckles and took her hand in both of his. "This is me, Deb. I love you. All I want is my family back. Are you really telling me you don't want that as well?"

"Please, Aaron, let me have some time." She slipped her fingers out of his grasp.

By the time Becca arrived with the groceries strapped to her sled—the same one she'd had since childhood—Aaron had already trudged out to return to the campaign office, and Deborah had begun making lasagna. Before she ladled sauce over the damp noodles, Deborah told her daughter about her plans to visit Liddie and about the talk with Aaron. Becca listened in silence with tears spilling down her cheeks. At some point she grabbed the grater and transferred whatever emotion she was feeling to the lump of parmesan cheese. She spent most of the afternoon in her room but came down to eat the lasagna with Deborah and listen to the news.

"Folks, if last week was Snowmageddon, this promises to be Snowpocalypse," the announcer on 94.7 informed them. "If you were planning to go out of town, unpack your bags. If your boss says you have to come in, tell him every respectable forecaster is ordering you to stay at home. Snuggle up or bundle up. Either way, my friends, stay safe."

Becca merely scratched at her food and restricted her comments to the storm, which she allowed to preoccupy her. Deborah watched some of her daughter's spunk return as she planned how to tackle the twenty inches of additional snowfall projected for that night and the following day.

"Don't wig out, Mom, but I'm going to set my alarm for every two hours so we don't get trapped in the house again."

"You really don't have to, sweetheart. Those groceries you bought will last for a week. And there's no way I'm going to the office tomorrow. Marquita will handle the media. As long as the power doesn't go out, I can take any overflow calls in my pajamas."

"You miss my meaning. Reporters are going to have to wait in line for you, because tomorrow, we sled."

Marquita called Tuesday morning, having ridden the bus for over an hour to the office.

"DB, more than snow is blowing in today. I'm talking a certified check for fifty thousand dollars from an anonymous donor, paid via Chase bank, just messengered to our office by a guy who told me he was from Buffalo and couldn't see what all the blizzard fuss was about. It came with a typed note on some official-looking Chase letterhead. Wait, you gotta hear this." Deborah listened as Marquita shuffled papers on the other end. "'The enclosed check has been given to you for the express purpose of helping to identify and support women who have been date-raped while attending college in the United States.' Then there's some legalese about us agreeing to use the check for that purpose and a number to call if we do, to activate the deposit."

"Unbelievable!" Deborah put the phone on speaker to share the news with Becca, who was warming up by the fire after her latest foray with the shovel.

"There's more," Marquita said. "The donor commends the three women who spoke out about Mr. William Quincy and thanks you for 'giving voice to so many of us'—you hear that?—'who have been silenced all these years.'"

Deborah pictured a woman her age or a little older, married to a financial bigwig or industrialist who had no clue about her history, someone who couldn't be bothered to track his wife's charitable donations.

"I'm saying Will Quincy is the gift that keeps on giving. We also got calls from two different researchers who want to update the 1985 study on date rape."

"That's the study that saved Liddie's life," Deborah said to Becca. "Wow! All these things are popping, and guess what my daughter wants me to do—go sledding!"

Marquita whistled. "Can you hear me, Becca?"

"Oh yeah." Becca rubbed her hands in anticipation.

"If you take your cell phone and snap a picture, I'll give you my doggy bag from Nora's Restaurant. Go, please, DB. I need the image, and you need to cut loose."

"Hey," Deborah said. "Don't count your doggy bags before Will does his perp walk."

Deborah gave in and spent Tuesday afternoon sledding with her daughter, under whiteout snow that transformed runs down the hill behind the middle school into something closer to bumper cars. Becca made sure they were both well padded and took on the task of steering. Deborah just hung on. "My mom never opened her eyes or shut her mouth the whole time!" was how Becca described it that evening in a call to Marquita. "Check out the photo. She had a blast!"

Will Quincy managed to stay out of sight until the following day at noon, when he organized an impromptu press conference with every reporter who could find a way through the snow. "CNN in five minutes," Marquita called from home to inform Deborah. They stayed on the phone while each settled in to watch. When Will came on camera with his wife glued to his side, Marquita let out a louder-than-usual whoop. "That's what I'm saying!" she shouted. "I want the pan-seared filet mignon and the I-just-died-and-went-to-heaven chocolate cake with ginger ice cream. And I want it soon—well, soon as you get back from Wisconsin."

Usually the camera added a few pounds, but Will looked as if he'd been on a crash diet. "Will you look at that!" Marquita said. "Whoever called themselves putting on his make-up should get booted, pronto. The man's a mess. If I didn't hate him so much, I might feel sorry for him."

On their third call of the day, Marquita commented on the huge advantage Aaron's candidate had inherited "without doing a speck of work to deserve it. Get ready for an earful from Amanda Pruitt"—here, Marquita shifted into Amanda's Texan drawl: "You mighta scored a goal against scuzz, but you may return women to the back alleys as a result."

Deborah was scouring the lasagna pan. "Can't I pass her to you?" she asked. "Tell her I'm off."

"She'd just lay it on you when you come back," Marquita said. "In her eye, I'm not important enough to yell at."

"Fine, you get Gillean Mulvaney, then. She's been leaving me serial messages."

"Why waste your chance to try the NFC response?"

"The what?"

"You know, Liddie's invention—No Fucking Comment."

Deborah left exactly that message for Gillean Mulvaney. Then she returned Amanda's call and allowed her to rant without interruption.

"What are y'all going to do when the newly elected Senator Plale votes against VAWA?" Amanda's pronunciation of the acronym for Violence Against Women Act made it sound like something sexual. "How are you going to feel when that lovely man stands with the Republicans while they filibuster a Supreme Court nominee because she believes that government shouldn't be slipping under the sheets with you?" She went on for another several minutes with barely a pause to breathe. "I hope righteousness tastes sweet, darlin'," she said as she wound down, "because reality is gonna feel real bitter—take it from me."

"I hear you," Deborah said. "I hate the collateral damage, too. But we're going to have to agree to disagree about this. Okay?"

Amanda's sigh filled the phone waves. "Doesn't mean I have to like it," Amanda said. "But it won't be the first time. Likely not the last."

Deborah cleared her throat. "Listen, there's something else, completely separate. I respectfully need to decline the Egalitarian Couple of the Year award. Confidentially, I'm not sure we're going to stay a couple. But, in any case, we don't meet your criteria."

The line went silent for more than thirty seconds. "Oof," Amanda said. "I'm sorrier than you know. In this area, anyway, you were my role model."

"I hope it's not a huge hassle." Deborah rubbed her fingers on the slender silver bracelet she'd worn since her wedding in 1988 and wondered whether or not to take it off.

"Not at all. The blizzard's backed everything up—nothing's printed yet. Plus, I've been around long enough to know you always have to have an alternate. We'll be fine. Hope you are, too."

The government and most everything else was still shut down on Thursday. By necessity, the board meeting scheduled for that day had morphed into a conference call. Before Deborah could introduce the minutes from the last meeting, Catherine Snyder, the board chair, invoked a point of personal privilege and asked that discussion of the Quincy incident climb to the top of their agenda. "I know I'm not the only one who would like Deborah to admit she was wrong in refusing to confront Will Quincy earlier," Catherine said. "While I applaud her changing her mind, I think we need some accountability here."

Yomara and Della both jumped in the instant Catherine stopped grumbling. Catherine asked Lian Shiu, the secretary, to take over as meeting chair. Lian queued up Yomara and then Della to make brief comments.

"In what universe does listening to survivors translate into refusing to act?" Yomara was talking so fast, the last words slid into each other. "This situation was a great example of what happens when we let women make up their own minds and give them a vehicle to operate in. Something big changed here—other women who'd been raped by this guy found us because of years of work on our part. Deborah was able to put her friend and these women together. And together they brought this *cabron* down."

Della delivered her motion more slowly. "I move as a board we applaud Deborah and Marquita for their outstanding leadership in this initiative."

Deborah wished they were all around a table so she could watch faces as Lian Shiu asked for and got a second.

"*Discussion*!" Catherine Snyder shouted. "With all due respect, I'd like to know how Marquita Reynolds became a spokeswoman here. She's Deborah's *assistant*, for heaven's sake."

Deborah cursed herself for not having taken this battle on months ago. "Actually, she's the chief of staff. Same position Rahm Emanuel holds for the president. Would you be so dismissive of him?"

"But all she has is an as-*so*-ciate degree," Angela Treat added.

"Go back and read our by-laws and mission statement." Deborah paced to keep herself from raising her voice. "Fortunately, we addressed the need to value experience, skills, and leadership above all. Marquita Reynolds is the perfect illustration of why we hold these principles. She shaped Project Quincy—set up the meeting, scripted my lines to get him in the room, organized the messaging afterward, is overseeing all the follow-up."

"I was involved in the planning and strongly agree," Yomara said, with a prompt "ditto" from Della.

"That came as no surprise to anyone on staff," Deborah said, "given that Marquita has run the office for some time. We're way overdue in giving her the title that goes with her actual responsibilities. I recommend Marquita be promoted immediately to codirector of Breaking the Silence. She's going to be in charge while I take some time off."

The first time Deborah had announced a promotion for Marquita, they hadn't discussed it in advance. "If you really know I earned it," Marquita told her, "don't make it feel like a gift." The codirectorship was something they'd been talking about for several weeks.

Lian Shiu called for a roll call vote, first on Della's motion and then on Deborah's recommendation. Both passed nine to six. Whatever other resolutions Catherine and Angela were planning to introduce, about adding donors to the board and shifting expenses away from organizing, never materialized.

The text signal on Deborah's BlackBerry lit up like the winning light on a slot machine. "Oh yeah," read Yomara's text. Della wrote, "Woo-hoo!" Marquita's message was the longest: "You've still gotta take me to Nora's. And Nora gets to pick out the wine."

Recounting these events to Liddie on Saturday afternoon as they hiked around Random Lake impressed on Deborah that, yes, this had all happened and it was all real. Liddie devoured every detail, laughing out loud several times and clapping her mittened hands together at the end.

"I have some news for you, too," she said, stopping so she and

Deborah could be face-to-face. "Kirsten Dawes forwarded me an email this morning from Stuart Mulligan."

The name sounded both familiar and unpleasant to Deborah, but it took a minute for her to hear the voice of Frat Boy Two at the hearing thirty years earlier, telling Randall Peters, "Everyone calls me Skip."

"Turns out his daughter is a sophomore at Northwestern," Liddie said. "Over winter break she came to him one night sobbing, said her best friend had been raped by some guy she was out on a date with. The daughter couldn't stop shaking. Skip wrote that he just held her while she wept, unable to say a word. 'I'd cut off my arm if I could take back what I did to cover for Will,' he said in the email. 'I knew all about the Senate race, of course—Will went out of his way to keep his fraternity brothers updated. After that night, I just had to do something to try to keep him from winning.'"

Deborah pictured a big guy at a computer desk, surfing the Internet until he found the name of that investigative reporter he'd seen on the news. "So that's who tipped off Gillean Mulvaney?" she asked.

"Yup."

"Wow—it's almost too much to digest." Deborah took off her left glove and slipped her hand into Liddie's roomy right mitten. "What's this all mean for you, Lid? How are you really—right now and when you get up in the morning?"

"I wish I were getting up only in the morning and not in the middle of the night." Liddie turned them so they'd take a shorter path back; daylight was already seeping into dusk. "But daytime's good, and evenings. And I'm really, really glad we knocked Will out of the race."

Charlie Brown tore out of the woods and circled them several times, tongue hanging as if he'd just run a marathon. For another few minutes, the only sound was Charlie's panting.

"In some ways, nothing's changed," Liddie said. "I'm still at my loom every day. I'll probably spend time with Helen and Marilyn again, but not soon. Don't look for me to head up a survivors' network."

Deborah stopped moving and squeezed Liddie's right hand.

"On the other hand," Liddie said, her nose and cheeks a lively pink from the cold, "there's what Richard said the other day." She was smiling so wide, her eyes crinkled.

"What's that?" Charlie Brown, back on his leash, was dragging them toward the house.

"He said, 'Welcome back, Liddie Golmboch. I'm so happy to meet you.'"

Thirty two

Danforth University: Wednesday, October 24, 1979

When Liddie returned from textile class, Deborah was still sitting on the floor of their room, legs sprawled out in front of her. In some part of her brain, she could imagine what a sight she must be, rocking slightly, hands rubbing her knees.

"Talk to me, DB, before you wear a hole in those jeans." Liddie dropped her coat and book bag on her bed. "Whatever truth you're seeking is not in that denim, I promise you."

"I know," Deborah said with an exaggerated sigh. "I'm hopeless. It's Brad. I'm supposed to marry this guy, and I'm not sure I even respect him. What's wrong with me?"

Liddie crouched down next to her roommate. "Maybe you should be asking what's wrong with Brad."

"Yeah." Deborah stowed away for future exploration the fact that she had to be reminded of this. "I've been sitting here too long," she said. "My back is killing me. I need something to lean against."

Liddie slid down to the floor and fitted her back to Deborah's. "Here. We can be each other's backrests. My favorite teacher, Mrs. Weiner, had us do this once on a field trip, when everyone was tired and crabby and there were no chairs in sight."

Deborah stretched her hand over her shoulder to thank Liddie, who grabbed on.

"Forget what I just said. Don't think about what bothers you about Brad. Focus on what you want in a relationship. If you had to make a list, what would be on it?"

Deborah thought back to a conversation she'd had with her grandmother the summer before Danforth. Deborah had been torn about how to decide whether to pursue some line of work that mattered to her or to settle down and be a wife and mother. "You know how you do both, *shana*?" her grandma had said. "Marry someone who wants you to be your own person."

"I can see why you loved her so much," Liddie said after listening to this story.

"See if this makes sense. What I want from a man who loves me is that he'll *want* me to shine. Not that he 'doesn't mind if I do better than he does.'" Deborah made fake quote marks with her free hand, even though Liddie couldn't see the gesture. "I want someone who doesn't think of life as a competition."

"Exactly."

Even though daylight savings time wouldn't end for another week and a half, the sun was already starting to sink and it wasn't even five o'clock. Deborah scooted closer to Liddie. "What about you?" Deborah asked.

"Me? Hmm . . . I want someone who likes the way I put my teeth together."

"That's your whole list?"

"Okay." Liddie sat up taller. "I want someone steeped in decency. I don't care what he looks like, but he has to be solid. Someone who says hi to people on the bike path, who always knows the name of his server, someone quick to laugh and slow to yell. A guy whose idea of success is waking up beside me every day."

The chimes began to play. Time to get ready for dinner, start their homework, write a letter home. Still, Deborah stayed where she was for at least another fifteen minutes, until Liddie broke the silence.

"I hope they have those little red potatoes tonight," she said.

Acknowledgments

I'm humbled and fortified by all the friends who read some version of this manuscript and said, "I need it now to give my daughters and their friends"; or "I need it for the daughters of my friends"; or "Now I understand what happened to me."

Huge thanks to my writers' group, Rachel Buff, Patty Donndelinger, and Jennifer Morales, who pushed me and rooted for me and made the book so much better.

A big shout-out to my beloved twin sister Lynne and surely-they're-sisters-too, Barbara Deinhardt and Zohreh Emami, who read and re-read and asked and answered and believed.

A special thanks to Esther Cohen and Rinku Sen, two amazing women whose literary skills and criticism are coupled with political wisdom and whose support meant the world to me. I am also dazzled by the other giants who agreed to write blurbs for me: Gloria Steinem, Alexandra Brodsky, Jacqueline Mitchard, Salamishah Tillet, and Mary Lowry.

I'm honored to have many friends who gave feedback, helped make connections, and spurred me on—abrazos to you all, including Janice Balsam Danielson, Cynthia Ellwood, Arvonne Fraser, Becca Holtz, Saru Jayaraman, Carol Joyner, Anita Kline, Linda Meric, Karen Nussbaum, Ai-jen Poo, Sandra Priebe, Barbara Zack Quindel, and Jessica Quindel. Much gratitude to Brooke Warner and the team at She Writes Press for shepherding this book into the world and creating a much-needed space for women authors.

Thank you above all to the Miller boys, Larry, Nat, and Craig, who said, "This is it. This is the one that will get published and get people to ask what other manuscripts you have stuffed away in a drawer." Your love and humor and belief sustain me in ways I can never express. You also prove what an insult it is to men to think rape is something they cannot condemn and combat.

About the Author

© Tamara Didenko

Ellen Bravo was born in Cleveland but has lived in Wisconsin long enough to be a diehard Green Bay Packers fan and say "c'mere once" and "you bet." A lifelong activist, she is the former director of 9to5 (the group that inspired the movie) and current head of Family Values @ Work, a network of state coalitions working for family-friendly policies. She is the award-winning writer of three nonfiction books, the most recent being *Taking on the Big Boys, or Why Feminism is Good for Families, Business and the Nation*. Bravo lives in Milwaukee with her husband; they have two adult sons.

SELECTED TITLES FROM SHE WRITES PRESS

She Writes Press is an independent publishing company founded to serve women writers everywhere. Visit us at www.shewritespress.com.

Vote for Remi by Leanna Lehman
$16.95, 978-1-63152-978-8
History is changed forever when an ambitious classroom of high school seniors pull the ultimate prank on their favorite teacher—and end up getting her in the running to become president of the United States.

Stella Rose by Tammy Flanders Hetrick
$16.95, 978-1-63152-921-4
When her dying best friend asks her to take care of her sixteen-year-old daughter, Abby says yes—but as she grapples with raising a grieving teenager, she realizes she didn't know her best friend as well as she thought she did.

Shelter Us by Laura Diamond
$16.95, 978-1-63152-970-2
Lawyer-turned-stay-at-home-mom Sarah Shaw is still struggling to find a steady happiness after the death of her infant daughter when she meets a young homeless mother and toddler she can't get out of her mind—and becomes determined to rescue them.

A Cup of Redemption by Carole Bumpus
$16.95, 978-1-938314-90-2
Three women, each with their own secrets and shames, seek to make peace with their pasts and carve out new identities for themselves.

Trespassers by Andrea Miles
$16.95, 978-1-63152-903-0
Sexual abuse survivor Melanie must make a choice: choose forgiveness and begin to heal from her emotional wounds, or exact revenge for the crimes committed against her—even if it destroys her family.

Wishful Thinking by Kamy Wicoff
$16.95, 978-1-63152-976-4
A divorced mother of two gets an app on her phone that lets her be in more than one place at the same time, and quickly goes from zero to hero in her personal and professional life—but at what cost?